OPEN WINGS

Lorna gave a little cry.

'Jimmy blind! How will he bear it?'

'There is only one thing I have to say,' the
Air Vice-Marshal continued. 'It may be a
little comfort to you later. I have personally
recommended your husband for the D.F.C.
He has been exceedingly gallant—not only
on this occasion, but on many others—and
there is no one under my command who
deserves it more.'

P9-APC-706

Arrow Books by Barbara Cartland

Autobiography

I Search for Rainbows
We Danced All Night

Polly: the Story of My Wonderful Mother
Josephine Empress of France

Romantic Novels

Barbara Cartland

OPEN WINGS

ARROW BOOKS

ARROW BOOKS LTD
3 Fitzroy Square, London W1

An imprint of the Hutchinson Publishing Group

London Melbourne Sydney Auckland ·
Wellington Johannesburg Cape Town
and agencies throughout the world

First published by Hutchinson & Co (Publishers) Ltd 1942
Arrow edition 1971
This edition 1976
© Barbara Cartland 1942

This book is published at a net price and
supplied subject to the Publishers Association
Standard Condition of Sale registered under
the Restrictive Trade Practices Act 1956

Made and printed in Great Britain
by The Anchor Press Ltd
Tiptree, Essex

ISBN 0 09 911660 x

I

'Can I help you?'

Lorna let her arching arms drop and turned her head. Looking over the fence which bordered the orchard she saw a young man and guessed that he was one of the convalescent officers from the Hall.

'Thank you but I've nearly finished,' she replied, pointing to where, at the foot of the tree, several baskets were filled with the ripe cherries which she had been picking for over two hours.

'Well, can't I come and help to eat them?'

Lorna laughed.

'Certainly not. Most of them are going to the Preserving Centre to be made into jam and a few—just a very few—I am keeping for ourselves.'

'All the same I feel I could be useful,' the stranger said irrepressibly.

Looking along the fence he selected a place which was sadly in need of repair and climbed over into the orchard. He was slim and tall, but as he came walking towards Lorna, she saw that he was limping and that his arm was in a sling.

'You must be hard up for a job, but if you really feel energetic, you can help me finish this bough. I've done the rest.'

She held out her basket invitingly. The newcomer came and stood beneath her, reaching for the cherries with his good arm and dropping the fruit into an empty basket. But

5

after a few moments Lorna perceived that he was not working very assiduously—instead, he seemed to be watching her.

The bough finished, she descended the ladder, feeling suddenly self-conscious and aware of her untidy hair and hot face. She pulled a handkerchief out of the pocket of her cotton overall and wiped her forehead.

'Was there really such a frantic hurry?' her helper asked.

'Well, they had to be picked before this evening—in fact, before teatime.'

'Good—you've time to spare!' he said reassuringly. 'Let's sit down for a moment and introduce ourselves. I know your name—it's Lorna, and you are the Vicar's daughter, but there are a lot more things I want to hear. Sit down and tell me about yourself.'

There was the trunk of an old tree lying on the ground only a few paces away. He sat down on it and smiled up at Lorna as she stood irresolute, a little shy, a little surprised.

'Come on,' he insisted. 'Don't look so frightened of me.'

'I'm not,' she protested instantly, flushing in spite of herself.

Reluctant, yet hardly knowing how to refuse, she moved towards the log.

'That's better,' he said. 'Now we can talk. My name's Braith—Jimmy Braith—and as you can guess I am here for the good of my health.'

'How were you wounded?' Lorna asked, her voice softening.

'I had a forced landing,' he answered. 'I thought I could get home in spite of the worst the Huns had done to us. Well, I did it, but we didn't land as comfortably as we'd have liked—hence the bumps and bruises. But they're not serious and I'm thankful to have come down in old England—I should have hated a watery grave!'

'Don't talk like that, it all sounds so dangerous.'

He laughed.

'I love every moment of it. I always wanted to fly, even when I was a small boy.'

'So the war gave you your opportunity!'

'Oh no. I did a lot of flying before the war and you're really talking to quite an important person, if you but knew it!'

'I'm afraid you didn't introduce yourself properly. You should have added your full rank or title!'

'I'm sorry. Squadron-Leader Jameson Braith—R.A.F.'

'That's much better—and I'm very impressed.'

'I'm glad. I wanted you to be. Some time you shall see me in my uniform—they always tell me there's nothing like a uniform to make a woman's heart beat quicker.'

'We in Little Walton will do our best to be appreciative,' Lorna said mockingly.

'I don't know what you mean by "we",' Jimmy Braith challenged. 'I haven't seen a woman under sixty in the whole village—I've never been in such a one-eyed place. If I stay here much longer I shall be flirting with our Commandante and goodness knows what will happen to me then!'

Lorna giggled. She knew Lady Abbott and the idea of her flirting with anyone was almost sacrilegious.

'I am sorry you find it dull,' she said, looking to where in the distance through a protecting screen of trees there rose the grey Norman tower of the village church.

'Don't you?'

Lorna shook her head.

'Good Heavens, no! I'm far too busy. And that reminds me—I must go now. Thank you for your help—or should I say your hindrance?'

There were dimples in her cheeks as she smiled. Jimmy noticed them as he got rather slowly to his feet.

'Don't go,' he said, 'or if you must, let me come too. I'll help you carry the baskets.'

'Oh, we can leave the big one,' Lorna replied. 'Peter—my brother—has promised to come down and fetch it as soon as he has finished a game of tennis, and I can manage the other two.'

'Nonsense! You'll strain yourself. I insist on taking one.'

There was no gainsaying his determination and Lorna gave up the struggle.

'Very well, in that case we might as well take the lot. We'll carry the big basket between us and put the smaller ones on top.'

It was quite a heavy load and they walked slowly through the orchard until they came to a wooden gate which led into the Vicarage garden.

'Peter ought to be very grateful,' Jimmy said.

'Oh, he will be,' Lorna answered. He hates having to fetch and carry. We'll tell him that we have done his job for him. By the way, if you talk to him, don't say too much about flying.'

'Why not?'

'He's so frightfully keen on it. He's only just seventeen but I have a feeling that any day now he will go off and join up —giving his wrong age. He'd have done it before if it hadn't been for Peke.'

'And who's Peke?'

'That's my sister.'

'What a strange name!'

'Oh, she was christened Patricia, but soon after they were born—she and Peter are twins—my mother had a sudden idea that one of them was dead. She sent my father hurrying to the nursery. When he came back to her he said briefly— "The boy's yelling his head off—the girl's snoring like a Pekinese." And, of course, the name stuck.'

'So you've got twins in the family,' Jimmy said. 'What an achievement!'

'What an expense you mean!' Lorna retorted.

'Are they alike?'

'You will be able to judge for yourself in a moment.'

They turned the corner of a mellow brick wall and in front of them was the Vicarage. The house was a low, rambling building, originally Elizabethan, now architecturally a pot-pourri of each succeeding generation.

The garden was untidy and badly in need of cultivation

8

and yet it had a wild beauty of its own. There were flowers everywhere growing profusely, unhindered and untrammelled, while shrubs and trees had apparently not been pruned or cut back for years.

The lawns were white with daisies; only the tennis court had been cut, but erratically, leaving high, thick grass growing beneath the dilapidated net.

There were two players, both wearing shabby grey flannel trousers and white open-necked shirts. As Lorna and Jimmy appeared, a ball lobbed high into the air, bounced off the court and disappeared from sight into the rhododendron bushes.

'Damn you, Peter! You've done it again.'

'Game and set,' was the reply.

Peter threw his racquet up in the air and caught it deftly.

'It wasn't really fair,' his twin started to protest; then, seeing Lorna, stopped.

'Hello!' she said. 'Peter's beaten me again and by his usual methods.'

'You should retaliate,' Lorna said.

Peke came across the court. At a distance she had looked like a slim, rather badly dressed boy, but as she drew nearer, it was obvious that she would one day be exceedingly pretty.

At the moment her hair was strained back behind her ears to prevent it getting into her eyes, and she was scowling in a childish manner which Lorna knew meant embarrassment at the presence of a stranger.

'This is my sister,' she said to Jimmy.

'How do you do.'

Peke made no attempt to hold out her hand but helped herself to a couple of cherries out of the basket.

'Refreshments! Just what I wanted,' Peter announced, coming nearer.

'No, you're to leave them alone,' Lorna commanded. 'I've had an awful job picking them while you two have been amusing yourselves, and Squadron-Leader Braith helped me carry them; so there's nothing for you to do, Peter, except

9

keep your hands out of the baskets!'

'Squadron-Leader!' Peter ejaculated, drawing in his breath eagerly. 'I say, are you up at the Hall?'

'I am.'

'That's fine! Then we shall see something of you, sir.'

There was no doubting Peter's enthusiasm and Jimmy grinned.

'You will,' he promised. 'In fact, I hope you will see a lot of me.'

'Well, we certainly hope so,' Peter said, 'don't we, Peke?'

Peke was not scowling now, her brow had cleared and she was smiling. It was obvious that her brother's enthusiasms were identical with her own.

'Will you help me carry the cherries as far as the house?' Lorna asked Jimmy, a warning note in her voice.

'Of course.'

'No, you must let me do it, sir,' Peter said.

After an argument they were all moving towards the house, everyone lending a hand with a willingness that would have surprised Lorna if she had not known only too well the underlying motive for such newly-acquired courtesy!

They took the cherries in at the back door, putting them in the cool, old-fashioned larder with its stone flags and white-washed walls.

'I say, Lorna, what about some tea?' Peter suggested. 'Perhaps Squadron-Leader Braith would like a cup. Wouldn't you, sir?'

'I'd love to stay if you would have me?' Jimmy answered.

He spoke diffidently, but somehow Lorna had the impression that he had intended to stay all along, and she felt slightly annoyed although she could not have explained why.

She led the way into the big sitting-room which overlooked the garden. It was a large room with french windows, and must originally have been intended to be the drawing-room of the house. It was certainly not worthy of the name now, and yet it had a homely charm in spite of its miscellaneous collection of furniture and its shabby, faded, chintz covers, all of which had been patched or darned.

'The twins will entertain you,' Lorna said, 'while I go and see about tea.'

'But look here,' Jimmy expostulated, 'I don't want to be any trouble. Can't I help?'

'I think I'm better on my own,' Lorna replied. 'You've been quite enough hindrance for one afternoon!'

Her smile took the sting from her words, and then she had gone while Jimmy still looked irresolute.

'It's all right, sir,' Peter said. 'You can't really do anything. Lorna always gets the tea.'

'It seems to me Lorna does a lot of things around here,' Jimmy replied, lighting a cigarette.

'Oh, I don't know,' Peter said vaguely. 'I think she likes doing it, don't you, Peke?'

'She always has.'

'Are there many more of you?' Jimmy asked.

'Only Beth,' Peke replied. 'She's at school at the moment, but she ought to be back about six o'clock.'

'And how old is she?'

'Fifteen or sixteen—I can't remember. No—she's two years younger than us—that would make her fifteen.'

'And Lorna looks after you all?' Jimmy said, looking at Peter.

'That's right, sir.'

'For Heaven's sake don't call me "sir"! It makes me feel as if I had one foot in the grave. Jimmy's my name.'

'Oh, thanks.' Peter was pink with pleasure. 'And I say, if it wouldn't bore you, tell us something about your flying experiences.'

When Lorna came back with the tea they were hard at it. The twins were sitting on the floor listening with tense, concentrated expressions, and they were obviously impatient of her interruption, as Jimmy got to his feet when she came through the door. She looked at him reproachfully.

'I'm sorry,' he said. 'I couldn't help it.'

'I've a good mind not to give you any tea,' she threatened.

'You don't deserve it!'

'Oh Lorna, how can you?' Peke exclaimed. 'What do you think? Jimmy's actually been over Berlin!'

Lorna raised her eyebrows.

'Jimmy?' she questioned.

'Your humble servant,' Jimmy Braith interposed.

There was a challenge as well as a teasing implication in his tone. Lorna was disconcerted.

'I think . . . ' she started, but Jimmy interrupted her.

'Don't be pompous,' he begged. 'I'm enjoying myself so much and two of the family have befriended me. Why should you hold out?'

There was something appealing, almost irresistible, in his dark eyes and in the soft tones of his voice. She realised that he had a most attractive voice, and it might be hard to deny him anything on which he had set his heart. Yet some inner caution told her not to surrender too quickly to his swashbuckling methods. He was going too fast.

It would be wiser to be more cautious, to hold him at arm's length, and yet it was difficult. Lorna hesitated and was lost. Other women, older and more experienced than she, had found it easier to arrest an avalanche than to defy Jimmy's headlong impetuosity, where his own desires were concerned.

So Lorna said nothing while the twins swept the conversation out of her grasp by pressing food upon their hero.

'Cucumber sandwiches. Do have one.'

'And shortbread biscuits! I say, Lorna's made an effort as we've got a visitor.'

'You're embarrassing me,' Jimmy said.

'You needn't worry,' Lorna replied gaily. 'It's really an effort to save our jam ration.'

'I'll bring mine with me next time I come.'

The door of the sitting-room opened and the Rev. Arthur Overton came in. It was easy to see from the first glance at him where the children got their looks. He had almost Grecian features, and a square forehead from which his silver hair grew luxuriantly.

He had broad shoulders, the build and carriage of an athlete, and, although he looked thin and overworked, there was a twinkle in his eyes and a hint of irrespressible humour at the corner of his mouth.

'Lorna, my dear,' he said, 'I've lost my engagement book. Is it to-night or to-morrow that the W.I. are having their Whist Drive?'

'To-morrow, darling,' Lorna answered. 'Come and have your tea.'

'Oh, that's a good thing. I was thinking that I couldn't go to the First Aid Lecture, but now I can manage them both. Yes, I'll have some tea—I've got five minutes I think. Why are we having it in here?'

'Because we've got a visitor,' Lorna answered. 'Daddy, this is Squadron-Leader Braith—he is convalescing at the Hall.'

'I think I saw you there yesterday, sir,' Jimmy said, holding out his hand.

'How do you do. I am very glad to see you. Yes, I was at the Hall yesterday. How do you like this part of the world?'

'I have only been here a few days,' Jimmy answered, 'but I am beginning to alter my first impressions.'

He looked at Lorna as he spoke and in spite of herself, she felt the blood rising in her cheeks.

'Well, I'm afraid you may find it quiet and rather isolated,' the Vicar went on. 'Two facts for which at the moment, we are sincerely grateful.'

'I can't quite believe that,' Jimmy replied. 'They were telling me how lucky you had been as regards bombs.'

'Touch wood!'

The twins shouted at him simultaneously, and he bent down and touched the leg of his armchair.

'Are you as superstitious as all that?'

'I should think we are,' Peter said. 'Why, if it hadn't been for Peke seeing a horseshoe, we'd never have got on board the ship at Marseilles.'

'Marseilles!' Jimmy looked bewildered.

'When we were coming back from Italy last April. We

13

were staying out there with our aunt and she got the wind up because people told her Italy might be coming into the war and decided to ship us off home. We motored into France, but we'd left it a bit late and the roads were pandemonium.

'Anyhow, we got to Marseilles and we were all tired and hungry after the journey. I wanted to go down to the docks and see if there was any likelihood of getting on to a ship, but my aunt and Peke wanted to go to a hotel first for a wash and some food. Well, we couldn't make up our minds.

'We stopped the car and just then Peke saw a horseshoe pointing towards the docks, so we picked it up and took that road right away, and it was very lucky we did. We got on the last boat that was leaving—a coal barge—the people who came down to the quay after us were left behind.'

'You should have seen them when they got home,' Lorna interrupted. 'They were absolutely black! It took us a week of scrubbing to get them the right colour again!'

'It must have been an awful trip,' Jimmy said. 'I heard a bit about those barges.'

'It was frightfully exciting,' Peke answered. 'We enjoyed every minute of it, although we were terribly hungry. The sailors were perfectly marvellous to us and yet—would you believe it?—there was an old couple who came on board with a huge hamper and they never shared a mouthful with anyone. How we hated them!'

'I should have pushed their hamper overboard,' Jimmy said sympathetically.

'We would have if we could have got them away from it, but they never left it—not for a second! They even brought it up on deck when we were summoned to the boat stations.'

'Well, let's hope they lose their ration books and have to go short for months.'

'Oh, those sort of people never suffer.'

'I shouldn't be too sure of that,' the Vicar said gently. 'But most people act through ignorance rather than because they are deliberately ill intentioned.'

Lorna rose to take her father's empty cup and bent down to drop a light kiss on his forehead.

'You always find the best in everyone,' she said. 'You are an idealist, darling, and I have come to the conclusion that they are the happiest people in the world. They find so much perfection everywhere.'

'And talking of perfection,' Peter interrupted eagerly, 'what do you think of the new Stirling bomber, Jimmy? Have you flown one yet?'

Lorna groaned.

'Oh dear, he's off again!' she said to her father. 'It was fatal to introduce an airman into the house!'

'Good gracious me!—is that the right time?' the Vicar ejaculated as the clock on the mantelpiece chimed the half-hour. 'I must be off. I'm afraid I shall be a few moments late for supper, my dear, but don't wait for me.'

'We will wait and you must try to be punctual, Daddy. Your meeting is at eight o'clock and you've got to have a proper meal before you go.'

'I'll try—I'll try, I promise you,' the Vicar said, 'but I've got a lot to do before then.' He got up hurriedly. 'Good-bye, Squadron-Leader, I hope we shall see you again.'

'Thank you, sir. You will certainly find me here pretty often if you can put up with me.'

'Delighted, of course—delighted. Come any time you like.' The Vicar reached the door and then turned back. 'Oh, by the way, Lorna, I nearly forgot. I saw Michael this morning, and he asked if you could give him supper to-night. He's coming to the meeting with me and will be out this way—he's got an operation, I think, at the hospital.'

'Oh goodness! I am glad you remembered to tell me. I can't possibly make shepherd's pie do for all of us.' Lorna put her hand to her forehead and stood thinking. 'I expect there are some eggs—the women will have to have poached eggs.'

'Don't look so worried,' Jimmy said, 'and who's Michael?'

'Michael Davenport,' Peke answered, before Lorna could

speak. 'He's our doctor and Lorna's young man.'

'Oh, he is, is he?' Jimmy said, in a tone that sounded as if he were not too pleased by the information.

'Don't be so ridiculous, Peke! Don't take any notice of her. Michael is a very old friend of the family—I have known him for years. The children like to tease me, that is all.'

Lorna wondered even as she spoke, why she was so emphatic. She thought there was an expression of relief in Jimmy's eyes, then was ashamed with herself for thinking such things. She felt at that moment annoyed and distrustful of this stranger, who seemed to have found his place so quickly in their lives. She looked at the clock.

'It's getting late,' she said. 'I don't want to hurry you, but I'm sure you ought to be getting back to the Hall, and I have a lot to do.'

'Why . . . Lorna!'

The twins looked at her astounded.

'I'm afraid that sounds like my marching orders,' Jimmy said, getting to his feet. 'The least I can do is to withdraw with a good grace.'

'I am sorry,' Lorna said. 'I'm not really being rude, it's only that there is a lot to do. Please understand?'

She was pleading with him now, a little frightened that she had been unforgivably abrupt.'

'I understand.' His voice was caressing. 'And I will forgive you if you will walk as far as the orchard with me. I want to ask you a favour.

Lorna looked irresolute.

'Can't you ask me here?'

He shook his head.

'You ought to see me safely off the premises. Good-bye, twins. I shall see you soon.'

'You won't forget about those books you promised me?' Peter asked.

'Of course I won't—I'll bring them down to-morrow.'

'What's that?' Lorna asked.

'Only something I have promised to lend him,' Jimmy

replied lightly. 'I can easily walk down with them.'

Lorna knew instinctively that this was only an excuse to come again, and yet there was nothing she could say. Meekly, because she did not wish to protest in front of the children, she let herself be led into the garden.

'Well,' she asked, when they were out of earshot of the house. 'What is this important matter?'

'Don't look so severe, you frighten me.'

'Nonsense!'

'It's true. When you smile you are the most adorable thing I have ever seen. When you frown you remind me of some of my more austere relations—they have just the same disapproving manner.'

'Perhaps they have very good reasons for showing disapproval?'

'That sounds most uncharitable. I can't imagine why, since you know me so little, you should assume that there must be defects in my character. A character, I assure you, with the highest recommendations!'

Lorna dimpled at him.

'Aren't you just the tiniest bit conceited?'

'Frightfully. And at this moment I'm being presumptuous enough to believe that you would like to see me again.'

'It seems as though it might be inevitable.'

'It is quite inevitable,' Jimmy spoke seriously, dropping the note of idle banter.

Lorna looked at him in surprise.

'Why?' she asked innocently.

'I should have thought you could have guessed that,' Jimmy said, and instantly she felt the warm blood flooding her cheeks.

They had reached the gate leading from the garden into the orchard.

'Your methods are too swift for this part of the world,' Lorna said. 'You must remember that in Little Walton we are slow but sure.'

'I'm sure, all right,' Jimmy said. 'When can I see you to-morrow?'

'I haven't the slightest idea. I'm terribly busy.'

'What are you doing this evening? After dinner?'

'Nothing out of the ordinary. Why?'

'Then meet me. I will walk down here and we can talk.'

'Certainly not!'

Lorna spoke almost violently.

'Why not?' Jimmy insisted, his voice low and appealing. 'Why are you frightened.'

'I'm not frightened—I don't know what you mean. It's just . . . there's no point in doing such a thing.'

'There's lots of point, and you are afraid.'

'I'm not!' Lorna insisted, but she wouldn't meet his eyes and she knew he had spoken the truth. 'I must go,' she said quickly. 'Good-bye.'

She would have left him but he caught her hand.

'Come to-night,' he said. 'I shall wait for an hour. We have to be in by ten but at nine o'clock I shall be here waiting.'

'You're being ridiculous,' Lorna said, trying to free herself.

'I will try to convince you that I'm not. Good-bye, Lorna. Until nine o'clock.'

He raised her hand to his lips but swiftly she snatched it away from him.

'Then you will be wasting your time,' she said. 'I shall not come.'

She did not wait for his reply but turned towards the house, running through the shrubs and trees until she reached the lawn. Then, conscious that her heart was beating, not only with the exertion but with some strange, unaccountable sensation, she walked slowly and soberly into the house.

'How ridiculous!' she said out loud, as she shut the french windows behind her.

2

'Tell me all about him!'

Beth burst into the room where Lorna was changing her dress. She threw her hat and coat on the bed and sat on the arm of a chair, swinging her feet in their dusty shoes.

'Tell you about whom?' Lorna asked.

She was hooking her black dinner frock into place and had not glanced up at the entrance of her noisy younger sister.

'The airman, of course! The twins told me he had been here but all they could talk about was what aeroplanes he had flown. I want to know about him. Is he good-looking? How did you meet him? It would be just my luck to be out!'

Lorna finished fastening her dress.

'I met him when I was picking cherries in the orchard if you want to know,' she said quietly.

'Lorna! You mean to say you picked him up!'

'I did nothing of the sort,' Lorna said composedly, 'and where you get those vulgar expressions I can't think.'

'Oh, tell me about it, don't be a pig, Lorna! You know I'm dying to know.'

'Why are you so interested?' Lorna asked, although she knew the answer.

'Don't be silly! I'm not interested—I'm thrilled!' Beth replied. 'Why, there might even be a dance and we could ask him to go with us, or at any rate he can make a four at tennis—you know the twins never let me play.'

'He's wounded,' Lorna answered. 'You seem to have forgotten that fact, or he wouldn't have been here. He limps and he's got an arm in a sling. I don't think he'll be much use to you athletically.'

'How disappointing! But anyway, I want to see him. When's he coming again?'

'I've no idea,' Lorna replied untruthfully, and consoled herself with the explanation that it was 'for Beth's good.'

Beth was likely to be the problem child of the family. She was excitable, demonstrative, and at an age when she had just begun to take an intense and somewhat over-enthusiastic interest in the opposite sex.

In the last six months she had already lavished her un-requited affections upon the cashier at the bank, the organist who came from another village, and a young farmer who frequently rode past the house on market days. The latter, however, had been a short-lived affair, for the twins had learned that he had a wife and four children.

Beth had been teased unmercifully and had quickly look-ed round for someone else on whom to focus the affections of her exceedingly resilient heart.

At times Lorna found it rather difficult to cope with Beth. On the whole her brother and sisters accepted her control and authority as a matter of course. The twins were easy-going and were so wrapped up in themselves that the out-side world troubled them very little; but Beth had begun to show signs of revolt, and Lorna was half afraid of what might happen in the future.

Besides, Beth was going to be the beauty of the family, Lorna had no doubt about that. Even at fifteen she was al-most flamboyantly attractive. Her hair was fair like Lorna's, but it had an extra sheen of gold which gave it a somewhat brazen look at times; her eyes were almost preposterously blue, and her pink and white skin was of that matt quality which resisted the fiercest rays of the sun.

Beth's only detraction at the moment was her plumpness. It was only puppy fat and would undoubtedly disappear as she grew older, but it worried her a good deal and Lorna had to be very firm in seeing that she ate the right foods, and did not starve herself at mealtimes—often to indulge later in an orgy of snacks and sweets when a healthy appetite was a stronger motive than vanity.

The fact that Beth was always quite frank about her enthusiasms somewhat alleviated Lorna's anxiety. She was incapable of deception, and her family were never kept long in ignorance of her latest escapade—on the contrary, they grew heartily sick of listening to her confidences. Her gaiety and good temper made her a lovable person and her physical attractions often disarmed adverse criticism.

Smiling now, Lorna good-humouredly gave her a short and somewhat abridged version of the afternoon's events.

'I think it's too thrilling,' Beth exclaimed, 'exactly like the beginning of a novel. Oh Lorna!—aren't you simply dying to see him again?'

'I'm not,' Lorna replied, 'and I think it exceedingly un-likely that he will bother about us. I expect it was just curiosity which made him come the first time.'

She spoke indifferently, yet at once realised that she would be disappointed if her words proved true. She wanted to see Jimmy Braith again—wanted it very much.

'And why not?' she asked herself. 'It isn't as if we see so many people here that there is anything surprising in being interested in a stranger.'

'Do you think he's rich?' Beth asked dreamily.

'I don't think about it at all,' Lorna said snappily. 'Go and get ready for supper. Michael's coming.'

'I know. Daddy told me.'

'When did you see him? Is he back?'

'Yes, he came in just now as I was coming upstairs.'

'Oh, why didn't you tell me? He's early, and I particularly wanted a word with him. Go and get tidy.'

Lorna ran down the stairs. She opened the door of her father's study and found him sitting at his desk.

'You are early, darling. I wasn't expecting you till supper-time.'

'I got through quicker than I thought I should,' her father answered. He put down the papers he was reading and turned in his chair to look at her. 'How smart you are! Are you expecting another visitor?'

'Only Michael,' Lorna answered, 'and this dress is over two years old.'

'Is it? I didn't realise I'd seen it before,' her father said absently, 'but I hope you don't want any more clothes. I've just been looking at the bills.'

'I was afraid you had, darling, that's why I came down early—to see you. They are up again this month, but I couldn't help it. Beth had to have some new things, and the twins have grown out of all their shoes.'

The Vicar sighed.

'I know, I know, but there's the repairs to the roof and I've had to have a new tyre for my bicycle—Robinson just refused to mend the old one again.'

'I will try to be more economical next month,' Lorna promised, 'but it is difficult.'

'I know it is, dear, and I'm sorry you should be worried by it. You ought to be enjoying yourself, instead of struggling with housekeeping accounts.'

'I don't mind struggling with them, you know that,' Lorna said. She put her hand affectionately on her father's shoulder. 'What a nuisance money is!'

'Or the lack of it,' the Vicar sighed. 'Everything seems to be getting more expensive—and by the way, Lorna, I want to speak to you about the twins.'

'Yes?' Lorna drew a sharp breath—she knew what was coming.

'I saw Mr. Maidstone this afternoon. He says that Peter is doing very badly indeed; he's not preparing his homework, and both he and Peke are inattentive and unpunctual. You know, Lorna, we were lucky—very lucky indeed—to get Mr. Maidstone to take the twins on. They really must make an effort.'

'I know, Daddy. I'm afraid they have been very tiresome

lately, but you see all Peter wants to do is to get into the Air Force.'

'But he's too young.'

'I know that, but he thinks he can get in if he lies about his age. I've said that if he does you will fetch him home again at once. It's the only way to stop him.'

'It's ridiculous, of course. Why, they're only just seventeen! He must wait a year. In the meantime, he won't pass the pilot's examination unless he works a bit harder.'

'I have told him that,' Lorna said, 'but he does work at the things he thinks will be useful. He and Peke study the most extraordinary books containing information on flying and aeroplanes, while for the ordinary lessons which Mr. Maidstone gives them, they have no interest, and therefore make no progress.'

'I'd better speak to them,' the Vicar said. 'Perhaps we should have been wiser to send Peter to school. If only they could have finished their education before this happened!'

'Yes, I know,' Lorna commiserated. 'It couldn't have come at a more inconvenient time.'

'After all, we'd always relied on your aunt. I remember when the twins were born she said to me—"I'm going to be Godmother to both of them and I'm going to be responsible for them all through their lives."'

'She knew then that she could never have any children herself, and she was generous, extraordinarily generous. As you know, up to now Peke and Peter have had advantages which I could never give you or Beth.'

Lorna sighed.

'If only Aunt Edith hadn't married an Italian it would have been all right. Do you think she will be all right in Italy? —it must be very uncomfortable for her, being English.'

'She's lived there for so many years,' the Vicar answered, 'but, as you say, it must be very uncomfortable for her and very hard. Her husband and all his relations will be fighting against us.'

'Uncle Leonie always hated the Germans. I wonder what he really thinks about it?'

'He was a member of the Fascist Party,' her father replied. 'He had to be.'

'Well anyway, they can't help us now. It's a blow, but we'll manage somehow. Don't you worry, darling.' Lorna bent and kissed her father, then looked at the clock standing on his writing desk. 'Supper will be ready in two or three minutes. I wonder if Michael's come?'

She opened the door and at that moment heard a car draw up outside.

'Here he is,' she called.

She moved towards the front door, but before she could get there it had opened and, without ceremony, Michael came in. He was not tall and he had the quick, agile movements of a man who is driven hard by his own eager vitality. He held out his hands to Lorna, hands which, with their long, sensitive fingers, were obviously those of a born surgeon.

'I'm sorry to be late, but I couldn't get away a moment sooner.'

'But you're not late.'

'From my point of view I am! I promised myself at least half an hour's rest in the garden—now we've got to swallow our supper and be off to this confounded meeting.'

'Must you go?' Lorna asked, sympathetically.

'I'm afraid so. They've sent down someone from headquarters to instruct the whole area regarding First-Aid Posts, Emergency Hospitals, and goodness knows what else! Your father and I have both got to be there.'

'What a nuisance! Never mind, come into the sitting-room. You look tired.'

'I am,' Michael put his hands up to his eyes.

'You smell of anaesthetic, too,' Lorna said, wrinkling her nose. 'Was it a bad operation?'

'Yes, rather tricky, but I think it's been successful, and that's the main thing.'

'The Bannister child?' the Vicar asked, as he came out of

his study and followed Michael into the sitting-room.

'Oh, hello sir! Yes, it was.'

'And the operation was successful? Good for you, Michael. I felt you were the one person who could save him.'

'Thank you.' Michael smiled at the compliment, and for a moment his tiredness dropped away from him. He looked young—almost boyish.

He was working, as were so many doctors all over the country, at a rate which was practically beyond the strength of any man, however resilient. Before the war Michael, attached to one of the great London hospitals, was also collecting for himself a growing practice of private patients. But his father, who had been the beloved General Practitioner at Little Walton for over fifty years, had had a stroke.

There was just a chance that the old man might recover —anyway, it would have been cruel to move him, or to let him think that his career was ended. Michael had come home to take his father's place, keeping up with some of his hospital work in London by going there twice a week.

Then had come the war, and the only other doctor in the neighbourhood had gone off to active service; on Michael had fallen, not only the general work, but the care of several convalescent homes which opened in the district, and also the medical attention needed by thousands of evacuees who had been brought to that part of the country from a great industrial town some thirty miles away.

It was certainly an experience, but it was doubtful if anyone could continue to work as Michael was working without a rest, and without some assistance. He was only thirty, but he looked at least eight or nine years older.

The Vicarage children had known him since they had been in their perambulators and Lorna had always looked on him as an older brother; at least, she thought she had, until just lately the relationship between them had seemed to enter a new phase. But she told herself that she was being fanciful—Michael had not changed, he was only tired and overworked.

The sound of a gong came booming to their ears. It was being beaten by Peter, who put all his strength into it. Peke, changed from her grey flannel trousers into a blue linen dress, came into the room as the gong ceased its reverberations.

'Minnie says supper's ready.'

'We gathered that,' Lorna said. 'I wish Peter wouldn't make such a noise.'

'Well, come along,' said the Vicar. 'We mustn't be late.'

As the little party moved towards the dining-room, Beth came down the stairs like a whirlwind.

'I'm not late,' she cried pantingly, as she jumped the last three stairs and landed at her father's feet. 'Hello, Michael! I've been making myself beautiful for you.'

'So I see,' Michael answered, looking with amusement at Beth's hair, which had been pinned laboriously into small curls on top of her head. Lorna did not say anything, but she noted with disapproval that Beth had been at her lipstick again, and that there was a plentiful coating of powder on her small, tip-tilted nose.

'I must remember to lock it up,' she thought, although once before when she had done that Beth, quite irrepressible, had used cochineal on her lips, and made the most of some flour stolen from the kitchen when Minnie was not looking.

There was a homely meal laid in the dining-room. A small —very small—shepherd's pie was waiting to be served in front of the Vicar's place, while at the other end of the table there were three poached eggs on very large pieces of toast.

'Lorna, my dear, can I offer you some of this?' her father asked.

Lorna shook her head.

'No, thank you, darling. That's for you, Michael, and Peter.'

She helped the girls to the poached eggs; Peter passed round the salad which was standing on the side table.

'It's a good thing you didn't come a few hours earlier, Michael,' Beth said. 'You'd have had your nose put out of joint. They had a visitor this afternoon—a real visitor.'

'What do you mean by "a real visitor"?' Michael asked. 'Am I not included in that category?'

'Of course you're not,' Beth replied scornfully. 'We know you so well it's no great treat to see you, but Lorna picked up an airman this afternoon. I wish I'd been at home.'

'A very nice young fellow, I thought,' the Vicar said. 'I hope we shall see him again.'

'You will,' Peter answered. 'He's coming down to-morrow with a book for me. He says he's got one with every type of plane in it.'

'Coming to-morrow!' Beth exclaimed. 'Ooh, Lorna!— and you said you didn't know when you'd see him again!'

In spite of a great effort to control it, Lorna felt herself flushing. She was conscious of Michael's eyes on her—eyes which seemed to hold some strange expression. She felt he was disapproving, and yet surely there could be no reason for that?

The children chattered on; Peter vainly trying to keep the conversation to airman and aeroplanes, Beth demanding whether she could stay at home in case the Airman came early—or leave school earlier than usual so as not to miss him should he come to tea—but Michael said very little.

It was only when the meal was over and they left the dining-room, that Lorna found herself alone with him in the garden.

'Who is this stranger that's caused so much excitement?' Michael asked.

'I know nothing about him,' Lorna replied, 'except that he's at the Hall. I wonder you haven't seen him.'

'I think I have,' Michael answered.

'His name's Braith—Squadron-Leader Braith.'

'Then I have seen him. I remember. His arm's damaged— nothing serious, but it will take a little time to put right.'

'You know how ridiculous the children are about anyone new,' Lorna said. 'I suppose they get tired of seeing the same people all the time.'

'And you—do you get tired of old friends?'

'Of course not. How ridiculous you are!'

'I don't know,' Michael answered, frowning as he would sometimes do when considering a particularly knotty problem. 'There's an old saying, you know—"familiarity breeds contempt".'

'And who is likely to arouse my contempt?' Lorna questioned. 'Daddy?—the children? I'm certainly familiar with them.'

'And with me,' Michael suggested.

'Oh, Michael, you know how we love you being here. Why, don't you remember when you came back—although we were awfully sorry about your father—what a welcome we gave you? The children planned for weeks. . . .'

'Never mind about the children,' Michael said. 'I was thinking about you. You haven't answered my question.'

'The question as to whether you are tired of seeing me—or whether you've got used to me.'

'I must be getting awfully stupid,' Lorna said, 'but I don't really see what you are getting at. How could I possibly get tired of you? Why Michael, you mean as much to me as . . . well, who shall I say? . . . as Peter—almost as much as Daddy. You are one of us.'

'So that's what you feel about me?' Michael's voice was low, and he didn't sound particularly pleased.

'I couldn't say anything more complimentary, could I?' Lorna asked. 'What's the matter, Michael?' She slipped her arm through his. 'Have you got a fit of the blues?'

'No, it's just . . .' He hesitated and put his hand over hers as it lay on his arm. She felt the warm strength of his fingers and then, just when he was about to speak, there came a call from the house.

'Michael! We must be going.'

'I've got to go, I suppose. Listen, Lorna. Some time I want to talk to you. There's something I want to tell you.'

'Well, any time suits me,' Lorna answered. 'I'm always here. Don't look so worried.'

'Come on, Michael. Daddy says you must go.'

It was Beth shouting now, and Michael started to run towards the house.

'Good-bye, Lorna.'

'Good-bye, bless you. Don't let Daddy be late.'

She watched him disappear through the french windows;
then she turned towards the tennis court, picking up a ball
from the long grass where it had escaped notice.

'I wonder what's the matter with Michael?' she thought.
'He seems queer to-night. Perhaps his father's worse. It must
be awful living in that house with the old man a helpless
invalid and only the housekeeper to look after them both. I
hope he isn't worrying again about going to the war—he
can't be spared.'

The church clock struck eight. Lorna went into the house
to find that the twins were already immersed in books on
aviation. Beth was looking at herself in the mirror over the
mantelpiece.

'Do you like my hair done like this, Lorna?' she asked.

'If you want my frank opinion, I don't,' Lorna replied. 'It
makes you look ridiculous—like a child dressed up in its
mother's clothes.'

'I thought it made me look older,' Beth said, somewhat
crestfallen.'

'It looks much nicer the way you do it ordinarily,' Lorna
answered. 'And, by the way, Beth, I wish you wouldn't bor-
row my lipstick—you know you're too young to make up.'

'It isn't really my colour. If you would give me enough
money to have one of my own it would look far better. I need
more of an orange shade.'

'You don't need any at all,' Lorna retorted. 'It looks ridiculous on a child of fifteen.'

Beth groaned.

'I wish you wouldn't be so old-fashioned, Lorna dear.
The prunes and prisms style is all right for you—in fact it is
rather becoming, but I'm quite different, and you can't expect to treat me in the same way as you treat Peke, for instance.'

'Thank goodness Peke doesn't want to mess about with herself,' Lorna replied, 'and she's two years older than you.'

'Oh, Peke wants to be a boy, we all know that. I've never wanted to alter my sex. I think women can have all the power they want in the world by guiding and inspiring a man. I mean to be the shadow behind the throne.'

Lorna laughed.

'Good gracious, Beth! Are you aspiring to Royalty? You'll have to hurry up—there aren't many kings left.'

'I'm speaking figuratively, of course,' Beth said with dignity, 'but I wouldn't expect you to understand.'

She walked out of the room with what she imagined was a dramatic exit of offended dignity.

Lorna smiled as she picked up her knitting, but a few seconds later her thoughts were not on Beth. She was thinking of Jimmy Braith, wondering whether he would keep his word, wondering if, when nine o'clock struck, he would be waiting in the orchard.

It was ridiculous, of course, even to think about it. It was unlikely that he would be there; unlikely, not only that he would be able to get away, but that he would trouble to hang about on the off chance that she might change her mind and keep the appointment which he had forced upon her.

The time went ticking by. Peke and Peter with their heads close together spoke in quiet voices. Lorna let her knitting drop on her lap.

She looked out of the window; the curtains were undrawn, there was a golden glow in the west, and the branches of the trees were silhouetted against a vivid sky. The first evening star glittered above the church tower.

Nine o'clock! As the hour struck she felt her heart beat quickly and her hands trembled. It was ridiculous, of course! She picked up her knitting and started to work feverishly, but at the end of the row she glanced up again at the clock on the mantelpiece.

It was only a few minutes past nine. She wondered if he were there. What would he do? Would he walk about or would he sit on the fallen tree trunk where they had sat that afternoon?

What a nice voice he had—soft and almost caressing in its tones, and somehow it was in complete contradiction to his eyes! Lorna knew she was half afraid of looking at him. No . . . not afraid exactly—shy. It seemed to her that no man had ever looked at her with that mixture of boldness and undisguised admiration.

It made her feel strange—gave her an inexplicable feeling of guilt. But that, of course, was ridiculous. There was nothing wrong in meeting—or, indeed, liking—this young man. Her father approved of him—why, he had said so at supper!

A quarter past nine! Surely time had never contrived to move so slowly. It seemed to her as if two or three hours must have passed since she had last looked at the clock. Would he really wait the whole hour? It would seem long to him. The mosquitoes might be bad in the orchard, too, but then he could smoke. . . .

The sun was sinking; soon it would be twilight—that mystical, magical moment before night came, when the sky would still be translucent, although the trees and shrubs would seem enveloped in purple darkness.

Lorna felt restless. She got up and walked about the room, re-arranging the flowers that she had picked that morning, tidying some books which had lain for several weeks on the table in the corner waiting for someone to put them away in the bookcase.

Half-past nine! The silvery chime of the clock quivered on the air and then she knew that she must go.

'To satisfy my curiosity,' she told herself; but her eyes were shining as she slipped through the french windows and walked slowly across the lawn towards the orchard.

3

There was no one there.

Lorna felt almost sick with disappointment. She stood looking at the fallen trees on which she and Jimmy had sat that afternoon; and the orchard was suddenly the emptiest and loneliest place she had ever known.

The darkness under the trees and by the overgrown hedge was no longer filled with mystery and romance, instead it seemed to her somewhat sinister, cold, and creepy. She felt herself shiver, then tried to be philosophical about it.

'It's only what I expected,' she thought.

Yet, as a sop to her outraged pride, she began considering the possibilities of a legitimate excuse to account for his non-appearance. Any reason rather than indifference.

'Well, I hope this will teach you a lesson—to be more sensible in future,' she muttered to herself.

She turned back towards the gate by which she had entered the orchard; then something attracted her attention. It was the crimson glow of a cigarette—a cigarette being smoked on the other side of the hedge.

He had come after all! She hesitated, and then making up her mind turned swiftly towards the gate—but it was too late!

'Lorna!'

She heard him call her name. The next minute he had climbed through the gap in the hedge and was striding across the intervening space between them, ducking his head every few steps to avoid the low boughs of the fruit trees.

'Why was I such a fool as to come!' Lorna thought to herself hotly.

Flight now would be undignified and she could only stand her ground with seeming indifference.

'So you did come.'

He held out his hand towards her invitingly.

'I might say the same to you,' Lorna retorted.

He had reached her now and she could see him smiling, and his eyes, bold and dark, looking down into hers.

'Are you angry because I'm late? Don't be—I couldn't help it. The Commandante fussed round me like an old hen after dinner—I couldn't get away from her.'

His voice was pleading. Lorna felt her anger evaporating.

'I didn't mean to come myself.'

'But you did.'

'Yes, I was curious. I couldn't believe that you really meant to wait here for a full hour."

'I was prepared to wait till midnight if necessary.'

'That's untrue. You've got to be in by ten o'clock.'

'That's where you're wrong,' Jimmy said triumphantly. 'Just in case you were kind to me, I got someone to promise to let me in whatever time I got back.'

'You mean you will creep in without the nurses knowing?'

'Exactly.'

'But won't you get into a terrible row if you're caught?'

'Terrible, I expect! But I won't be. I'm very lucky.'

'You mustn't take risks. It isn't worth it, really it isn't.'

'That's for me to judge. Come and sit down. I want to talk to you.'

'Oh . . . I can't stop, I've got to see the children go to bed. At any rate, I don't want to be responsible for your playing truant. You must go back.'

'Still afraid of me?' Jimmy asked, his voice amused.

Lorna did not answer; instead, she walked across the grass towards the fallen tree. She sat down determinedly.

'Five minutes,' she said.

'We'll see about that. Round one to Jimmy Braith!'

'I'm not fighting you—I'm only trying to be sensible.'

'Do you always do the sensible things in life?'

He sat down, stretching out his long legs.

'Don't we all try to?'

'Most emphatically, no! I, for instance, dislike all sensible things, all things that are good for me, and all the people who tell me things that they think I ought to know. I like excitement, irresponsibility, adventure, and, of course—love.'

Lorna was silent.

'Well,' Jimmy challenged, 'haven't you got anything to say to that. What do you think about love?'

'I don't know much about it.'

'No? What about your doctor friend? Isn't he in love with you?'

'Of course he's not!' Lorna spoke emphatically. 'Why, Michael's one of the family, he's like a brother to me—funnily enough, I was telling him that this evening.'

'And what did he say? Was he pleased?'

'Yes . . . I think so . . .' Lorna hesitated.

Had Michael been pleased? Supposing, just supposing, he hadn't wanted her to think of him as a brother? But no —it was absurd. She mustn't let this newcomer put ridiculous ideas into her head.

'I've known Michael since I was a baby.'

'And doubtless he appreciated you at that age,' Jimmy answered, 'but you know, Cherry Ripe, you're a very beautiful young woman now.'

Lorna was glad that the deepening twilight hid the colour which came into her cheeks.

'Thank you,' she said shyly. 'I wish I believed you.'

'But Good Heavens!—are there no men in Little Walton? —or are they all blind? Don't you really know how lovely you are?'

Jimmy bent towards her; he was looking into her face, his eyes were compelling hers. Suddenly Lorna was frightened . . . he was too near. There was a growing tension between them, a feeling of breathlessness, which she half desired, half feared. . . . She sprang to her feet.

'I must go,' she said. 'The children will wonder where I am. It was nice of you to come, but I'd feel terrible if you got into trouble over it. Do go back—please.'

She was speaking quickly, the words coming almost wildly from between her lips. She had a feeling that Jimmy was enjoying her agitation. He put out his hand and took hers.

'If I let you go now, will you come again to-morrow night?'

Lorna shook her head.

'We mustn't make a habit of this.'

'You darling little prude, we won't. There will be lots more amusing things I shall want to do with you than sitting in an orchard; but for the moment—well, just for the moment—the orchard must serve.'

Lorna felt as if everything he said and did was beyond her comprehension. Everything was moving too fast; she seemed to be completely losing control of the situation.

'Anyway, I must go now,' she persisted obstinately.

'I am afraid,' Jimmy said quietly.

'Afraid?' Lorna was genuinely surprised.

'You're like the will-o'-the-wisp—I think that you'll vanish and I shall find that I've been dreaming. Was it only this afternoon we met under this very tree? It seems as if I must have known you for centuries, that you are a part of my life, and yet I am afraid of losing you—of finding when to-morrow morning comes, that you have disappeared.'

His words seemed to wind a spell of enchantment around her.

'I shall still be here.' Her voice was low, hardly above a whisper.

'You promise me that?'

She was looking up at him, her head thrown back a little. It was getting dark; their features appeared blurred and indistinct, and yet both were so intensely conscious of the other's physical presence that the rest of the world was forgotten. Only they remained—man and woman, face to face.

'You won't forget me? Promise that too.'

'I promise.'

'I shall dream of you, Cherry Ripe.'

His voice was like the murmur of the waves, she felt hypnotised by it, drawn towards him by some magnetic force stronger than her will-power. They were so near to each other; Jimmy's hand had tightened on hers until his grip was almost painful. Lorna knew she was trembling, she knew, too, that she was waiting . . . waiting. . . . Then the church clock struck!

Boom! The first note broke the spell. Abruptly she drew back from him.

'I am going now.'

Her voice sounded strange to her own ears yet it was no longer a whisper, no longer pulsating in harmony with the throbbing of her heart.

'Good-night, Jimmy. I hope you get in safely.'

She was gone. There was a faint murmur of her skirts over the long grass and then she was lost in the darkness of the shrubs. He heard the gate shut behind her and he was alone.

He stood for a moment watching the shadows into which she had vanished, then with some difficulty he lit a cigarette with one hand, climbed from the orchard into the field, and started off towards the Hall. He was smiling, and after a little while, he began to hum tunefully one of the latest dance tunes.

Lorna stood on the terrace in front of the house. She looked across the garden towards the church tower, dark and solid against the sky. The chimes of the clock were silent now, and yet they still seemed to vibrate on the air. Ten o'clock.

The world was silent and still, the only movement in the garden was the swooping and circling of the bats. Lorna stood motionless. She was not thinking, she was feeling for the first time in her twenty-one years the awakening of her own heart.

Never before had she been aware of such emotions. She

36

was half ashamed, half afraid, and yet a wonder and a glory had appeared in the world which would not be denied.

'Is this wrong?' she asked, but felt that nothing so poignantly lovely, so utterly beautiful, could be anything but right and good. It was beyond words, it defied expression.

Lorna turned towards the house because she felt she could bear no more. She must get back to normality. She opened the french windows. The twins were where she had left them, sitting on the sofa, books scattered around them.

'Where's Beth?'

'I think she's gone out—for a walk or something,' Peke answered.

Lorna started. Supposing Beth had seen her go to the orchard and then followed her? But it was unlikely. It was silly of her to be afraid.

'It's the first time,' Lorna thought, 'that I've ever had a secret. I want to keep it to myself.'

'Bedtime,' she said aloud. 'And put away your books to-night. I had an awful job clearing them up this morning.'

'All right.'

Obediently the twins started to collect their things.

'I wonder where Beth is?' Lorna worried, but at that moment the door opened and Beth came in. 'Oh, here you are. I've just been talking about you—where have you been?'

'For a walk.'

'You sound mysterious. Where did you walk to?'

It was impossible for Beth to keep anything to herself.

'If you really want to know,' she said defiantly, 'I walked up towards the Hall. I thought I might get a glimpse of the handsome Squadron-Leader.'

'Which way did you go?' Lorna asked, not looking at Beth. She was unnecessarily tidying the ornaments on the mantelpiece.

'By the road, of course, and up the drive. If I'd met any-body I should have said I was taking the right-of-way through to Great Walton.'

Lorna felt herself relax in relief.

'Well, did you meet anyone?' she asked gaily.

'Not a soul,' Beth replied. 'It's my belief that they put those wretched men to bed at nine o'clock, tuck them up and pull down the blinds.'

'You'd better tell Michael to give strict instructions that they are to be paraded for your inspection every evening,' Peter said. 'Honestly, Beth, I wish you'd lay off. You've got the whole village laughing at you as it is.'

'I don't care what the village think,' Beth retorted, 'and if you were a decent sort of brother you'd have some boy friends to bring home, instead of hanging around with a twin sister all the time.'

'Well, Peter's friends wouldn't think anything of you,' Peke said hotly, rising in gallant defence of her twin. 'Any friends we have would be interested in sensible things—not taken up with a lot of silly lovesick little girls!'

'Now, children, that's enough,' Lorna interposed, knowing of old that these arguments generally ended in blows and tears. 'Leave her alone, twins, and come to bed. And Beth, as you're late you'll have to hurry—you know you're supposed to be in bed at a quarter to ten.'

'I'm sick of all the things I'm supposed to be!' Beth was despondent now—the inevitable reaction from buoyancy and defiance.

'Oh, come along, old thing.' Lorna put her arm round her shoulders. 'I tell you what we'll do. If you undress quickly we'll look through my Weldon's Pattern Book and see how you want that new cotton dress made up. I've got the material—it arrived this morning.'

'What—the one with the little red berries on it? Could they get it? I am glad.'

'Yes, that's the one.'

Lorna walked upstairs. She was not listening to Beth's eager and detailed description of how she wanted her new dress made, she was thinking of Jimmy's voice when he called her 'Cherry Ripe'.

'Now hurry,' she said absent-mindedly to Beth, as they parted at the top of the stairs. 'Come along to my room when you're undressed and don't forget your teeth.'

'You'd think I was five instead of fifteen!' Beth grumbled, but calling, 'I shan't be a jiffy.'

She swung into her bedroom, slamming the door behind her. The twins were half-way up the stairs.

'Did you remember to bolt the windows?' Lorna asked. That was recognised as being Peter's job.

'No, I forgot.'

'I'll do it,' Lorna said, 'I want to go down again. I've got to leave a note in the kitchen to remind Minnie that Daddy's got an early service to-morrow—she always forgets Wednesdays. By the way, did you stoke up the boiler this evening?'

Peter nodded.

'Right to the top. It ought to last till the morning easily.'

'It will if you don't draw off too much to-night. Don't forget, Peke, and tell Beth she can't have a bath. It's no use trusting her, and Daddy likes a bath in the morning, even if it is only lukewarm.'

'Right-oh!' Peke said, going towards Beth's room.

Lorna bolted the drawing-room windows.

'I'd better draw the curtains in the study,' she thought, 'in case Daddy goes in there.'

She knew that her father, in his usual absent-minded way, was quite capable of working till late at night with the lights full on and the windows unscreened. The wardens were used to his idiosyncracies, and on more than one occasion had hurried to warn him; but Lorna was always afraid that sooner or later they would be fined.

She had just finished when she heard Michael's car outside, and a moment later her father opened the front door.

'Here we are, my dear!' he said. 'We're not too late, are we. Fortunately, our lecturer was staying with the Colonel and was warned that we were early birds; so he stopped on the stroke of nine-thirty.'

'What have you been doing since?' Lorna asked.

'Gossiping,' Michael said, coming through the front door, 'and it's made me thirsty. Is there such a thing as a glass of beer about.'

'Of course there is, and Daddy, I'll get you your milk. Will you have it hot or cold?'

'Cold, please.'

'Well, go into the sitting-room and I'll get it for you.'

'Let me come and help you?' Michael suggested.

'Yes, do,' Lorna replied. 'The beer's in the cellar because it's cool down there and, quite frankly, I'm terrified of fetching it! Minnie said she saw a rat yesterday which was as big as a rabbit!'

'Nonsense! Minnie must have been sampling the beer herself.'

'Oh Michael!' Lorna exclaimed. 'You know Minnie's a lifelong abstainer!'

'I shall take the greatest pleasure in prescribing a strong dose of alcohol three times a day next time she calls me in,' Michael answered. 'She deserves a few pleasures in her old age after taking care of you children all these years!'

'Forty-two next month,' Lorna interposed. 'At least, she's been with the family that time. Now don't make a noise or Minnie will think it's burglars. You go down to the cellar while I get Daddy's milk from the kitchen.'

Lorna poured out a glass of milk from the big muslin-covered jug in the cool larder. Michael met her at the door of the cellar; he was brushing a cobweb from his eyes and in his hands he was holding a bottle of beer.

'You'll find a glass in the dining-room,' Lorna said. 'Do you want anything to eat?'

'No thanks, I'm only thirsty.'

'Thank goodness for that! I don't think there's a thing in the house! The children are like locusts these days—I can't keep a thing.'

Michael was in the dining-room.

'I can't find any glasses.'

'In the sideboard, silly!' Lorna called. 'Look, I'll show you.'

'I've found them!'

He held up one triumphantly just as she came through the door.

'You ought to know where they are by this time,' she said teasingly; but he was not attending—he was looking at her and there was once again that strange expression on his face which she did not understand.

'A new dress?' he asked. 'I like it.'

'What's the matter with everyone round here?' Lorna questioned in genuine surprise. 'I've worn this dress for two years and if you've seen it once, you've seen it a hundred times, and yet Daddy thought it was new this evening, too.'

'Perhaps it's our clumsy way of paying you a compliment!'

'In which case—"Thank you kindly, sir, she said."'

'Do you like compliments, Lorna?'

'Sometimes. It depends who makes them.'

Lorna's face was serious now, her thoughts wandering far away from Michael. They were both silent, then Michael spoke.

'Lorna.' His voice was sharp.

Lorna jumped.

'Good gracious!' she said. 'How you startled me! I nearly upset Daddy's milk. Come on—he's waiting for it.'

She hurried away. Michael followed her; he was frowning.

'Here you are, darling,' Lorna said, putting the milk down beside her father. He was sitting in a deep armchair, and he looked tired.

'I wish we hadn't had to give up the car,' Lorna said suddenly. 'All this bicycling is too much for you, Daddy, isn't it Michael?'

'Far too much,' Michael agreed. 'I've been reading your father the Riot Act all the way from the meeting, but he won't listen.'

'I am a little tired this evening,' the Vicar confessed, 'and yet there seems to be more to do every day, and this idea of a Nursery Hostel is going to take a lot of organising.'

'What's that?' Lorna asked.

'The authorities at Melchester have approached us with the idea of forming a Nursery Hostel here where the workers can leave their children—some of the mothers who go daily to work or those who return for the week-ends. There will be two or three resident nurses, but the rest of the assistance must be found locally.'

'What a good idea!' Lorna exclaimed. 'I'd love to help. Do you think I could?'

'You are doing quite enough as it is,' Michael said gravely. 'You are the mainstay of the family, Lorna; that ought to be enough for you.'

'Oh, but the twins and Beth are nearly grown up now,' Lorna replied. 'It was different when Mummy first died. Beth was small, then, but now I feel they don't want me, except to see that their meals are on the table and their clothes mended, and Minnie can do that.'

'And what about your Girl Guides, the Sunday School, the Knitting Party, and all those other miscellaneous organisations to which you belong?'

'You make me sound indispensable.'

'You are.'

'That's only too true,' the Vicar interposed. 'My eldest daughter is rather a wonderful little person, Michael.'

'I appreciate that, sir.'

The two men's eyes met for a moment and the Vicar sighed.

'Sometimes I wonder if I ought to let her do so much. I'm sure her mother would have disapproved of my allowing her to shoulder so many responsibilities.'

'Will you stop talking about me as if I weren't here?' Lorna interrupted. 'Daddy darling, I couldn't be happier or enjoy life more if I tried—and as for you, Michael, you are a croaking old woman! You're always saying—"Don't do too much,"—"Take things easy,"—"Have a quiet lie down with an aspirin." It's becoming second nature to you—in fact, it's an infectious bedside manner. Just stop it for once and say—"Go ahead, Lorna, do anything you like!"'

Michael laughed.

'All right, you win. But I warn you if you volunteer for the Nursery Hostel, I shall say that I consider you an unsuitable and irresponsible person to take over the care of innocent children.'

Lorna turned to her father.

'Darling, he's slandering me!'

'I'm afraid I support him in this,' the Vicar answered. 'You've got quite enough to do at home, dear.'

Lorna would have protested, but at that moment the telephone rang.

'Oh bother? Who do you think that is for?'

'Me, I expect,' Michael said wearily.

'I suppose so,' Lorna answered. 'Triplets, at least! All right, don't either of you move—I'll answer it.'

She went into the hall and took the old-fashioned receiver off its hook. A moment later she reappeared.

'We're wrong, it's for Daddy. Lady Abbott wants to know if you can lunch on Sunday. Say yes, darling—she's a bore—but her food is good!'

'I'll go and talk to her,' the Vicar said.

Lorna sat down on the sofa.

'You must be relieved it isn't for you, Michael. You do look tired.'

'I'm all right. Lorna, if I get a chance to come in about tea-time to-morrow, will you be alone?'

'I expect so,' Lorna replied; yet instantly wondered if Jimmy would be there.

'There are too many children in this house,' Michael went on. 'I never get a chance to talk to you.'

'Well, the twins get back about four. I'm always alone immediately after lunch.'

'That's hopeless for me. Surgery hours.'

'Yes, of course. I'd forgotten. What do you want to tell me?'

'I can't tell you in a hurry. If I can't manage to-morrow afternoon, what about the evening?'

'Oh, I don't think that's any good,' Lorna answered quickly, 'the children are always here then.'

She felt guilty even as she said it, for already she was eagerly looking forward to the next meeting with Jimmy in the orchard.

'Well, I'll try to be here about tea-time,' Michael said. 'I'm sorry to be vague, but you know what it's like these days.'

He spoke hastily, for the Vicar's voice had ceased and there were sounds of his footsteps crossing the oak floor.

'I'll be waiting—full of curiosity,' Lorna promised.

'And now I must be going.' He got to his feet. 'Good night, Lorna.'

'Good night.'

The Vicar hadn't come in, something must have kept him in the hall. Michael hesitated a moment and then—as if he could not help himself but did it against his better judgment —he raised Lorna's hand sharply, almost roughly, to his lips. He kissed it and turned abruptly towards the door.

She heard her father's voice in the hall.

'Good night, Michael.'

'Good night, sir.'

She stood still, looking at the open door, bewildered and disturbed.

4

'Beth was late starting for school again to-day.'

Lorna spoke to Minnie, who was rolling out the pastry for a tart at the other side of the kitchen.

'I know she was,' Minnie replied. 'She was fiddling about with her hair; trying a new style, she told me.'

'Oh dear!' Lorna sighed. 'I wish she'd leave her hair alone. Even Daddy noticed how peculiar she looked the other day.'

'I said to her this morning—"Beauty's only skin deep, and if you paid as much attention to your soul as you do to your body the world would be a lot better off"—but for all the good it did, I might have been talking to a stone wall!'

Lorna laughed.

'Poor Minnie! Beth's the only one of the family who doesn't heed your sermons.'

'Where she gets her airs and graces from I can't think,' Minnie went on. 'Your darling mother was the loveliest girl I ever saw, and as natural as a baby. She never worried about her looks, and never wasted her time fiddle-faddling in front of a mirror!'

'And we certainly can't say Daddy's conceited. Just look at these shirts! He really will have to have some new ones.' Lorna held up the shirt she was ironing to show the darns near the collar, and how the cuffs had frayed past all repairing.

45

'Your father's a saint,' Minnie said, slapping the pastry over on the board and flouring it.

'I wish he weren't so worried about money,' Lorna sighed. 'How are we going to manage, Minnie, with everything getting more expensive every day? And that reminds me—you've been paying for things again. I won't have it, Minnie! You can't afford it any more than we can.'

'I don't know what you mean,' Minnie grunted.

'Oh yes, you do, you old humbug! This isn't the first time, and when I looked at the grocery bill I missed several things which I knew we had eaten; the pears, for instance, and those pots of shrimp paste we had for tea; so I asked Mr. Colbert and he told me the truth. Minnie, you're an angel, you always have spoilt us, but I won't allow you to beggar yourself. Heaven knows you get ridiculously small wages as it is!'

'And I don't want them. I told your father so, but he wouldn't listen.'

'I should think not, indeed.'

'Well, children have to eat—growing creatures need their victuals.'

'We get enough to eat, all right, and I won't have you spending your money on luxuries—but thank you, Minnie, all the same.'

She smiled across at the old woman, and there was no mistaking the affection in that glance.

Minnie had been nurse to the Vicarage children from the time they were born. Now it would have been difficult to imagine the household without her. Stout and grey-haired, she had an immense amount of energy, and the work she managed to do would have made many a younger girl hand in her notice.

Everyone, from the Vicar downwards, consulted and ultimately obeyed Minnie; and yet she never overstepped her position or neglected to impress upon the children that Lorna must take their mother's place as best she could and assume authority as the eldest of the family.

Peter was Minnie's favourite—for she made no secret of preferring boys to girls—and Peter was the only one who could coax her into changing her mind or altering what was in most cases an inflexible decision.

Minnie had been almost broken-hearted when the war had prevented the twins from continuing to enjoy the advantages of their aunt's generosity.

Minnie's efforts to provide them with more luxuries by paying for them herself, was in some way meant to atone for the privations Peter was experiencing by living in straitened circumstances at home.

Peter and Peke were still far better turned out than the rest of the family. Ironing Peke's exquisitely made underclothes, Lorna felt almost a pang of envy when she compared them with the inexpensive, home-made ones, which furnished her own wardrobe.

'Look at that embroidery,' she said to Minnie, holding up a lawn nightgown, beautifully worked in a drawn-thread design. 'The Nuns made that at a convent in which Aunt Edith was interested. Peke told me that even the smallest children could embroider too beautifully.'

'It's a pity she didn't learn to do it herself,' Minnie replied sharply, putting her pie carefully into the oven.

'Peke ought to have been a boy. Do you think she'll ever marry anyone and settle down? I can't imagine Peke without Peter perpetually in tow.'

'Time enough to think about that!' Minnie replied. 'You are the one that should be considering marriage.'

'I?' Lorna questioned. 'No chance of that Minnie, I've got too many other things to do.'

'There's nothing so important that it can't be put on one side for a husband—especially the right man.'

'I've got to meet him first.'

'Are you quite sure you haven't?'

Lorna put down the iron and looked up in surprise.

Why. Minnie, what are you hinting at? Whom are you suggesting that I should marry?'

'If your heart doesn't tell you, no words of mine will be any use,' Minnie replied, enigmatically.

'But I don't know any men. At least . . . there's Michael.'

'Exactly!'

Lorna laughed.

'Oh Minnie, how ridiculous you are—you're as bad as Beth! You know Michael doesn't think about me in that way. Why—he's like a brother!'

The words seemed to echo round the kitchen and come back to her. They had a familiar sound. Surely that was the second or third time she had said those very words in the past twenty-four hours? Lorna picked up her iron again.

'If you start match-making I shall run away and join the A.T.S. What is more, I shall tell Michael what you've said and make him laugh.

'I should,' Minnie said stolidly. 'See what he says to that!'

Lorna didn't reply. She was thinking that perhaps it might not be so easy to tell Michael. He had been strange, lately, and there was that something he kept wanting to tell her. She wondered what it was. Oh well, he was coming to tea—she'd know that evening.

Poor old Minnie, she loved a wedding, but not even for Minnie's sake could she consider Michael as a prospective lover. She might as well think about marrying Peter or Daddy!

She moved the iron and realised it was too hot. She turned to switch off the power and then stood staring at a sudden apparition in the doorway—Jimmy!

'Can I come in?' he asked gaily. 'I've been ringing the front door bell for some time, and as nobody answered, I thought I'd do a bit of exploring.'

'There now!' Minnie exclaimed. 'I meant to telephone the electrician yesterday, and forgot all about it.'

'I'm sorry,' Lorna stammered, but Jimmy was smiling at her and she regretted the fact that she was wearing the faded overall and silk handkerchief round her head in which she

48

did her housework in the mornings.

He came into the kitchen.

'I've never seen anyone so industrious. You're always working!'

'There's a lot to be done. We don't usually expect visitors till the afternoon.'

'I know, but as an excuse I have come bearing gifts. I thought you might like to ask me to lunch, and anyway I'm coming to tea, so I have brought my rations. Wait a minute.' He went out of the kitchen into the passage. 'Hi, driver! Bring in that hamper.'

His voice echoed down the stone-flagged passage. Lorna met Minnie's surprised eyes and felt inexplicably guilty.

'He won't be a minute,' Jimmy said, coming in again.

'By the way,' Lorna said quickly, 'I don't think you've met Minnie before. She's much the most important person in the household. Minnie, this is Squadron-Leader Braith. He's convalescing at the Hall.'

'How do you do?' Jimmy held out his hand and smiled at Minnie who, like most of her sex, found it impossible not to smile back.

'May I stay for lunch?' he asked her. 'I realise you are the person from whom I must beg an invitation.'

Minnie looked at him appraisingly.

'It's rissoles,' she said warningly, but there was a twinkle in her eye.

'Oh no it isn't!'

There were heavy footsteps in the passage and a chauffeur came staggering into the kitchen carrying a large wicker hamper.

'Put it down there,' Jimmy commanded, 'and thank you for your trouble.' He slipped something into the man's hand, then turned to Lorna. 'Won't you unpack it?'

'But what is it?' Lorna questioned. 'I don't understand—what does all this mean?'

'Exactly what I've said,' he answered. 'I want to stay to lunch and I realise that you and Minnie won't welcome an

49

extra mouth in wartime, so I've been shopping this morning
—by telephone, I must admit—but I wasn't allowed out of
the Home until after the doctor had seen me.'

'By telephone!' Lorna ejaculated, and looked at the label
on the hamper. 'Why, it's from Forts, in Melchester! That's
a terribly expensive shop.'

'Well, let's hope the things will be good then.'

Lorna knelt down beside the hamper and raised the lid.
Inside, wrapped in greaseproof paper, was a whole turkey,
trussed and ready for cooking. Lorna stared in amazement,
then slowly she took out the other packages around it—
a brawn of some sort, a chicken already cooked and stuffed,
preserved fruits, honey in the comb, a tin of chocolate
biscuits, a grouse in aspic, and finally a large pot of caviare.

Lorna stared at them in bewilderment, then she raised her
face to Jimmy.

'But you're not going to eat all this for lunch and we can't
take it. It's impossible!'

'I'm afraid you must,' Jimmy replied. 'The taxi's gone
now.'

'Taxi!' Minnie spoke from behind them. 'Do you mean to
tell me, young man, that you had a taxi out from Melchester
with these things? Well, that's a fine waste of money, and
I'm ashamed of Forts for letting you do it, when the twelve-
thirty bus would have brought them just as easily and left
them at the bottom of the drive.'

'I was impatient, Minnie. I wanted them at once. Besides,
I was thinking of my lunch. Which is it to be—the turkey or
the chicken.'

'Neither,' Lorna said decidedly. 'We can't let you do this,
can we, Minnie?'

Minnie looked from Lorna to Jimmy and then at the
pile of foodstuffs on the kitchen floor.

'And to think that we couldn't afford a turkey at Christmas,' she said, 'and it's Peter's favourite dish.'

'Turkey it is, then,' Jimmy said.

'The meal will be late,' Minnie replied, 'but you shall have it, if I have my kitchen to myself. I can't work with a lot of people about.'

'Come on, Lorna, we're dismissed until luncheon-time.'

Jimmy held out his hand, but Lorna turned away from him and picked up the clothes she had been ironing.

'Are you quite sure you can manage, Minnie?' she said, hesitating near the door. But Minnie was holding the turkey in her hands.

'It's a fine bird,' she exclaimed admiringly, 'and I'm sure they asked a wicked price for it!'

Jimmy laughed.

'I'll tell you if it was worth it after lunch,' he promised. He shut the kitchen door and followed Lorna down the passage which led into the hall. 'What do we do now?' he asked.

'We—nothing,' Lorna replied. 'You go and sit in the garden and I'll finish my work.'

'That's not fair!'

'But I've got a lot to do—I have really.'

'Well, forget it and talk to me instead.'

She hesitated, looked into his eyes, and was lost.

'All right,' she said weakly, 'but give me time to take off my overall and this awful handkerchief.'

'Three minutes then,' he said, 'but only three—or I shall come and fetch you!'

Lorna fled up the stairs and into her own bedroom. She put the ironed clothes down on a chair, snatched off the shapeless overall, and searched in the cupboard for a clean cotton dress. She put it on and turned to the dressing-table. She combed her hair, curling the ends over her fingers, and was glad that it framed her face naturally like a halo of gold. She powdered her nose and picked up her lipstick.

She had been quick—but not quick enough.

'The three minutes was up long ago,' said a voice at the door.

'Jimmy!' She turned swiftly.

'Well, don't look so shocked,' he said. 'Is it forbidden at

the Vicarage to enter a lady's bedroom—even at eleven o'clock in the morning?'

'It most decidedly is,' Lorna replied. 'Go away at once!'

'I won't! I want to see where you sleep. Yes, I like your room—it's simple, cool, and, shall we say—very virginal?'

He looked round at the white walls, at the oak beams holding up the low ceiling, at the narrow divan bed with its white linen cover, and at the pale blue casement curtains, faded but freshly laundered, drawn back from the diamond-paned windows. There was an armchair also covered in blue, a simple oak dressing-table, and a very lovely old Italian *prie-dieu*, which had belonged to Lorna's mother.

'Without you in it—I'd say it was the bedroom of a nun,' he said, 'but when I look at you Cherry Ripe, I'm quite certain it's nothing of the sort.'

'Why are you so certain?'

'I will show you.'

He walked across the room and, putting his hand on her shoulder, turned her round to face her reflection in the mirror.

She saw her own face—the cheeks slightly flushed, the eyes wide and starry, her lips parted; and behind her she could see Jimmy, his sunburnt skin in vivid contrast to her own; his dark eyes looking into the reflection of hers. His mouth was smiling, yet his whole expression was not that of amusement. Lorna looked away. She was shy and a tiny bit afraid.

'Do you understand now?'

There was a throb in Jimmy's voice. Swiftly Lorna stepped aside.

'Come downstairs,' she urged. 'What would the children think if they found you up here—or Minnie?'

'I can't answer for any of them,' Jimmy replied, 'but I know that most people would say I was a very lucky young man.'

The meaning in his words made Lorna blush.

'Don't be absurd! Come on.'

'You're very young,' Jimmy said, following her to the top of the stairs.

'I don't know what you mean by that remark, but I'm not old enough to take it as a compliment.'

'Don't apologise for your lack of years—I appreciate it. In fact, I like you just as you are!'

'As if I would apologise to you,' she said scornfully. 'You get more conceited every time I meet you!'

'Haven't I every reason,' he asked. 'Why, here's the most beautiful girl I've ever seen prepared to have luncheon with me and to spend the whole day bringing happiness and amusement into my lonely existence.'

'You're impossible!—and I'm prepared to do nothing of the sort!'

Nevertheless, she found herself sitting lazily in the garden, talking and laughing, while an unpleasantly active conscience told her there were a thousand and one things she should have been attending to both in the house and in the village.

Yet she had not the strength of will to resist temptation. It was a happiness she had never experienced before—to let the hours drift by light-heartedly.

Time passed so quickly that Lorna, far from the practical, stolid earth, was suddenly brought back to realities by the church clock chiming one. There was the chatter of voices as Peter and Peke came bounding out through the house, back from their lessons. They rushed up to Jimmy and she got to her feet.

'Good Heavens! I haven't laid the lunch yet and Daddy will be back at any moment.'

'Hello, my dear, what's the hurry?' he asked.

'Jimmy's here and there's turkey for lunch,' Lorna answered incoherently, and disappeared into the dining-room.

'Good gracious me!'

The Vicar stared after his eldest daughter, then walked through the sitting-room into the garden.

53

Jimmy got up out of the deck chair as the Vicar approached.

'Good morning, sir. I have taken you at your word and inflicted myself upon you again.'

'I'm delighted,' the Vicar answered. 'I gather that Lorna realises you are staying to lunch?'

'I think so, sir.'

There was a smile at the corner of Jimmy's lips.

'Good. Then that's all right. Lorna is very dependable.'

'She's a marvel!'

There was something in Jimmy's enthusiasm which arrested the Vicar's attention. He looked sharply at the young man standing beside him and spoke instinctively, without reflecting on his words.

'I can't think what we should do without her!'

The telephone was pealing shrilly. Lorna hastily put forks and spoons down on the half-laid table and ran from the dining-room to the hall.

'Hello!'

It was Michael.

'Listen, Lorna, I've been called out to Godsdean this afternoon, so I shan't be able to come to tea, but can you come with me? It's a lovely drive. I'll pick you up at three-thirty.'

'Oh, I can't.'

'Nonsense!—of course you can.'

'No . . . honestly, Michael, it's impossible.'

'Why?'

'Well—there's so much to do. . . . I've got to be here.'

'Don't argue—there's nothing to keep you at home. If there is, chuck it, please, Lorna!'

'Oh Michael!—it's so difficult.'

Lorna was feverishly seeking for words, for any explanation that would sound a genuine one. Through the open door of the sitting-room she could see Jimmy talking to her father in the garden.

Michael was getting angry—she knew that cold, impatient note in his voice. He was talking rapidly.

'. . . you do too much and worry too much about unimportant details and unimportant people.'

How could she explain about Jimmy? How could she tell him that to be at home this afternoon was of vital importance.

'I can't stop now, Michael, lunch is ready.'

'I'll pick you up at three-thirty.'

'No, please be sensible. . . . I can't come—I can't.'

'I don't understand. I was coming to see you, anyway.'

'Don't be angry, Michael.'

'Angry? Yes, I suppose I am—but you're usually a reasonable person.'

'Yes, I am,' Lorna thought—but to-day everything was unusual. So unusual and so strange that she couldn't express what she felt, even to herself.

'I'm sorry—very sorry. I'll explain when I see you . . . to-morrow.'

She was playing for time.

'Shall I come in this evening, if I get back in time?'

'I. . . . Yes . . . of course . . . do.'

'You don't sound very enthusiastic—what's the matter? Is anything the matter?'

'No, of course not . . . it's just . . . well, . . . oh, I can't tell you now.'

'Tell me.'

'I can't, Michael, I must go. Lunch is ready and I haven't laid the table.'

'Damn the table! Lorna—I want to see you.'

'You will see me . . . this evening . . . or to-morrow.'

'Come with me this afternoon?'

'I can't—I can't! Good-bye, Michael.'

'Listen, Lorna ! . . . Lorna !'

She had gone—he heard the click of the receiver and the line was dead.

5

The 'best laid schemes' go astray quite often. Lorna felt more than once during the afternoon that the Fates were against her.

To begin with all went well; luncheon was an unqualified success. The turkey was excellent; they all enjoyed it and the Vicar was kept busy carving.

'I say, this is a present!' Peter exclaimed. 'You should have heard what I said at Christmas when Lorna wouldn't buy us one! We had a couple of chickens instead, but that didn't seem right, somehow.'

'We had a plum pudding, though,' Peke said, 'and Beth got the thimble. She was furious, and said Lorna had done it on purpose, but, of course, it was just chance.'

'Who got the ring?' Jimmy asked.

'Lorna,' Peke replied, 'and she was quite coy about it.'

'I wasn't anything of the sort,' Lorna contradicted.

'Doesn't that mean she'll be married before the year is out?'

'Yes, it does,' Peke agreed. 'Daddy got the bachelor's button.'

But Jimmy wasn't listening to the second half of the sentence; he was looking at Lorna, who refused to meet his eyes.

When luncheon was over, Lorna expected to be alone with Jimmy. She sent him out of doors with her father while she cleared the table and helped Minnie with the washing-up, then she rushed upstairs to comb her hair and powder her flushed face.

It was nearly half-past two—when she came out of the house; but to her surprise, her father was still there. It was the first time in weeks that she had known him linger on after the mid-day meal. Usually as the clock struck two, he would hurry off, either on his bicycle or on foot, but now he was sitting in one of the deck chairs talking eagerly with Jimmy.

She drew near, and, hearing the tail end of a sentence, learnt that they were speaking about cricket.

'Hello, my dear.' Her father looked up at her as Jimmy rose to his feet. 'I have just been discovering that this young man's father was at Oxford with me. We actually got our Cricket Blues the same year. Of course, I remember him well. Douglas Braith was one of our most promising cricketers—I always expected that he would play for England.'

'He couldn't afford it,' Jimmy said. 'He had to work, and work jolly hard—my grandfather was a martinet.'

'And he was successful?' the Vicar asked.

'Very,' Jimmy replied. 'I suppose our business is one of the largest of its kind in the world—certainly in England.'

'And for that he had to sacrifice cricket . . .' the Vicar said with a sigh. 'Well, many people would feel there was no reason for regret; but if you are a cricketer you understand that nothing could replace the thrill of representing England.'

'I'm not a cricketer—not what you'd call one, anyway—but I can understand that, sir. My father brought me up in the old tradition.'

'He was happy at Oxford,' the Vicar said. 'Yes, now I can see that you are like him. He was very gay—he seemed to have a greater capacity for enjoying life than most people.'

'I've been told that before, but I'm afraid you'd find he has changed since those days.'

'I'm sorry to hear that. There's too little laughter and happiness in this world.'

'And too much hard work,' Jimmy added. 'At least—for my liking. That's why I'm always in trouble—or was until the war started.'

'You're in your father's business?'

'Supposed to be, but factories have never been my line of country. Now, I ask you—do I look like an industrialist?'

Jimmy looked at Lorna as he spoke and he laughed.

'You don't,' she admitted.

'Nor did Douglas Braith when I knew him,' the Vicar said quietly.

'It's funny but you make me feel sorry for my father. I've never been that before—too busy seeing my own point of view, I suppose.'

'That's an obstacle to many of us.'

'Yet if Father was as you remember him,' Jimmy said, reflectively, 'you'd think he'd find it easier to agree with me. Frankly, I want to enjoy life while I'm young. I'm sure it's better for one's character to stand on one's own feet and be one's own master and all that sort of thing; I've heard those arguments since I was eighteen; but I wonder if Father's character is so very much improved by what he's been through? You'll have to meet him, sir, and give me your honest opinion.'

'I should be very pleased to meet your father again,' the Vicar replied, 'but not for the reason you suggest. Anyhow, please remember me to him when you write. I have the happiest memories of my friends at my Alma Mater.'

'I will,' Jimmy promised.

The Vicar looked at the church clock and got to his feet.

'I'm late,' he said. 'And I don't care—I've enjoyed our talk. Thank you, my dear boy, for an excellent luncheon which was due to your generosity. It was a kindly thought.'

'If you knew what a relief it was to get away from the Hall, even for a few hours,' Jimmy replied, 'you'd know that I'm the one to be grateful to you.'

The Vicar touched him on the shoulder as he passed.

'Then come again soon.'

'I will.'

'Now don't hurry,' Lorna exhorted her father, 'it's terribly hot.'

As the Vicar entered the house, Jimmy sat down again in the deck chair. He held out his cigarette case to Lorna.

'Will you light one for me?'

She opened the case, offered him a cigarette, and held the match cupped between her hands. He put his hands on hers to steady the light and she thrilled for a moment at the touch of his fingers.

'Now,' Jimmy said, with a sigh of content, 'tell me lots of things. Have you been thinking about me?'

'Of course not!'

'The Vicar's daughter should never tell a lie,' he said reproachfully.

'How do you know it's a lie?'

'I'm quite certain of it. You've been thinking about me just as I've been thinking about you. That's the truth, isn't it?'

Lorna dropped her eyes before his. She wanted to be gay, she wanted to talk amusingly, teasingly, but instead Jimmy's voice was submerging her in the wave of ecstasy and magic from which she recoiled, afraid of its power to carry her out of her depth.

'You're very sweet.' He spoke caressingly. 'I wonder how you would look if you lived in London.'

'Why should I look any different?'

'Dressed by Molyneux, your hair done by Antoine, your finger-nails varnished, jewels by Cartier . . . you'd be stunning, Cherry Ripe—yet it might spoil you.'

Lorna stretched out her fingers and looked at her polished but untinted nails.

' "Penny plain" seems more suitable,' she said, 'but you can have them "tuppence coloured" if you like.'

'Bless you!' Jimmy sat up suddenly and reached across to her with his hand. 'Darling, you're perfect. I don't want you altered in any way. I'd hate you to be sophisticated, painted, and over-dressed. I adore you just as you are.'

Lorna was still looking at her hands.

'I shall have crimson talons next time you see me.'

'Lorna . . . didn't you hear what I said?'

She turned to face him and, as their eyes met, her answer was lost. . . .

There was the sound of voices, they both turned swiftly—out from the house, escorted by Minnie, came the two Miss Piggotts. Spinsters of uncertain age, they were the backbone of every organisation and parochial activity in the village; they had come to see Lorna, bearing a list of things they wanted arranged or altered. They settled themselves down in deck chairs and talked for over half an hour.

Lorna showed no sign of the impatience she was feeling. The Miss Piggotts were of inestimable help to her father and without them, a great deal more work would fall on her shoulders. She disregarded a slight sullenness which was beginning to show itself in Jimmy's manner; she ignored the fact that he had become morose, answering in monosyllables when he was included in the conversation.

At last they showed signs of going, but even as they rose to say good-bye, yet another visitor arrived. This was Colonel Summerfield, Squire of the parish, who was in command of the local Home Guard. His mission was to notify the Vicar that in future the Home Guard would use the church tower as an observation post.

He wanted the key and also the use of the Vicarage garden that following Sunday, when a mock battle was to take place against the adjoining village of Great Walton.

By the time the Colonel and the Miss Piggotts had been finally speeded on their way, it was after four o'clock and, even as Lorna turned to the exasperated Jimmy, the twins came hurrying through the sitting-room window, delighted to find their hero still there and ready to continue discussions of the inexhaustible subject of flying.

'We were afraid you'd have gone!'

'And there was something we particularly wanted to ask you!'

'What is it?' Jimmy asked, rather curtly.

'It's about the cannon on the Stirling bomber,' Peter said. 'I was talking to an airman in the village yesterday and he was saying. . . .'

Lorna interrupted.

'Don't you think you'd better go and change first? It's awfully hot and I expect you will be playing tennis after tea.'

It was an understood thing that the children should not wear their best clothes for messing about in the garden. Their more respectable garments had to last a long time; and when the twins came back from their lessons or Beth from school, they nearly always changed—generally into something already old and shabby.

'Oh, wait a minute!' Peter said, but Jimmy turned away. 'I'll tell you about it later.'

The twins hurried into the house—obviously impatient to be back again.

'Do you always live in this hubbub?' Jimmy asked. 'It's like camping on Victoria Station. People incessantly coming and going! Am I never to have a moment alone with you?'

'It doesn't seem like it,' Lorna said ruefully. 'I suppose things are often like this but I've never noticed it before. You see, I've never wanted to do something else.'

'And what do you want to do now?'

'Talk to you,' she said frankly. 'But I won't be able to— it's nearly tea-time and the twins won't let me get a word in edgeways.'

'Good Heavens!' Jimmy ejaculated. 'And I thought the country was dull!'

'Well, you wouldn't exactly call it a whirl of gaiety.'

'I'll get a car and take you out of this, if I have to do it forcibly!'

Lorna laughed at the vehemence of his tone.

61

'We can't go joy-riding in war-time. Think of the bad example I should set!'

'I see now why most clergymen's children are born with adenoids, pimples, and defective eyesight.'

'Why?'

'So that they shouldn't be tempted from the straight and narrow path of good works. You're the exception, darling, and therefore you can't expect people to behave normally with you. Example or no example, you've got to be kind to me or I shall go mad!'

'Aren't I being kind?' Lorna smiled at him provokingly, but before he could answer, Minnie came out from the house carrying the tea-table.

Lorna jumped to her feet.

'Oh, Minnie, is tea ready? . . . and I haven't laid it! I am sorry.'

'It's been waiting for you.'

It was obvious, even to a stranger, that Minnie was upset; her usual kindly mouth was set in a straight line, and there was an air of repressed ill-temper about her.

'I will go and get the tray.'

Lorna ran towards the house.

'It's so nice out here we forgot the time,' Jimmy said.

'So I noticed!' Minnie answered shortly, and walked away, her back eloquent of disapproval.

'What's the matter?' Jimmy asked, as Lorna came back with the tray.

'I can't imagine.'

'Something must have stung the old girl. She looked at me as if I was something the cat had brought in!'

'I'll find out!' Lorna hurried back to the house again.

Minnie was pouring hot water into the tea-pot. Lorna picked up a plate of sandwiches, then said coaxingly:

'Are you cross, Minnie? What have I done?'

'You've done nothing. That's just the trouble.'

'What do you mean?' Lorna asked. 'Don't talk in parables, Minnie. You know I hate you to be upset.'

She was used to Minnie's moods and knew that far the best way of handling her was to force her into the open; otherwise she would glower sullenly at the offender for hours —perhaps days.

'It's not for me to interfere with your actions,' Minnie said. 'You must make your own decisions and stand by them.'

This was obviously serious. Lorna put down the sandwiches and, moving close to Minnie, put an arm round her shoulder.

'You're being a beast to me,' she said. 'What have I done? Tell me at once, Minnie, otherwise you'll make me unhappy.'

'You'd better take the tea to your visitor—it will be getting cold.'

'Who's been here?' Lorna asked. 'Who have you seen this afternoon?'

Minnie hesitated.

'Martha Bates dropped in as she was passing, but only for a few moments.'

'Mrs. Bates!' Lorna began to see daylight. 'And I suppose she had a little talk to you about Michael.'

'She told me how he'd asked you to go out to Godsdean with him,' Minnie admitted, 'and how disappointed he was when you refused.'

'Now how did Mrs. Bates know?'

Minnie looked embarrassed.

'He may have mentioned it to her.'

'Or she may have listened to his telephone conversation!' Lorna said slowly. 'That's more likely. I hate that old woman, Minnie, she's always prying and sneaking around the place. Why, Michael can't cough but she spreads it all over the village! What's it got to do with her if I go motoring with him or not.'

Minnie seemed taken aback by Lorna's violence.

'It would have been nice for him and nice for you, dear,' she said. Her tone had mellowed, she was melting.

'How could I go?' Lorna asked. 'There's so much to do here, and anyway, what's it got to do with Mrs. Bates? Tell her to mind her own business—or I will tell her myself if you are afraid to!'

'I'm afraid of nobody,' Minnie said stoutly. 'But Dr. Davenport's a fine man—you'll go a long way to find his equal. It isn't those who put all their goods in the shop window that make for happiness and security in life.'

'Who's putting their goods in the shop window?' Lorna asked crossly. 'Honestly, Minnie, I don't know what you're talking about, and as for Mrs. Bates—you wait till I next see her!'

'Now, dearie,' Minnie said soothingly, 'you wouldn't be making trouble between me and an old friend. I've known Martha Bates for over thirty years. She's a gossip, I'm not denying that, but she's a good woman, and she'd take the eyes out of her head and give them to Mr. Michael if she thought he wanted them.'

'Even that doesn't excuse eavesdropping,' Lorna said. 'And what's more, if she tells you she'll tell the whole village —you know that, Minnie. Not that I care what she says. My friendship with Michael isn't going to be affected one way or the other by any chattering old woman; and you can tell her that, too!'

Lorna picked up the teapot and the sandwiches, and flounced out of the kitchen. She was angry, not only with Mrs. Bates but also—although she didn't dare to say so— with Minnie.

'She resents Jimmy being here,' she thought. 'Minnie's always been the same. If she took a dislike to one of our friends when we were children, she would make trouble about them until we gave them up. Michael's always been a favourite of hers, and I suppose she's jealous of any other man that comes here. Well, she's just got to lump it!'

She walked into the hall, as Beth came through the front door.

'Beth!' Lorna exclaimed in surprise. 'Why are you home so early?'

'Is he here?' Beth asked.

'Answer my question.'

'I got excused,' Beth said easily.

'Well, that's very naughty of you,' Lorna scolded. 'You know quite well you're not supposed to leave school until half-past five—and what's more, I shall write to the head-mistress and tell her so!'

'I wouldn't do that,' Beth retorted. 'I told her you wanted me particularly.'

'I shall most certainly inform her that you told a lie. I don't want you, you'd no right to ask permission to leave early.'

Beth wasn't listening; she was peeping through the sitting-room door.

'He is here! Oh, Lorna, how exciting! I'm going to change my dress.'

She threw her school books down on the hall table and was scampering up the stairs three at a time, before Lorna could say anything. It was hopeless, Lorna thought, as she went into the garden.

'I couldn't manage the cakes, Peter,' she said. 'They're in the kitchen. Make yourself pleasant to Minnie—she's in a foul temper.'

Peter got up from where he had been sitting at Jimmy's feet.

'Oh, Lord!' he ejaculated. 'What's upset her now?'

'Never mind that,' Lorna replied. 'Get the cakes and soothe her down if you can.'

'What a life!' Jimmy exclaimed jokingly.

'It certainly is,' Lorna responded. 'And now Beth's come home an hour earlier—just to see you!'

'I'm flattered!'

'You needn't be,' Peke said. 'Beth runs after anything in trousers. She makes us all sick, but we can't do anything about it. In the last war you'd have called her a flapper, but Heaven knows what's the name for them these days!'

'You talk as if you were middle-aged and past the follies

of youth,' Jimmy teased. 'Are you never interested in young men?'

Peke shook her head.

'I haven't got time for them. There are such a lot of things to do with Peter.'

'But one day Peter will get himself a wife, and then what are you going to do!'

Jimmy spoke lightly, but Peke answered him seriously.

'I don't know. I've often thought about that, but somehow it seems as if it could never happen. I can't imagine my life without Peter—I can't even imagine sharing him with another girl.'

'If he goes into the Air Force, you will have to do without him.'

'I know,' Peke said in a low voice, 'but that's different. He'd be leaving me for England—not for another person.'

'Well, you needn't face that difficulty yet,' Jimmy said cheerily. 'You've got him for another year.'

'Have I?' Peke asked a question, but her voice held a note of resignation, and her eyes, with a dreamy, far-away expression, seemed to peer into the future.

'Here they are!' Peter came up with the cakes. 'Minnie's all right now. I couldn't find out what was the matter, but she's beginning to smile again.'

'Thank goodness for that!' Lorna cried fervently. 'Hand the sandwiches to Jimmy, Peke.'

She started to pour out the tea. A few moments passed, then Beth appeared. She was wearing one of her new dresses; it was longer than last year's and gave her a more sophisticated look. She had brushed and combed her hair till it shone like burnished gold, and used Lorna's lipstick and powder with a heavy hand.

'She is pretty,' Lorna thought reluctantly, as she watched her sister approach them. 'If only she'd be unaffected and natural like Peke.'

But that was the one thing Beth could never be.

'I'm simply thrilled to meet you,' she said to Jimmy, in

what the family knew as her society voice. 'There's been quite a conspiracy to keep us apart.'

'I'm sorry to hear that, for I've been equally anxious to make your acquaintance.'

'Have you really?'

'Really,' Jimmy said, and Beth looked superciliously at the family, as if mentally asserting—'That's one in the eye for you!'

'How do you like it at the Hall?' she asked.

'Not very much,' Jimmy replied. 'That's why I'm planning to spend a good deal of my convalescence here.'

'Oh, that will be lovely, won't it, Lorna?'

'Will it?' Lorna asked, non-committally.

'We think so,' Peter said. 'And look here, Jimmy, as we were saying. . . .'

He sat down between Beth and Jimmy and turned the conversation once again to aeroplane engines.

Beth was furious. She got up and crossed to the other side of the table, seating herself beside Jimmy.

'You must excuse my little brother,' she said, 'his manners are appalling. Also, as you may have realised, he is mechanically minded—he has no other assets or interests. Unfortunately his brain works on two cylinders and one of them is missing.'

Jimmy laughed.

'I say, Beth, you are awful!' Peter said, crimson in the face; but Beth had scored a point and she knew it.

'Are there any other interesting men at the Hall?' she asked

'One or two,' Jimmy replied. 'I'll bring them down for you to see.'

'Oh do—that would be fun!'

'Don't encourage her,' Lorna interrupted. 'She's supposed to keep her mind on her lessons.'

'Supposed to!' Peter growled. 'That's about all!'

'You see how I'm bullied at home,' Beth said, raising large blue eyes to Jimmy, and making a gesture which she had copied from one of her favourite film stars.

'You are evidently very down-trodden,' Jimmy said.

'Perhaps you could make them more sympathetic to me,' Beth murmured.

This was a new bit of acting.

'In another minute,' Lorna thought grimly, 'she'll be implying that we ill-treat her, and that she's a modern Cinderella, bullied by her ugly sisters!'

It was amusing, but at the same time Lorna was apprehensive. However would she be able to manage Beth in another two years?

'More tea?' she asked Jimmy.

He shook his head.

'No thank you. I shall have to be getting back soon.'

'Oh, must you?' Beth asked plaintively.

'I'm afraid so. I've got to have a special treatment on my arm before dinner.'

'Well, if you've all finished,' Lorna said, 'you can help me carry the tea-things in. Not Jimmy, of course, he's a visitor—but you'll help, please, Beth, and no scrim-shanking!'

'I always help,' Beth answered. 'In fact I do a great many things around here, but nobody notices it.' She addressed herself to Jimmy.

'I believe you,' he said gravely. 'It's pathetic to see a person as attractive as you are having to stoop to menial tasks.'

'Don't encourage her,' Lorna begged, as Beth carried the tray into the house. 'She'll take you seriously—she will really. You don't know what trouble I am having with Beth.'

'I shouldn't worry,' Jimmy said lightly. 'She won't be on your hands for long. She's going to be a raving beauty.'

'I'm afraid she is.'

'Like her elder sister, only in a different way.'

'If you mean me,' Lorna replied. 'I've never pretended to be a beauty.'

'There's been no reason for you to pretend, but the difference between you and Beth is the difference between a masterpiece and a very skilfully executed poster.'

'If we see much more of you we shall all have swelled heads,' Lorna said, laughing.

'But I want you to see a lot of me,' Jimmy replied. 'Now I've got to go, but you'll meet me to-night, won't you?'

'I can't promise,' Lorna temporised. 'You see how things are—anything might crop up and prevent me coming.'

'You've got to come!' He rose from his chair and slipped his arm through hers. 'Walk as far as the orchard.'

There was the sound of a car coming up the drive. They both stopped to listen.

'I wonder who that is?'

'More callers! My God, what a house! Come on, quick!'

They turned towards the orchard. In spite of Jimmy's limp he managed to move surprisingly quickly; they were concealed by the shrubs and bushes before they heard the car stop at the front door.

'How ridiculous we are!' Lorna said breathlessly. 'It may be Michael. I shall have to go.'

'He can wait,' Jimmy replied grimly. 'Lorna, I shall go crazy if I never see you alone!'

They reached the wooden gate which led into the orchard, and both put out their hands towards the latch. Their fingers met. Jimmy's covered Lorna's. Slowly, very slowly, his pressure tightened, then almost roughly he released her hand and put his arm round her shoulders. She gave a little gasp, and was still, imprisoned within his arm.

'My darling!'

Jimmy's words were hardly above a whisper. She threw back her head and looked up into his eyes. For a moment they were both spellbound, then Lorna knew that she was trembling. She gave a tiny convulsive movement as if she would escape, but it was too late.

Jimmy's arm held her like a band of steel. He bent his head and she felt his lips on hers—fiercely, passionately, and triumphantly making her his.

69

6

Michael opened the front door and walked slowly into the hall. He was tired and his head was still vibrating with the noise of the engine.

He had driven very fast from Godsdean—unusually fast for anyone, but especially so for Michael, who was a steady driver, erring if anything, on the cautious side. It was hot, and for the last twenty miles he had been thinking longingly of a cup of tea.

How often he had watched Lorna pouring out for the family! The grace of her movements and the beauty of her hands—which no amount of housework seemed to coarsen —were indelibly etched upon his mind.

There were so many pictures of Lorna stored in his memory. He could visualise them until they were as vivid and real as actual snapshots kept in an album or pigeon-holed in a desk; Lorna flushed and laughing from romping with the children; Lorna, standing by the bedside of some invalid; Lorna, crouched by the fire, her eyes on the glowing coals, her thoughts far away in a world where he could not follow her.

Always for Michael there were these pictures; but they remained a secret possession testifying to feelings and emotions which he was too inarticulate and tongue-tied ever to express in words.

In the hall he encountered Beth returning from the kitchen.

'Hello, Michael! We've just cleared away the tea but Minnie will put some on a tray for you. I'll go and tell her.'

'I'll go myself and make my apologies for being late.'

'Did she know you were coming? Did Lorna know?'

Yes, I told her. Why?'

Beth looked knowing.

'I only wondered.'

She walked into the sitting-room. Looking into the garden she saw it was empty, Lorna and Jimmy had disappeared. Beth gave a little whistle, a habit she had learnt from Peter.

'Hiding!' she said aloud.

In the kitchen, Peter and Peke were stacking dirty cups and plates in the sink, while Minnie was putting away the uneaten cakes in a tin.

'Will you give me a cup of tea, Minnie?' Michael asked from the doorway.

Minnie beamed all over her plump face.

'I certainly will. Peke, get that tray from behind the door, there's a good girl.'

'Hello, Michael!' Peter said. 'I didn't know we were going to see you this afternoon.'

'You sound surprised.'

'He's nothing of the sort,' Minnie said briskly. 'There's nothing surprising in seeing someone who comes most days —or should do if he knew where a welcome was waiting him.'

'Thank you, Minnie.'

'Are you hungry?' she asked, deftly buttering a loaf of bread.

Michael watched her.

'Very,' he replied. 'Something went wrong with the range this morning, and I had a beastly lunch.'

'Martha Bates told me,' Minnie said. 'It's time you had a new range in that house. Things won't last for ever. They're like bodies, they wear out with old age, and who should know that better than you?'

'So Martha's been here. What did she come for?—a good gossip?'

71

'She came to see me,' Minnie parried.

'And to have a little talk about you, I expect, Michael,' Peke said meaningly. 'I bet we none of us had any reputations left by the time the old girls had talked us over. I've heard them!'

'That's both unkind and unfair,' Minnie exclaimed, but there was no anger in her voice.

She liked being teased, but whatever imputations might be made against Martha Bates she herself was a model of discretion. No one had ever managed to make Minnie discuss the Vicarage, although she was always prepared to be a good listener where the rest of the village was concerned.

'Your tea's ready,' she said, 'and if you want any more hot water the children can fetch it for you. Come on, Peke, carry it out into the garden for the doctor and see he eats every bit of it—the man looks starved!'

'I shall tell Martha you said that,' Michael threatened. 'I know of nothing which would annoy her more. She takes it as a personal insult that I'm not one of the fat sort.'

Minnie snorted.

'And well she might,' she retorted. 'Martha never could cook!'

Michael laughed.

'I'll give you the last word, Minnie.'

Peke had already picked up the tray and he followed her down the passage and out into the garden. Beth was sitting alone, the empty chairs clustered round her.

'Where's Lorna?' Michael asked.

'She's about somewhere,' Beth replied. 'She was here just a few minutes before you came.'

Her eyes were bright and as perceptive as those of a small bird. She watched Michael as he settled down in a deck chair, helping himself to a sandwich.

Peter came strolling out from the house.

'Where's Jimmy?' he asked. 'Has he had to go?'

Michael looked up sharply.

'Jimmy Braith?'

72

'That's right,' Peke said, 'he's been here all day.'

Only Beth noticed the effect of these words on Michael.

'And I say, Michael, he's topping,' Peter went on. 'He's brought us down the most marvellous books on flying. I'll show them to you if you like.'

'I'd like to see them,' Michael said quietly.

'But one learns so much from talking to him,' Peter said enthusiastically. 'There were lots of things I didn't understand which he made clear in a few words. He's put me on the right track, I can tell you that. He's jolly decent to us, too. Did you hear about luncheon?'

'No. What about it?'

Peke and Peter both began to speak at once, but they had hardly begun when they were interrupted by Beth.

'Oh, you pigs!' she exclaimed. 'Fancy you having all that when I'm not here! I do think that's mean, don't you, Michael?'

'There'll be lots of other things,' Peke said. 'There's some in the larder now. You can go and look. Minnie showed them to us after lunch. And Jimmy said he was going to give us some more too! He was terribly tactful about it, in case Lorna or Daddy should get upstage—called it "contributing his rations" to the party.'

'The more the merrier was what we thought,' Peter added.

Michael was silent. He poured himself out a cup of tea and proceeded to finish up the plate of sandwiches.

'After all, it's very nice for us to see somebody new for once.'

It was Beth who spoke. There was a challenge in her voice and Michael, glancing up at her, was aware that she had rightly interpreted his resentment.

'Of course it is.' He tried to speak naturally and smoothly.

'It's a great handicap, you know, to be one of three girls in a family. Think how much better it would have been if Peter had been the only girl and we had all been men. What a time we could have had!'

'What on earth are you talking about?' Peter asked rudely.

'I wasn't talking to you,' Beth retorted.

'It's a good thing you weren't,' Peter said. 'I'll go and get those books, shall I, Michael?'

'Yes, do.'

'I'll help you,' Peke said.

They went into the house. Beth bent forward and spoke hastily.

'You don't think, Michael, that Lorna's really keen on him, do you?'

Michael put down his cup with a little clatter on the saucer.

'I think that's a question that Lorna must answer for herself, Beth.'

Beth looked disappointed; then there was a mischievous expression on her face.

'Well, here she comes,' she said in a piercing whisper. 'You ask her.'

Lorna was coming towards them, moving slowly across the lawn. She was not looking at them and was quite near before she saw Michael. She hesitated—there was no doubt about that—then turned in the direction of the house.

'I shan't be a moment,' she called; her steps quickened, finally she ran the last few yards over the terrace and into the sitting-room.

'What do you think of that?' Beth questioned.

Michael, who had half risen in his chair, sat down again.

'Aren't you home rather early to-night?' he asked.

'I got back at half-past four,' Beth answered. 'I wanted to see the handsome Squadron-Leader. I expected to be disappointed—they'd talked so much about him—but I wasn't. Oh Michael, he is good looking! Don't you think so?'

'I hadn't thought about it.'

'I like his black eyes—they are nearly black, you know—and the way his hair grows off his forehead. I think he's got a slight—a very slight—look of Clark Gable.'

'I wonder if he'd be flattered by the comparison?'

'Oh, I think any man would,' Beth answered seriously,

'but of course he's better looking in a way—more English and gentlemanly. Do you think he's rich?'

'I've no idea!' Michael got to his feet abruptly.

He walked away from Beth and stood looking along the gabled roof of the Vicarage to where one wing of the building, with its black and white cross beams joined an ancient wall of red brick.

Lorna's room was in the black and white part. He looked up at her window and thought he saw a movement.

'Lorna!' he called.

For a moment there was no answer, then she came to the window.

'Hello, do you want me?'

'Yes, of course I do. Come down.'

'I'm just coming. Have you had some tea?'

'Minnie fed me, but I am feeling neglected.'

'Poor Michael! But you've got all the rest of the family to console you.'

'Come down!'

'All right!' She moved from the window.

Inside the bedroom she stood for a moment looking at herself in the mirror of the dressing-table. Her ˢˢ were shining; even to herself she looked different. There was an aliveness about her as if every hair on her head were magnetised and her whole being supercharged! She put her hands up for a moment to her cheeks. They were burning, but her hands were icy cold.

She gave a little exclamation; a sound of rapturous joy escaped from between her lips—forced open by the excess of happiness within. Then she opened the door and went downstairs.

'Sorry, Michael dear.' She smiled at him and slipped her arm through his. 'How did you get on at Godsdean? I've had such a busy afternoon—a lot of people have been here—the Miss Piggotts, Colonel Summerfield, and of course, Jimmy. I expect the children told you.'

'Yes, they told me.'

'The twins are mad about him—he's been so kind to Peter.' She looked across the garden. 'Oh, I see he's brought out his books to show you. Come and look at them.'

'There's no hurry. Peter can wait. Tell me what else you've been doing—you sound as if you've been enjoying yourself.'

'I have. Oh, Michael, I have—so much!'

'That's fine.' He led her away from the lawn and through a blistered green doorway into the kitchen garden. With Lorna's arm through his they walked slowly down the overgrown path between the currant bushes.

'Why have we come here?' Lorna asked suddenly.

'Because I want to talk to you.'

'Oh yes, of course. I felt mean that I couldn't go with you this afternoon—but you understand, don't you?'

'I'm afraid I do,' Michael answered. 'No . . . I won't say that. I don't want to understand your reasons—I wanted you to come, that was all.'

'Dear Michael!'

Lorna pressed his arm with her other hand. She was happy and the world was full of joy. She wanted Michael to be happy too, she wanted everyone to share this wonderful happiness.

Michael suddenly stood still. He put his hand over hers and held it prisoner.

'Lorna,' he said steadily, 'will you marry me?'

He was conscious of the shock that his words gave her. He felt first her surprise, then the tense tightening of every nerve and muscle.

'Michael!' His name was a cry.

'Listen, Lorna. I've been wanting to tell you this for a long time, only it has been impossible. I thought—perhaps stupidly—that you had some idea that I cared for you, that the one thing I've wanted for years was to ask you to be my wife. It's been impossible with my father so ill, with my affairs muddled as they have been, to consider marriage; then, two days ago, I had a talk with my father which changed everything.

'I've always kept up the pretence that I was only doing his work as a stop-gap. But he said to me

' "I realise that I shall never recover. I've known it for a long time, but hope dies hard, especially in the very old. I shall not be here much longer, Michael, and there's one thing I'd like to see before I go—your wife."

'Lorna, when he said that, it cleared all the obstacles from my path. It's been difficult to keep silent these past two years —it's been hard to see you day after day and not tell you for what I've been hoping—for what I've been praying.'

'Oh, Michael!'

It was a piteous cry now. Lorna was not looking at him. Her hands had dropped to her sides.

'You don't love me, perhaps,' Michael went on, 'not yet. I'd wait for that—I'd wait for ever—if necessary! Lorna, will you try to think of me, not as a brother, but as a man who loves you—who wants, more than anything else in the world, the privilege of protecting and caring for you?'

'I can't—oh, Michael, don't you understand that I can't?'

Lorna made a hopeless gesture with her hands, then raised her face to him; her eyes were full of tears.

'Why not?' Michael asked the question sharply.

'I don't know. I've never thought about you like that. You've always been one of the family. I love you as I love Peter, but that isn't the sort of love you want. I never thought . . . I never realised. . . .'

'I know.' Michael reached down and put a hand on both Lorna's shoulders. 'I know all that,' he said. 'Why Lorna, you're trembling! Don't be upset—I'd hate to upset you in any way. Oh, my dear, I love you so!'

'But you mustn't! Please, Michael, you musn't love me!'

Michael smiled.

'It would be easier to harness the tides than stop loving you. I love you because I can't help it. I think I've always loved you since we were children together and you would insist on toddling after me when I was a schoolboy and had no use for girls!'

'I remember how ashamed you were of me,' Lorna said.

She tried to speak jokingly, but her voice was unsteady.

'And I watched you grow up,' Michael continued gently. 'I watched you change from an irresponsible child into a very capable young woman; I watched you grow lovelier year after year; I watched you take up the burden of the family when your mother died. Lorna, have you any idea how wonderful you are?'

She shuddered as if his words had the power to hurt her.

'What am I to say to you, Michael?' she said. 'I can't bear to be unkind—but oh, my dear, it's impossible!'

'Why? Why should it be so impossible?' Michael protested. 'You'll get used to the idea and then gradually, very gradually, I'll teach you to love me. Lorna, let me try?'

His voice was deep with emotion. He was very near her now—he had only to make one movement and she would be within his arms. As if she guessed the danger, Lorna put out her hands and laid them against his chest.

'Forget this, Michael—please forget it,' she pleaded. 'I suppose . . . you couldn't love Peke . . . or Beth, instead?'

'I'm afraid I couldn't. But you're not to distress yourself. I've told you, in time you'll get used to the idea.'

'Never!' Lorna said vehemently, and turned away.

Michael was very still—she was alarmed by the silence. She turned to look at him. There was something in his eyes which made her afraid of him for the first time in her life.

'I suppose there isn't anyone else?'

The question quivered in the air, then seemed to her like a physical blow. She had known that he would ask it, she had felt instinctively that she could not escape.

'No . . . no . . . of course there isn't!' she said. Her lips seemed dry and her voice was unreal, even to herself.

She was conscious of Michael's relief. She felt him relax.

'That's all I wanted to know,' he said. 'Lorna, you're not to worry your head about this. I want you to go on loving me in your own way. Let me continue to be one of the family.'

'That's what you've always been,' Lorna replied. 'I can't think why you've had to spoil our good friendship!'

She was like a petulant child and Michael smiled.

'I haven't spoilt anything,' he said soothingly. 'I promise you that.'

'But it has. Don't you understand? I feel strange with you, I can't tell you things. I can't come to you for advice, and I've always done that, haven't I, Michael?'

'You always have and you always will, please God!' he answered. 'Nothing's changed, Lorna. Can't you see that? I've loved you like this for years, and because you haven't known it we have been happy together, therefore there's nothing to stop us going on being happy.'

'I don't know. . . . I'm afraid. . . .'

'There's nothing to be afraid of.'

'You won't tell anybody?'

'No one, unless you wish it. It's our secret—yours and mine.'

'I think Minnie guesses, but no one else has any idea. I couldn't bear it if the twins knew or Beth. Think how awful Beth would be!'

'No one shall know.'

'We'd better go back, then. They'll think it strange for us to wander off like this.'

'Nonsense!' Michael replied. 'We've wandered off a thousand times before and you've thought nothing of it, but now you expect suspicion because there's something, if you like to put it that way, to be suspicious about.'

'It complicates things,' Lorna sighed, 'and I don't want my life to be complicated. I want it to be simple and straightforward. Oh Michael, why did you have to tell me!'

'Because I love you, Lorna,' he said simply.

There was a throb in his voice and her petulance fell from her. Somehow his words were not disturbing, instead they gave her a feeling of security and confidence. Michael was there . . . Michael, steadfast and reliable. Impulsively she slipped her hand into his.

'I do love you, Michael, although it isn't in the way you want.'

His fingers tightened until hers were lifeless in the force of his grip. Just for a moment she felt afraid again; for a moment she wondered if there were some force within Michael which would prove too powerful for her. She looked up at him apprehensively, but there was nothing to arouse fear in the dear familiarity of his face.

'We'd better go back,' Lorna suggested. 'Peter won't be happy until he has shown you his book of aeroplanes.'

'This fellow Braith seems to avail himself pretty frequently of your hospitality.'

The statement was unexpected. Lorna was suddenly very still. She was afraid that her expression might betray her, but Michael was not looking at her.

'Daddy knew his father at Oxford—they were cricketers together. It must be pretty boring at the Hall too—I can imagine nothing more ghastly than undiluted doses of Lady Abbott.'

'That's true,' Michael said. 'All the same, if he's here too much I shall get jealous.'

Lorna didn't answer. Her heart was throbbing now, throbbing with the memory of Jimmy's lips on hers, and his last words as he left her in the orchard :

'To-night, Cherry Ripe. It's a long time to wait until then, so don't fail me—I couldn't bear it!'

7

Lorna got out of bed and drew back the curtains. Outside, the newly-risen morning sun was touching with golden fingers the opening flowers. There was the glimmer of silver from the stream winding its way slowly through the village and under the ancient grey stone bridge. Beyond it Lorna could see Bredon Hill, blue against the distant horizon, blurred and mystical in the morning mist.

She loved the view from her window; she had always loved it, but this morning its beauty affected her almost unbearably.

'I must still be dreaming,' Lorna thought.

But it was not a dream! This morning there was no awakening to the dismal knowledge that such ecstasy had only been part of the imaginings of the night. For once the truth was more wonderful than a dream had ever been!

'I'm in love!' Lorna said to herself. 'And—please God— let it last for ever!'

She felt exalted, yet humble—proud, yet a supplicant.

How long she stood at the window she did not know. Dimly in her subconscious mind she knew that she should be helping Minnie lay the breakfast—but she could not move, could not break the spell which bound her. She was still half afraid and apprehensive that it might, after all, be a dream from which she had not yet awakened.

At last, as one in a trance, she walked towards her dressing-table. She saw in the mirror her own familiar features, but with a changed expression.

'I'm beautiful,' Lorna thought. 'I'm beautiful for him. He has done this—for I have never looked like this before.'

Her mood of exaltation continued while she dressed, and when she descended to the dining-room to lay the table and welcome the others down to breakfast, some of it radiated from her so that the children looked at her curiously, not understanding what had happened, but conscious of a change.

'Somebody left you a fortune—you're pretty bright this morning?' was Peter's observation.

'Are we doing anything exciting to-day?' Peke asked.

It was Beth whose shrewdness enabled her to point in the right direction.

'When are you going to see your airman again, Lorna?'

Lorna tried to look reproving.

'I don't know what you mean, Beth, and eat your breakfast—you'll be late for school.'

But somehow she couldn't keep it up, couldn't be dignified or fault-finding to-day.

'It's a lovely morning,' she said, 'I wish you hadn't got to do lessons.'

'Not half as much as we do,' Peter said.

The Vicar opened the door.

'Good morning, children. Good morning, Lorna, my dear. I'm sorry to be late, but I must have overslept.'

Lorna looked guilty. It was her habit in the morning to knock on her father's door as soon as her alarm clock had wakened her. She hurried to pour out his coffee and help him to porridge. Even in these little actions she felt as if she were pouring out herself—giving to those she loved something of her own happiness.

She herself ate nothing. She felt as if never again would she eat anything so humdrum, so ordinary, as porridge or toast!

So found it difficult to hurry the twins and Beth as she

usually did. The words of command would not force themselves from her lips; but, at length, they left. Chattering noisily, they picked up their school-books, collected their bicycles, and disappeared down the drive, a cloud of golden dust following in their wake.

By the time Lorna had shut the front door behind them, her father had gone too. She saw him striding across the lawn towards the church; and watched through the sitting-room window as he opened the gate into the churchyard, moving slowly among the ancient gravestones towards the porch. She followed him with her eyes—but her thoughts were with Jimmy.

Somewhere she had read that one could think of two things at once. It was true. She had been thinking of getting up, of washing and dressing, of breakfast, of the children, and now of her father; but behind these surface thoughts, these trivialities of everyday existence, she was thinking and feeling only of Jimmy.

'I love him!' she whispered, and then heard the telephone ringing.

For some seconds it went on ringing; she could not force herself to heed its interruption—to drag herself from the exquisite contemplation into which her mind had flown on enchanted wings. Then at length its imperious summons was too much—she was forced to obey. She picked up the receiver.

'Hello, is that you, Lorna? It's Sally.'

'Sally! How lovely to hear your voice! We'd not heard from you for so long we thought you must be dead!'

'I very nearly am—no joking. The house was hit last night.'

'Oh, I'm sorry!'

'I thought I'd come down to you for a few days. I've got week-end leave—but I've got to be back on Monday. Mother's going to Devonshire and it's not worth going with her for so short a time. Will you have me?'

'Of course—you know we will. But I'm sorry about Charles Street. Is it bad?'

'Well, most of the ceilings are down and the drawing-room is a shambles. I've managed to rescue some clothes, though, otherwise I'd have had nothing but my uniform. I'm going to start now—I should be with you by luncheon-time.'

'You're going to motor?'

'Yes, I shall have just enough petrol. Anyway, the trains are impossible. Good-bye, Lorna. Thanks awfully for having me.'

Lorna hung up the receiver and ran towards the kitchen.

'Minnie, who do you think is coming here? Sally! The house in Charles Street has been hit by a bomb and Aunt Julie is going to Devonshire.'

'No one was hurt, then?' Minnie asked.

'Sally didn't say so,' Lorna replied. 'It can't be too bad because she's managed to rescue her clothes.'

'Lady Serena would see to that all right,' Minnie said. 'It would have done her good to be without her frills and furbelows for a bit!'

Lorna smiled to herself. Her cousin Sally was not one of Minnie's favourites; she distrusted her sophisticated ways and was inclined to resent her periodical visits to the Vicarage.

Sally had not been to see them for a long time. Lorna knew she found them dull and old-fashioned in Little Walton, and she only came if she had nowhere else to go—which was not often—or if she really needed rest and quiet after an abnormal amount of exhausting gaiety.

'Aunt Julie will be angry about this,' Lorna said. 'She only did up the house from top to bottom just before the war.'

'Oh, I dare say she'd have found it old-fashioned by this time,' Minnie said with heavy sarcasm. 'Your aunt had always "more siller than sense".'

This was an old family joke, introduced many years ago by a Scotch member of the Vicar's congregation. Lorna laughed dutifully and turned towards the door.

'I'll clear the table,' she said, 'and then I'd better get the blue room ready. We must try and make Sally as comfortable as possible.'

'She must take us as she finds us,' Minnie said stoutly; but Lorna knew that she, too, would make an effort.

It was impossible, she thought as she hurried away, not to take people at their own valuation and to assess that valuation by their position in life. She and Sally were first cousins, her mother and Sally's mother had been sisters; but while Mrs. Overton had been the wife of a poor country vicar, her sister Julie had married the Earl of Lothe.

When Aunt Julie came to stay, she was given the best room, meals were specially ordered for her, and everyone, from the Vicar downwards, danced attendance and tried to gratify her merest whim.

It was very different when one of the Overtons visited the Lothe house in Charles Street, Berkeley Square, or spent a few days at Burnley Castle in North Devon. There they were inevitably the most insignificant and unimportant members of the party.

They were, of course, treated courteously and with affection, but even the servants knew they were of no consequence, and they themselves would often leave with a sigh of relief— conscious only of an unspoken apology for the smallness of the tips they disbursed.

Lorna felt thankful that Aunt Julie had not elected to come to them. In her old age her aunt, once pretty and attractive, had become pompous and not without austerity.

Lorna often wondered if she were happy with her distinguished husband; for the Earl of Lothe was a strange man, given to moods of deep depression, and interested mainly in his model farm and orchid houses, which were the best of their kind in the country.

It was strange indeed to think that Sally could be the child of such parents.

'How lovely she is!' Lorna thought, almost with a pang of envy, as she ran to the front door four hours later, when her cousin drove up in a long blue two-seater.

Sally's hair fell like dark curtains on either side of her expressive face. She was very thin and vividly alive with a nervous and seemingly inexhaustible energy. No one could remain quiet or static when Sally was about, she galvanised everyone she met into activity.

'Hello, darling, here I am.'

She climbed out of the car, revealing as she did so a long expanse of perfectly shaped legs encased in superfine silk stockings.

'I've had a marvellous run—three and a half hours—but it was pretty exhausting—especially after last night. Can I have a cocktail?'

Lorna kissed her cousin.

'Sorry, Sally, you know we don't run to such things. There's some sherry.'

'Well, that'll have to do. Can someone carry in my bags?'

'I'll do it,' Lorna said, lifting Sally's suitcases out of the dicky.

Sally, standing in the doorway and peeling off the wine coloured suède gloves which matched her coat and shoes, watched her cousin. It would never have occurred to her to carry her own luggage.

'I'm glad you could have me,' she said. 'I felt I couldn't stand the Castle this week-end with Mummy moaning and groaning about Charles Street. She's particularly annoyed because Daddy wanted to move the furniture months ago and she wouldn't let him. She'd got it firmly into her head that she was immune from bombs—specially protected or something. Anyway, she's been disillusioned, and I hate people to cry over spilt milk.'

'Poor Aunt Julie,' Lorna said sympathetically. 'But I'm glad you came to us.'

'Has anything happened since I was here last?' Sally asked.

'Nothing much. The Hall's been turned into a Convalescent Home.'

'Oh, that's interesting. Anyone exciting there?'

'It depends on what you call exciting,' Lorna said cautiously. 'Go into the garden—you'll find some chairs on the terrace. I'll go and get the sherry.'

It took her a few moments to find the decanter hidden at the back of the cupboard in the sideboard, to put it on a tray and polish two glasses. When she came out on to the terrace, Sally was not alone.

Lorna felt her heart leap, she steadied the tray by a great effort of will-power, and moved slowly towards them. The colour was rising in her cheeks; she had wondered all the morning when she was going to see him again and here he was! Sally saw her first.

'Why Lorna,' she exclaimed gaily, 'why didn't you tell me Jimmy Braith was down here? I was simply stunned to see him come walking across the lawn.'

'I haven't had much time to tell you anything,' Lorna said with a smile, then turning her face to Jimmy—'Good morning.' A simple enough word—but she felt as if it revealed everything she felt for him.

'Let me take the tray.' Jimmy put out his hand and she felt his fingers touch hers.

'No, no,' she exclaimed, 'it's too heavy—you can't manage with one hand.'

Together they put it on the table. Lorna felt a pulse hammering in her throat. She was happy—ridiculously happy.

'You'll go mad if you stay here long,' Sally said.

It seemed to Lorna as if her voice came from a long distance away.

'Why do you think that?' Jimmy asked.

'This is the last place God made,' Sally answered, taking her cigarette case out of her bag. 'Nothing happens from one year's end to the other. If you're here long enough, you'll learn the truth of my words.'

'It has its compensations,' Jimmy said.

He was looking at Lorna as he spoke—she felt her lips quiver.

'I've yet to find them then,' Sally retorted, 'but it's a haven of peace after London. Last night was hell, and yet I wouldn't have missed it for a thousand pounds. Can you understand that?'

'I can,' Jimmy said. 'I've felt that way myself.'

Lorna suddenly felt alone, a creature apart. She had not yet experienced danger—these two had a comradeship which she could not share. They went on talking.

Sally was in the A.T.S.—she spent most of her days driving an ancient but exceedingly important General—yet it seemed she had time for other things as well—for her friends, for evenings of gaiety, for cocktails at all the most fashionable places. She and Jimmy spoke the same language—they discussed scandals, jokes, and the idiosyncrasies of mutual acquaintances.

Presently Lorna went into the house to get luncheon ready. She thought that they did not notice her departure. As she laid the table, some of her happiness evaporated—yet sharply she chid herself.

'I can't be so stupid as to be jealous of Sally,' she said, and yet she knew that she was afraid of her cousin.

Sally was so attractive, there had been hundreds of men in her life; men who had loved her and whom she had loved, men who had devoted themselves to giving her a good time, men whom she had apparently only tolerated because they were useful.

'She's got so much,' Lorna whispered, 'and I . . . I have only Jimmy.'

She was afraid, however much she tried to put the thought from her.

'I'm ridiculous—a fool!' she told herself. 'Sally has been here only twenty minutes and already I'm making mountains out of molehills.' Yet how short a time had she known Jimmy and how much he meant in her life now!

She went into the kitchen.

'Squadron-Leader Braith is here,' she said to Minnie. 'I suppose he will be staying for lunch.'

'He'll have his own chicken, then,' Minnie replied. 'There's that and cold turkey. Lady Serena will be pleased—she likes a man about.'

In spite of the fact that she was ready for such a remark, Lorna felt as if Minnie had hit her.

'I'll tell them lunch is ready,' she said, 'I heard the twins come back a moment ago.'

She walked into the garden. Jimmy and Sally were still talking.

'Lunch is ready,' Lorna interrupted.

Sally put down her empty glass.

'I must wash. Which room am I in, Lorna?'

'The blue room.'

'Thank Heavens for that! It's the only decent bed in the house.' Sally walked away.

Lorna paused to pick up the tray and the decanter.

'Darling!' Jimmy was standing very close to her. 'I thought about you all night. Did you think of me?'

The world was suddenly radiant again—radiant with a glory that was almost blinding.

'All night,' Lorna replied.

'Do you love me?'

His eyes were on her mouth, his voice caressing as a kiss.

'You know I do,' she whispered tremulously.

'I want to be alone with you, darling. Damn your relations!—you've got too many of them.'

Lorna felt as if such joy was unbearable. Nothing and nobody, she felt, could destroy it now.

They went into lunch. The Vicar was late, but both surprised and pleased to find Sally when he did arrive. In contradiction to what might have been expected, he was exceedingly fond of his very wordly niece. She teased and argued with him, trying vainly to shock him by pretending to hold the most revolutionary views on human existence, and painting her own character as black as possible.

'You'll really be pleased at the change in Mayfair, Uncle Arthur,' she said. 'Physically, it's "damaged goods"—morally, it's too busy to have time for sin.'

'I can hardly believe that,' the Vicar replied.

'You'd be surprised,' Sally said. 'Adultery has quite gone out of fashion, hasn't it, Jimmy?'

Jimmy looked startled and for once seemed at a loss for words. The Vicar saw his predicament and smiled.

'My niece,' he explained, 'considers it her duty to educate me when she stays here. She tells me that in my conversation and knowledge of the world I am very much behind the times, therefore Biblical words such as she has just used are quite common at this table when Sally is our guest of honour. For her sake and because it gives her pleasure, we pretend that by listening to them we are adding to our vocabulary.'

'All right, Uncle Arthur, touché,' Sally laughed. 'You always get the better of me when it comes to a war of words. That's what education will do for you. I was dragged up in the best schools—the result is, I'm an ignoramus!'

The Vicar looked pleased at the compliment.

'There are different sorts of learning. But one thing I do admire is your pluck, Sally, my dear.'

'Thank you, Uncle Arthur. When the war's over I will take you to the gayest and most fashionable night-club in gratitude for those few kind words. I wish you'd make Mother see things that way. She's furious because I haven't got promotion—thinks I ought to be a General at least by this time!'

'Your mother was always an ambitious woman.'

'Darling Uncle Arthur! That's the only catty thing I've ever heard you say about anyone.'

The Vicar looked apologetic.

'I'm sure I didn't mean it that way.'

'Too late—you've said it,' Sally replied. 'It's so very true—but the truth is often unpalatable.'

'Did you ever try it?' Jimmy asked.

Sally made a grimace at him.

'He's being rude to me, Lorna,' she said. 'We met in somewhat unusual circumstances. He helped me to escape from a very disreputable night-club when it was being raided. All my party except one man and I were caught—we were quicker than the rest and slipped out through the kitchen. Jimmy had the same idea, and we clambered down the fire-escape together.

'Unfortunately, we met the next week-end, staying with the O'Connors. You remember them, Uncle Arthur? The Judge is a great friend of Daddy's. Well, somebody had let out that I was at the Club—a reporter had seen me, but I'd given a false name and of course I wasn't among the people arrested.

'I had to swear both to the Judge and to Daddy that I'd been somewhere else the whole evening. I warned Jimmy to be very careful. It was a beastly week-end; they were suspicious, but they couldn't prove their suspicions, and I got away with it.'

'Thanks to the best bit of acting I've ever seen,' Jimmy said. 'She looked like an aggrieved angel all the time she was being questioned. I've never believed since then in the old theory that a criminal can't look you straight in the eye and tell a lie. Sally can do it all right. I'd never believe anything she told me without concrete and tangible proof.'

'Don't you be too sure of that,' Sally said mischievously. 'I shall have to get even with you one day.'

'Get even with me?' Jimmy questioned. 'What on earth for? I'd like to remind you that I've done you a favour!'

'In which case I'm entirely justified in having a feeling of resentment,' Sally said. 'There's nothing more infuriating than being under an obligation.'

'Perverted sense of values I'm afraid, sir,' Jimmy said, turning to the Vicar.

All through luncheon Sally and Jimmy continued to rag each other. Lorna sat silent. She felt out of it and yet she did not care. She was content to know that once or twice Jimmy's eyes rested on her.

It was almost amusing that Sally was being her most attractive for Jimmy's sake. Lorna knew all the little gestures and intonations of voice which Sally used when she was anxious to be particularly seductive.

'He's mine,' Lorna told herself, 'mine . . . and I'm the luckiest person in the whole world!'

She left them on the terrace while she cleared the table and hurried the twins off again for their afternoon instruction. When she had finished, she found that her father was gone. Sally and Jimmy were alone.

Sally looked exquisite as she lay full length on a rug, her head tilted back against an orange coloured cushion. Her figure was perfect and she knew it, and no man could be expected to ignore those beautifully-modelled legs.

But Lorna, conscious that her dress did not compare favourably with Sally's, and that her stockings had cost perhaps one tenth of the price, was not perturbed. She was ashamed now of these few moments of depression when Sally and Jimmy had first met.

'He must have known so many girls in Sally's set,' Lorna thought wisely. 'If he'd wanted them there was no reason to want me.'

Jimmy got to his feet as she drew near. It seemed to her that his eyes held a message for her alone.

'I was just coming to look for you,' he said. 'I've got to go now. Your doctor friend didn't turn up this morning—he was doing an operation, I believe—so we are expecting him this afternoon. May I come back for tea?'

'And for supper, too,' Sally said. 'Lorna, ask him to supper. I've thought of a lot of annoying things I might say to him in the rays of the silvery moon.'

'You'll have to wait till next week for that,' Jimmy said.

'Well, the gloaming will do just as well,' Sally replied. 'Come and cheer us up—it's good for the Vicarage to be enlivened.'

Jimmy looked at Lorna.

'Of course,' she said. 'We'll have the caviare. I felt it needed a special occasion.'

'Caviare!' Sally said. 'Do my ears deceive me—or has Uncle Arthur been robbing the missionary box?'

'Jimmy gave it to us,' Lorna replied.

'I wonder you accepted it,' Sally exclaimed. She turned to Jimmy. 'Usually, when you offer Lorna a luxury she asks you to change it for a pair of good stout boots for the children, or some new vests for her father. Mummy and I gave up choosing her Christmas presents years ago. We write and ask what she needs and it's always something revoltingly domestic.'

'Then she shall eat three-quarters of the caviare to-night herself,' Jimmy said.

'Oh, no she won't!' Sally replied. 'Not while I'm about.'

'Abstinence would do you a lot of good, my girl!' Jimmy retorted. 'Good-bye, Lorna. I'll be back for tea.'

'Good-bye.' Lorna wondered if he realised how much she wanted to go with him as far as the orchard. She watched him move away.

When he was out of earshot, Sally sat up.

'You're cleverer than I thought, Lorna. I take my hat off to you.'

'What do you mean?'

'What do you think I mean?—Jimmy Braith, of course. Caviare, indeed! You take it, and anything else you can get'

'I didn't want to,' Lorna said hastily, 'but he wanted to come here to meals, and insisted on making some contribution towards them.'

'I should think he did, and why not? He can well afford to.'

'Can he?'

'The innocent abroad!' Sally exclaimed. 'My dear, he's Douglas Braith's son—Sir Douglas Braith, head of the Amalgamated Oxygen Industries. Surely you've heard of him? Why, I suppose he's one of the richest men in England—a millionaire, even in these days—and Jimmy's his only son.'

Lorna felt as if her elusive happiness were retreating again;

she could almost feel it ebbing away, despite her efforts to hold it close, to imprison it within her heart.

'It doesn't make any difference,' she thought, 'how rich his father is!'

But she was afraid—desperately afraid.

8

Lorna, tramping along the country road, was both wet and cold. It had been raining steadily all day, and it was impossible to see more than the distance of a field away; the rest of the world was shrouded in grey mist, and the blinding force of driving rain.

Yet nature's mood seemed to match Lorna's, for she, too, was lost in the mist of her own feelings. She was sad, and felt as if her physical coldness was but an echo of an icy misery within her heart.

Everything, she told herself, seemed to have gone wrong since yesterday evening. Jimmy had come back to tea but he had brought the news that he was leaving Little Walton the following morning for London.

'Your doctor friend wants Sir Alfred Dormer to look at my arm. He's the big bone specialist. They got him on the telephone and he's promised to see me to-morrow despite it being Saturday.'

Just for a moment the thought had come to Lorna, that Michael might have another motive in sending Jimmy to London, and then, even as the thought crystallised, she had dismissed it as unfair—and unworthy of Michael. He would never stoop to such a thing, she told herself.

'When will you be back?' she asked.

'Monday, I expect,' Jimmy replied, 'unless the old boy wants to see me again. I can't face Sunday trains—they're quite impossible.'

It was difficult for Lorna to say how much she minded him going, although, for so short a time. When she had crept out after Sally, and the children had gone to bed, and they were alone at last, she found it impossible to express her varied emotions.

All the afternoon, she had kept reassuring herself that money could make no difference to what they felt for each other, and yet even in the magic darkness of the orchard with Jimmy's arms round her, with his lips pressed against hers, the knowledge of his wealth and social position was like a barrier between them.

It impeded the happy words she would have spoken, it checked the soft whisperings of love which came to her lips, to die away unsaid.

She had been so completely happy in the wonder of her love, she had been so sure that Jimmy loved her as she loved him—yet now the feeling of apprehension was there. Was she merely a new interlude in his life, when for her he was the awakening of life itself?

Even when he held her passionately in his arms, when his kisses grew fierce and possessive, she found it difficult to surrender herself to the ecstasy which had been hers before. It was as if some critical, controlled part of herself watched him and waited.

'I love you, Cherry Ripe . . . you are adorable . . . kiss me . . . oh, my darling ! . . .'

Lorna returned his kisses, and for a moment doubts were swept away by an overwhelming flood of love and tenderness. Then she remembered.

'I must go.'

At last she spoke, recalled to realities by that independent, cold, reasoning part of her mind. She shivered; there was a drop in the temperature and the wind blowing softly through the orchard was chill.

'I don't want you to go—I don't want to go myself—I want to stay. Oh, my sweet ! Can't you understand how much I want to stay with you? I want you so !'

She could not disbelieve his need, could not doubt his urgent desire, or be deaf to the words he was whispering hotly against her hair. But then she was alone—creeping back through the darkness towards the Vicarage, letting herself in through the french window with cold and trembling hands.

She reached her own room and sank down on the bed hiding her face against the pillow. She had to face it; she had to look the truth in the eyes and know that, while he had voiced his need of her again and again, he made no mention of marriage.

She wondered how long she would have gone on without realising the truth had not Sally come to show her so clearly that Jimmy was not 'her sort' but the product of a very different world.

Only circumstances created by the war could have brought about their meeting, or—Lorna told herself bitterly—resulted in his being attracted by her.

Walking along the road now after a sleepless, restless night, Lorna felt that it was a pity Jimmy could not see her and realise, once and for all, how vastly their lives differed. In her old mackintosh and battered felt hat she felt drab and uninteresting.

The big leather shopping bag she carried contained the month's supply of Church Magazines which were to be delivered to one of the district visitors who would distribute them.

She thought of Jimmy. Perhaps now he was still lingering over luncheon in some smart restaurant. War or no war, she had learnt from Sally's conversation that social London would still gather together for meals, would still laugh and talk lightly; despite the devastation in the streets outside.

Jimmy would be back amongst his friends—was it likely, in spite of his assurances, that he would give more than a passing thought to the girl he had kissed clandestinely in the orchard of a Vicarage garden?

'I will ask Sally to tell me what he does in civil life,' Lorna thought. 'Does he really spend all his days running round with her crowd?'

She felt completely alien to them, not that she was antagonistic, but because it was impossible for her, with her upbringing, to be familiar with their slick sophistication.

But Lorna was not to have the opportunity of questioning Sally. When she rose in the morning, heavy-eyed and listless, she remembered that she had a Guide meeting at nine o'clock. Sally was still asleep and Lorna hurried off, telling Minnie to take up her breakfast when she rang, and exhorting the children to be as quiet as possible leaving for school.

It was after twelve when Lorna got back to find that Sally had gone.

'She left a note for you on the hall table,' Minnie said. ' "Recalled from leave," she said she was, and knew you'd understand.'

'I hope there wasn't a very bad raid last night,' Lorna exclaimed. 'It sounds as if there might have been. I wonder how we can find out.'

'We'll hear about it soon enough—bad news travels fast,' Minnie answered grimly.

Lorna went to get Sally's note. It was effusive and full of thanks for her hospitality, but it told her nothing. Yet, taking off her Guide uniform, she thought wearily perhaps that was for the best. What was the point of wounding herself still further?—of increasing her doubts and unhappiness?

She changed, and was ready for the children when they came back to lunch.

'Where's Sally?' Peke asked.

Lorna explained.

'Oh, bother!' Peter said. 'She's promised to take us out in her car this afternoon. I wanted to try it. I'm sure it could absolutely whizz along.'

'Did any of you see her this morning before you left?' Lorna asked.

'Yes, I did,' Beth said. 'Just as I was going out of the front door, she shouted at me from the landing to bring her up the papers and the telephone book. I went up—and oh, Lorna! you should have seen her nightgown! Pale pink chiffon and real lace. And what do you think she gave me?'

'I've no idea.'

'A lipstick!'

'Well, I think it's too bad of her, and you are not to use it, anyway. If you do I shall tell Daddy.'

'Don't be a pig,' Beth said coaxingly. 'It's a lovely one, Lorna, and must have cost at least seven-and-six, and it's got the cutest little green case. I'll show it to you—you'll be as envious as anything—and what's more, I'll use it very discreetly. Can't afford to waste it unless something exciting turns up.'

In spite of herself Lorna had to smile. Peter was still grumbling about missing the promised drive.

'If she'd waited until after lunch we could have gone with her some of the way, and got the bus back.'

'Well, it's too late now to think of what we might have done,' Lorna said, speaking as much to herself as to Peter. 'Incidentally, what are you all going to do this afternoon?'

The discussion as to the best means of passing the hours until tea-time carried them through the whole of luncheon. Only one thing emerged really clearly—which was that nobody wanted to accompany Lorna into the village with the magazines.

Little Walton was a widely distributed parish. The Hall, the Vicarage, the Doctor's house, and about a dozen cottages were grouped near the church; but the general store, the Post Office, and the larger portion of the village were nearly a mile away.

Lorna left her magazines at the cottages; then, passing the Doctor's gate, she hesitated. Should she go in? There was just a chance that Michael might be at home and somehow she wanted to see him urgently. She felt lost and lonely, and the thought of him and of his sane, sensible, reliability was a comfort she could not resist. She walked up the drive.

As she reached the door a car came speeding up behind her. It was Michael! His face gladdened at the sight of her. He opened the door and jumped out.

'Lorna, my dear, what brings you here?'

'I thought I'd like to see you,' Lorna said. 'I brought the magazines for Mrs. Browning, and then wondered if you were at home.'

'I am,' he said.

He opened the front door and drew her in. 'You're wet. Leave your mackintosh here. There'll be a fire in the study.'

He helped her out of the mackintosh and, putting his arm in hers, drew her through the low oak-beamed hall into his own sanctum. It was a large room lined with books and from it a passage ran to the back of the house, where the surgery was situated.

'Sit down,' he said.

Lorna did as she was told. He threw a log of wood on to the fire and she leant back in the big armchair and shut her eyes. She suddenly felt exhausted—worn out by her own emotion.

'You're tired.' His voice was gentle, and then she felt his hands raise her feet.

'Don't worry about me,' she said.

'I'm going to take off your shoes—they're soaking. You must be crazy to walk about in the wet with soles like these.'

She smiled at him without arguing. It was pleasant to be bullied by Michael, to let him scold her as he had done ever since she was a tiny child. He propped her shoes against the low fender to dry.

'Now your hat.'

She pulled it from her head.

'Thank you, Michael.'

'You look tired. What have you been doing to yourself?'

'Nothing.' She turned her head away from him, shutting her eyes, conscious that in some degree she had found peace.

'Well, you wait quietly here while I go and see if there is anyone in the surgery,' he said. 'I had to go over to Great

Walton immediately after luncheon, so if there are any patients they'll have been waiting. I shan't be long and when you've had a cup of tea I'll take you home.'

'I don't want any tea. I shall have to get back for that.'

'I shan't be long,' Michael said again. He opened the door which led to the surgery.

'Why not sleep?' he suggested, and was gone.

Lorna sat still in her chair. There was no sound in the room save the crackle of the flames as they licked appreciatively the fat log Michael had given them. Lorna had known this room ever since she was a child—it was untidy and it lacked in many ways artistic cohesion, yet it was a lovable room.

It was a room where generations of people had come, not only to find a cure for their physical ills, but often for their mental ones.

'The Doctor's a better priest than the Priest's a doctor,' Lorna had often heard her father say, and she knew that old Dr. Davenport had healed as many hearts as he had limbs.

She wondered if Michael listened to confessions here, and if people stammered out their unhappiness when they came to consult him about something quite different.

It was warm and cosy in front of the fire. Lorna closed her eyes wearily. When she opened them again Michael was sitting there looking at her.

'I've been asleep.'

She was dazed, and for a moment could not think clearly. At the back of her mind there was something she was trying to remember, but the sharpness of it had gone and it took her some minutes to recall that it was her own unhappiness she was striving to re-create.

'You look better.'

'How long have I been asleep?'

'Not long.'

'I hope I didn't snore!'

'Why were you so tired?'

Michael's question was casual, yet Lorna knew him well

enough to know that he was asking professionally rather than sympathetically.

'Because I'm a fool—if you want to know!'

He raised his eyebrows.

'That's the last way I should have described you.'

'It's the truth, nevertheless,' Lorna insisted.

'Would you like to convince me of that, or is it a secret?'

Lorna hesitated.

'Haven't you any idea?' she asked.

'Perhaps.'

'You know, then, that I lied to you the other day.'

'I suppose I might have guessed you would. The question wouldn't have occurred to me unless there'd been a reason for asking it.'

'Michael, I suppose really I oughtn't to talk to you like this but there's no one else. I'm so unhappy.'

'I gathered that watching you sleep. Do you know what you looked like?'

'No . . . what?'

'A child that was lost in a strange wood and sleeping from sheer exhaustion.'

'Sounds nice and poetical,' Lorna said. 'The first part's true enough. Why do these things have to happen?'

'To make one grow up, I suppose.'

'It's a hard way of having to do it. One minute it's so wonderful—and then one's afraid.'

'I know.'

'Has it ever happened to you?'

Even as she asked the question, Lorna wondered if he'd reply that it was happening to him.

'There was a poem I read once,' he said at length. 'I can't remember who wrote it. It started—"Open your wings and fly." I think that's what we all have to do sooner or later. Some of us only when we are forced; but for each one—the adventurous, the reluctant, even the coward—there must be that dizzy moment, half exaltation, half fear, when one soars off, flying for the first time.'

Lorna drew in her breath.

'Perhaps some people,' she said in a very small voice, 'start flying before they realise it, before they are wise enough to know what it's all about.'

'Whatever the reason,' Michael answered slowly, 'the act of opening one's wings is worth it and is inevitable.'

'You are certain it's worth it?' Lorna asked.

'Quite certain,' he said steadily.

They were both silent, Lorna thinking of herself, of her own wings opening to carry her out of the security and the quiet peace she had always known, into the emotional conflict from which at the moment she could not escape. Yes, Michael was right, it was worth it!

'Open your wings and fly' . . . she would always remember those words, she thought. She looked across the hearth at Michael.

'Thank you, Michael.'

He got to his feet.

'What for?' he asked gravely. 'For receiving what I consider the biggest compliment you can pay me—turning to me in trouble? I thank you, Lorna, my dear. It's what I want more than anything else—to be there when you need me.'

'You always have been,' Lorna said.

Michael turned away towards his desk.

'Thank God for that!'

9

'Lorna! Lorna!'

Lorna stirred uneasily, turned over and woke up.

'What is it? What's the matter?'

She opened her eyes and saw Beth was standing in the room. The curtains were closed, but Lorna recognised the dim figure outlined in the doorway.

'I want something for my throat—it hurts awfully!'

'I'll get you something. What time is it?'

'Nearly seven o'clock. I've been lying awake for hours, but I didn't like to disturb you.'

'Sweet of you, but I shouldn't have minded.' Lorna jumped out of bed and pulled back the curtains. 'Now, what's the matter? Have you got a cold? I thought your eyes looked a bit funny last night.'

'They hurt too. It may be hay-fever.'

Beth's voice was husky. Lorna looked at her in the clear morning light, and gave an exclamation.

'You do look awful! Why Beth, you've got a kind of rash. Let me look at your chest.'

Beth obediently undid the front of her nightgown. She certainly looked miserable; all her flamboyance and superficial glamour had disappeared, leaving only a sick and very sorry little schoolgirl.

Lorna took one look at her chest.

'Measles!'

Beth gave a cry.

'Oh Lorna, not measles—it can't be! Besides, it's in my throat that I feel bad—sort of choked.'

'Your glands are swollen.'

'They do hurt—frightfully.'

'It is measles, then,' Lorna said firmly. 'I only hope they're the real sort—not German. We've all had the ordinary kind.'

'Oh, it can't be!' Beth wailed. 'I can't stay in bed—there's such a lot of things I want to do.'

'I'll get Michael to come and look at you, but don't be silly about it, Beth. If it's measles it can't be helped. Anyway, you've got to keep warm. Hurry back to bed.'

'It's just a bad cold, I know it is!' Beth insisted plaintively, but she obeyed nevertheless.

'Oh dear!' Lorna thought, 'I hope she's not going to be bad. Measles can be horrid and result in complications if one is not careful.'

Lorna put on her dressing-gown and went to look in the medicine cupboard for some lozenges to ease Beth's throat.

'I won't ring Michael for an hour,' she thought. 'He might have been out late on a baby case; or even if he hasn't, he's entitled to a full night's rest, with all he's doing these days.'

She found the lozenges and took them along to Beth, who was in bed with the sheets pulled up to her chin.

'Lorna,' she said in a husky whisper, 'you don't think I'm going to be really ill, do you? I feel ghastly!'

'You'll be all right, darling,' Lorna replied. 'I expect you've got a temperature. Michael will give you something to take it down as soon as he comes.'

She tidied the bed, and started picking up Beth's clothes, which had been thrown in untidy confusion on to a chair the night before.

'Supposing,' Beth said suddenly, 'just supposing I died—do you think anyone would mind very much?'

'You're not likely to do that,' Lorna replied, 'so I shouldn't worry about it.'

'I was thinking about it in the night,' Beth went on, 'and wondering who'd come to my funeral. The village would

turn up as a kind of peep-show—you know what they are!
—but among the real mourners there'd only be you and
Daddy. I don't believe the twins would mind a bit.'

'Why this sudden morbidness?' Lorna asked. 'It would
take more than an attack of measles to knock you out, Beth.'

'I think you're very unsympathetic,' Beth said plaintively.
'If Mummy were here she'd understand.'

Lorna was hurt. She tried so hard to fill the empty place
left by her mother. She knew it was impossible, and she felt
only an inadequate substitute; nevertheless, when either
Peter or the girls mentioned a lack of maternal love or sympathy, she was hurt and slightly resentful.

She could think of nothing to say in answer to Beth now,
and kept silence while she hung dresses in the wardrobe and
straightened shoes beneath the dressing-table. After some
moments, a somewhat ashamed little voice behind her
croaked :

'I'm sorry, Lorna darling. I didn't mean that.'

Instantly Lorna was disarmed. She walked across to the
bed.

'It's all right,' she said, 'I understand. I often feel like that
myself when things go wrong.'

'Do you really?' Beth looked surprised. 'Yes, I suppose
you must miss her too—perhaps more than any of us. I've
never thought of that. Sorry I'm such a beast, Lorna. You're
wonderful to us and we don't deserve it.'

'Rot!' Lorna was embarrassed now. She bent and kissed
her younger sister's flushed cheek. 'I'm going to ring up
Michael. I'll come back in a few minutes to see if you want
anything.'

'I'm all right,' Beth replied.

As Lorna went downstairs to the telephone she was thinking that Beth's words had echoed her own recent longing for
a mother's help and advice. In these last days, when she had
been feeling so utterly miserable and lost, she had cried out
in her loneliness for the love and sympathy which had never
failed her in childhood.

'I've been selfishly absorbed in myself,' she thought now—somewhat guiltily. 'I ought to have noticed that Beth wasn't well yesterday. Mummy would have immediately suspected that she was too quiet to be healthy.'

She picked up the telephone, dialled the Davenport number, and a moment later heard Michael's voice.

'Am I too early?' she asked. 'I hoped you'd be awake.'

'I'd forgive you anything,' he replied, 'even to waking me up from a really deep sleep.'

'I'm sorry,' Lorna said contritely, 'but I think Beth's got measles.'

'What makes you think that?'

Michael was wide awake now. It was funny, Lorna thought, how his voice changed when he was talking professionally. She explained how Beth was looking and feeling.

'It certainly sounds suspicious,' Michael said at length. 'I'll be round within an hour. Keep her warm and don't try any of your patent medicines on her.'

'I won't,' Lorna promised.

She ran upstairs to tell Beth the news. The twins were already awake and were fighting for the first bath. Lorna dressed, and knocked on her father's door, before hurrying to the kitchen to tell Minnie the news and warn her that Michael might be there for breakfast.

By the time breakfast was finished and Michael had come and gone they had learnt the worst! Beth had got measles — and the only redeeming feature was that they were the proper sort.

'I wonder where you picked them up?' Michael said, reflectively, at Beth's bedside. 'I've only had one other case in the neighbourhood this month, and that was one of the men at the Searchlight Battery at Great Walton.'

'Well, he can't be contagious all that distance away,' Lorna said, and then noticed Beth's face—there was an expression of guilt on it which could not be misinterpreted!

She said nothing at the time, but when Michael had gone and she had helped wash up the breakfast things, she went upstairs. Beth was looking cooler and more comfortable.

The blinds were half drawn as a protection for her eyes, but the room was not dark and the sunlight made golden patches on the floor near the windows.

Lorna sat down beside her sister.

'How are you feeling?' she asked.

'Better,' Beth replied. 'I always did think Michael was a good doctor.'

'Are you well enough to tell me how you met that member of the Searchlight unit?' Lorna asked.

Beth's already flushed face grew even more rosy.

'I was bicycling that way, so I took them some books. After all, it's pretty deadly for them, stuck out in a ploughed field. They're over two miles from the village.'

'Where did you get the books from?'

'Out of Daddy's study. They were some old novels and I knew he'd never want them—you know he hates novels.'

'Oh Beth . . .' Lorna started, and then she stopped. 'I don't know what to say to you. You're hopeless, you are really. Why can't you behave like other girls of your age?'

'I can't think,' Beth replied cheerily. 'I expect there's bad blood in the family somewhere. Look at Sally. Perhaps I shall be like her when I grow up. I hope so, anyway.'

'Sally's different,' Lorna said.

'I don't see that she is,' Beth retorted. 'She runs after men —you can't say that she doesn't—why, she made a dead set at your Jimmy.'

'Don't talk like that. He isn't "my" anything. I suppose there's nothing I can say to make you see sense. Anyway, I hope you feel that your interest in the welfare of the troops has been rewarded by having to spend at least ten days in bed!'

'You needn't be sarcastic. And if you want to know, they weren't awfully pleased with the books. I expect they thought them a bit old-fashioned.'

'I'm not surprised. Daddy must have collected them when he was at Oxford. If you wanted to go as much as all that, you could have gone with Miss Lawson. She takes them books and magazines from the W.V.S. at least once a fortnight.'

'As if I'd want to go with that old trout!' Beth said scornfully.

'Well, it might have been better than getting measles.'

'Perhaps she'll get them too,' Beth said mischievously, 'and then it will look suspicious.'

Lorna's mouth twitched at the corners in spite of trying to look grave : but it was difficult to be cross with Beth when she was such a pale shadow of her usual exuberant self.

Nevertheless, she made a mental note that she must speak to her father and get him to have a really serious talk with Beth before she was up again.

'If only she had some other interest,' she thought to herself. 'Now, Peter and Peke are no trouble.'

Then she wondered whether sooner or later Peter's passion for flying might not result in some hasty and ill-considered action.

She put on an overall, tied a handkerchief round her head and brushed out the drawing-room. Jimmy should have returned from London yesterday, and yet she had heard nothing from him.

'I'm a fool!' she told herself sharply. 'And I'm making myself miserable. I expected this and yet now it's come I can't face it.'

Of course Jimmy would have enjoyed himself in London, he would have forgotten her in the excitement of meeting his friends again, of going to all the familiar places with the people he knew so well. He had been bored and lonely here —that was why he was prepared to spend the time amusing himself in the best possible way—but now she must realise the truth.

A short flirtation to while away some empty hours was all that Jimmy had asked of her; it was she who had made the fatal mistake of asking more, of demanding serious feeling when she had been offered light-hearted frivolity.

Lorna finished the drawing-room and, taking the vases to the scullery, emptied them of their overblown flowers; she washed them, refilled them with fresh water, and put them back in the drawing-room. Fetching her garden scissors and basket, she went out into the garden.

'Lupins,' she thought, 'on the table in the window, roses on the writing-desk, and a big bowl of pinks by the book-case.'

Her task was nearly finished when the sound of Jimmy's voice startled her.

'Do you ever stop working for a moment?' he asked.

She turned round quickly, unable to stifle a little cry of joy. Then, as he held out his hand, she stepped back.

'You mustn't come here,' she said, 'we're in quarantine.'

'What for?' he asked.

'Beth's got measles—real ones.'

'I've had them, so that's all right. Now welcome me properly—I hate these shocks.'

'What do you want me to say?' Lorna prevaricated. 'It's a bit late for "Hello!" or "How do you do".'

'You might kiss me,' he suggested.

'In full view of the house?' she asked. 'You must be crazy!'

'No, only impatient,' he answered.

Her eyes fell before his and she stooped to pick up her basket.

'You've come far too early in the morning. There's a lot of work to do yet.'

'I'll come and help you.'

'You wouldn't like to sit in the garden and wait till I've finished?'

'I should loathe it. Besides, you can talk to me while you are arranging the flowers.'

Lorna turned towards the house.

'I haven't time to argue. Tell me about your arm.'

'Oh, that's splendid. It will be all right in a far shorter time than we expected.'

Lorna felt a sudden pang, but she managed to ↑
steadily: 'I'm so glad. You want to get back so much, ↑
you?'

'Of course I do—I hate being out of it—but I shall also
hate leaving you—you know that, don't you?'

'I hope you'll give me a thought occasionally.'

Lorna tried to speak lightly and in what she imagined
was the right tone of flirtatious response. They walked
through the open french window into the sitting-room.
Lorna put her basket down on the table in the window; as
she did so she knew that Jimmy was just behind her and
waited, not daring to turn her head—scarcely daring to
breathe.

'Look at me, Cherry Ripe.'

She trembled and dropped her head lower, her hands
moving aimlessly about the flowers. Then she felt his hand
on her shoulder. She yielded to his touch and turned round
to find herself imprisoned. He bent his head and his mouth
touched hers. He kissed her, first gently, then passionately.

'Now say you are glad to see me,' he commanded.

'So glad! . . . so very glad!'

His magnetism captured and enchained her—she could
think of nothing save his nearness and the fact that she loved
him.

'You're so sweet, so unspoiled, so perfect after . . . London,' he hesitated before the last word—he had been going
to say something else.

'I expected you yesterday.'

Lorna had not meant to say that but, somehow, she could
not prevent herself.

'I know, darling, but I didn't get down till late; by the
time I had handed in Sir Alfred's report and seen the Commandante and all that sort of thing, I was just about ready
for bed.'

'Of course! Only I wanted to see you.'

'And I wanted to see you—I can't tell you how much.
Have you thought about me while I've been away?'

f course I have.'

'here's nobody like you. I love you—you know that, don't you, Lorna?'

'I want to believe it,' Lorna said. 'How much do you love me, Jimmy?'

'More than anything in the world. And you?'

'More than I have words to tell you.'

Jimmy's grip tightened round her shoulders, his mouth was very close to hers.

'Then what are we waiting for?' he asked. 'I want you . . . I want you to belong to me. Is there any point in going on waiting?'

'What do you mean?' Lorna's question was hardly above a whisper.

'What do you think I mean, you little Puritan?' Jimmy asked. 'Don't you want to be my wife?'

It was as if some tension snapped within her. She went limp and hid her face against Jimmy's shoulder. She was conscious that his coat smelt of tweed and tobacco, she felt the rough hairiness of it against her cheek, and within her a voice was singing in utter rapture. He did love her! . . . he did mean it! . . . he wanted to marry her!

Never afterwards could she remember clearly the happenings of that next half-hour—what she said was lost in a golden ecstasy through which she could remember only the wonder and beauty of being loved. At last she drew herself from his arms and going to the mantelpiece raised herself on tip-toe to look in the glass.

'Why did you have to propose to me when I was looking like a housemaid?' she asked, pulling the silk handkerchief from her hair and pushing up its curls with her fingers.

'I'm sorry,' Jimmy replied, sitting on the edge of the table watching her. 'Shall we consider it unsaid?'

'Yes,' Lorna answered. 'I want to be wearing my best dress, I want a full moon and a nightingale, the scent of syringa, and perhaps a Strauss waltz playing quietly in the distance.'

'You ridiculous infant! Come here!'

For a moment she did not obey him.

'Don't you hear me?' he asked. 'I want you.'

Slowly she came towards him until at last his arm could reach her. He put it round her waist and drew her close.

'You look about twelve years old,' he said. 'You make me feel as if I were cradle-snatching.'

'You talk as if you were a Methuselah.'

'It isn't only years, it's experience. So far as that's concerned I'm a very old gentleman, in fact I'm not certain that I'm not a dirty old man! While you . . .'

Lorna put her fingers to his lips.

'I refuse to be abused,' she said. 'As to being inexperienced, I'll prove an apt pupil.'

'And I'll adore teaching you.'

He bent and kissed her neck. She put her arms round him.

'I do love you, Jimmy.'

'Oh, my sweet . . .'

The door opened suddenly and they started apart. Minnie came in.

'Good morning, sir. I had no idea you were here.'

Lorna recovered herself and ran towards the old woman.

'Minnie darling, congratulate us. We're so terribly happy.'

Just for a moment Lorna thought Minnie was going to express disapproval; then she smiled, let Lorna kiss her affectionately, and held out her hand to Jimmy.

'You're getting one of the finest girls that ever stepped, sir,' she said. 'You will make her happy.'

It was a command, not a question.

'I promise I will do that,' Jimmy answered.

'And when are you thinking of being married?' Minnie asked.

'Just as soon as I can get a special licence.'

Lorna gasped.

'Oh, but I can't . . . You didn't tell me . . .'

'But of course,' he said. 'Why should we wait? I have got to go back to my Squadron—I might be sent abroad. The quicker the better, darling. We want to be together, don't we?'

'Yes, of course,' Lorna replied; but she was startled and in some inexplicable way, a little afraid.

It was one thing to love Jimmy and to be happy in the knowledge that he loved her; it was another to decide in a few minutes to leave her old life, to sever the ties which bound her and start off into a new existence with someone who was almost a stranger.

And yet how could she find him strange?—she loved him.

Just for a moment, the feelings she had experienced when he and Sally were together came back to her in almost overwhelming force; then they were dispersed and vanished completely beneath the magic touch of Jimmy's hand on hers. She clung to him. There was nothing to be afraid of —the future which lay before her was glorious beyond expression.

'I came to see,' Minnie said, 'what Beth is to have for lunch.'

'Beth!' Lorna looked stricken. 'I'd forgotten all about her! Do you think she wants anything? There's no bell in her room—I'd better go and see.'

She released Jimmy's hand and ran up the stairs with an almost desperate haste, arriving breathless and panting at Beth's door. She went in quietly. Beth was drowsy but she opened her eyes.

'I'm sorry I've been so long,' Lorna said. 'Is there anything you want?'

'No, I'm all right,' Beth answered. 'I'm awfully hot though.'

Lorna touched her.

'Yes, you're sweating,' she said. 'I'll change your nightgown.'

She got a fresh one out of the drawer, Beth sat up in bed and Lorna helped her change. Then, as she lay back against the pillows, Lorna could keep her secret no longer.

'Beth, I'm so happy,' she said, 'I'm going to marry Jimmy.'

'I say, how thrilling! Has he proposed to you? When did it happen?'

'Just now,' Lorna replied. 'He arrived while I was in the garden cutting some flowers.'

'It would be my luck to be up here with all this going on. I always miss all the fun.'

'Well, darling, it would hardly have made any difference if you'd been up. It isn't a theatrical performance.'

'I know—but I'm out of it up here.'

'He'll come up and see you,' Lorna promised. 'He's had measles so it doesn't matter. Oh Beth, it's so marvellous!'

'What do you feel like?'

'I can't explain. Just happy . . . and awfully excited.'

'What will you wear, and can I be a bridesmaid?'

'Oh, I haven't thought of all that,' Lorna said, 'we're going to be married very quickly—almost at once.'

'Almost at once!' Beth echoed. 'But if you do that, what's going to happen to us?'

Lorna stared at her.

'I don't know,' she said slowly, 'I hadn't thought . . . Oh Beth!—you'll be able to manage, won't you?'

'I suppose we shall have to,' Beth answered cheerily, 'but it'll be awful without you.'

'And there's Daddy, too,' Lorna said. 'He's so absent-minded. I've got to marry Jimmy, but I shall hate leaving you—it will make me miserable.'

She turned away abruptly from the bed and walked towards the window. There were tears in her eyes and she didn't want Beth to see them. For the first time she realised just how much her home meant to her—how much she loved her father and the children.

Here at home she knew security. For a moment she hated the idea of going away . . . she wanted to stay . . . she wanted life to go on as it always had. . . . And then she remembered Jimmy, and she felt the warm strength of her love for him course through her veins.

How could she be so silly as to doubt that marriage would

bring her perfect happiness? She must find him now. Only his presence could dispel the doubts which were besetting her. She wanted him near—she wanted the reassurance of his love.

She walked from the window towards the door.

'Where are you going?' Beth asked.

'Downstairs—to find Jimmy.'

'Don't go. There are such a lot of things I want to ask you.'

Lorna paused with her hand on the door knob.

'About what?'

'About your marriage; what are you going to do? Where are you going to live?'

'But I don't know any of the answers myself yet.'

'Sally says that Jimmy's awfully rich. Won't it be wonderful, Lorna, not to have to scrimp and save with every penny. You'll be able to have clothes just like Sally's —pink chiffon nightgowns with real lace!'

'I don't think they'd suit me,' Lorna said, doubtfully.

'Nonsense! Of course they would. After all, you can't go about in the things you wear now. You'll be the rich Mrs. Jimmy Braith. Think of it!'

'Don't, Beth . . . don't talk like that!' Lorna spoke sharply, so sharply that Beth looked at her in surprise.

'I'm sorry,' she added, 'I didn't mean to shout at you, but can't you see that I don't want all that sort of thing? I love Jimmy for himself, not because he's rich. I wish he hadn't got a penny!'

'Like Michael?'

'Like Michael!' Lorna repeated the words absently.

'Are you going to tell him when he comes to-night?'

'Yes, I'll tell him, I suppose.' Lorna's voice was disturbed and unhappy.

She opened the door and walked slowly, very slowly, down the stairs.

10

To Lorna's surprise her father was unexpectedly firm about making plans for the wedding. She was so used to looking after him herself, and finding him absent-minded and at times almost as child-like as Peter, that it was strange to find him taking up a very firm paternal attitude.

'The first thing we must do, my dear boy,' he said to Jimmy, 'is to write to your parents. You, of course, would do that anyway, but I would like, with your permission, to send a note to your father suggesting that we might meet and discuss the future of you young people.'

Lorna was well aware that Jimmy was impatient of this old-fashioned attitude.

'I've worked it out like this, sir,' he said to the Vicar. 'My arm should be all right in about ten days—perhaps sooner. I shall then get leave—a week at least. It was my idea that Lorna and I should get married the day I get my discharge from the Home. In that way we could squeeze in a honeymoon—a difficult enough problem in wartime.'

He smiled at Lorna over her father's head and she smiled back, conscious of the thrill his words gave her. A week alone with Jimmy!—nothing could sound more wonderful.

But the Vicar would not agree.

'Why on earth is he like this?' Jimmy asked Lorna as soon as they were alone together. 'Doesn't he approve of me —or what?'

'Of course he does,' Lorna said soothingly. 'It's just that he isn't used to the modern way of getting married and telling people afterwards. He and Mummy were engaged for three years.'

'Good Lord! He isn't expecting us to follow his example, I hope?'

'No, of course not; but I expect, if we're too hurried about it, he's afraid that your father and mother will think I'm a scheming adventuress out to catch a rich young man!'

This was the first reference Lorna had made to Jimmy's money and she felt embarrassed, even as she forced the words lightly from her lips.

'They will only have to look at you to know that's untrue,' Jimmy said. 'You'll get on famously with them, and I'll tell you who you will like—my sister.'

'Your sister!' Lorna exclaimed. 'I'd no idea you had one. I suppose it's silly of me, but I've always thought about you as an only child.'

'Well, I am, to all intents and purposes,' Jimmy replied.

'Muriel's my half-sister—my mother was a widow when she married Father. Muriel's older than I—why, she must be nearly forty—but she's a jolly good sort in her own way. You two will hit it off together—I'm sure of that.'

'And your mother?' Lorna asked. 'Do you think she'll like me?'

Jimmy hesitated.

'Of course she will,' he said—not very convincingly.

'You don't sound very certain,' Lorna challenged.

'Well, Mother's a queer person—she's so busy organising and running things she's almost a machine. You'll understand when you meet her. She's a bit overpowering and gives the impression that one's been put down in her engagement book to absorb just so much of her time and no more.'

'It sounds terrifying!'

'Oh, I shouldn't worry,' Jimmy answered. 'She'll give us her blessing and that's all there'll be to it. She means well. Mother's intensely conscientious but, as I say, she's got so

much and so many people to be conscientious about that in-
dividually one doesn't get much of a look in.'

'Do you think your parents will come and stay here?'
Lorna asked.

'I'd take a bet of a thousand to one against, but, if it
pleases your father to ask them, let him go ahead with it.
I'm all for keeping in with the old boy—after all, he's giving
me the most valuable thing he has.'

'Thank you.'

Lorna smiled. At the same time she felt uneasy and a
little apprehensive. Jimmy's family sounded formidable.
More than once she wished that she could rush off and get
married to him and tell no one; it was difficult to make so
many arrangements.

The twins took the news of the engagement calmly, offer-
ing Jimmy a very sincere welcome into the family. Peter,
indeed, had so much to say to his prospective brother-in-law
that Lorna, looking out of the scullery window while she was
washing-up after lunch, was horrified to see him still in the
garden talking animatedly to Jimmy instead of having left
for Mr. Maidstone immediately luncheon was finished.

'Peter!' she called. 'You're late. Go at once.'

'All right,' he shouted back, but still made no decisive
movement.

'Really, Peter is naughty!' Lorna said, and she wondered
if Minnie would be strong-minded enough to hurry them
when she had gone. But Minnie had so much to do. Lorna
wished they could afford a girl to do the scrubbing.

'If Jimmy's really rich,' she found herself thinking, 'what
a lot of money I could spend here.'

She made a mental list as she dried the plates. New covers
in the drawing-room . . . new curtains in her father's study
. . . new clothes for the children, and a fur coat for Minnie
next winter. She suffered terribly from the cold and her
winter coat was absolutely threadbare.

'And if we're millionaires,' Lorna thought, 'there could be
a curate for Daddy, a finishing school for Beth, and a hard

tennis court for Peter and Peke. Oh dear! that would all cost a terrible lot and I don't suppose for one moment Jimmy would let me do it.'

Nevertheless, she could not help thinking it would be rather wonderful to play the benevolent fairy Godmother to her own family.

At the present time there was the pressing need of some sort of trousseau for herself. Lorna wondered if Aunt Julie would help her but she shrunk from asking her.

'I shall have to buy a few new things,' she thought desperately, reviewing with her mind's eye the contents of her pitiably small wardrobe.

She finished the plates and went into the hall, just in time to hear the front door slam and to see through the window Peter and Peke rushing away on their bicycles.

'Half-past two!' she exclaimed. 'It's too bad of them! Mr. Maidstone will complain to Daddy again.'

She went into the garden prepared to scold Jimmy, but he was lying on the grass, his hat tipped over his eyes, nearly asleep.

'Come and sit near me, darling,' he said to Lorna, 'and let me hold your hand. I want to feel you are real and to be quite certain you won't vanish and leave me inconsolable.'

'I'll never do that,' Lorna said seriously.

'You're certain?' he questioned. 'Oh, I know you're going to take me "for better for worse", but if I get worse won't you be like everyone else and seek refuge in the Divorce Courts?'

'Jimmy! How can you say such a thing!'

'Don't look so shocked, Cherry Ripe. As a parson's daughter, I suppose you must disapprove of divorce. At the same time aren't you just a tiny bit afraid of getting yourself tied up to somebody for ever?'

'Of course I'm not,' Lorna said hotly. 'Do you think I'd marry you unless I was quite certain—quite sure, that I wanted to be your wife, not only when things went right, but when they went wrong as well

'Bless you!' Jimmy lifted her hand to his lips, kissing first her fingers and then the soft centre of her palm. 'You're perfect, but you frighten me.'

'Why?'

'You feel things so intensely—you've got such hard and fast rules as to what is black and what is white. Most of us are morally indecisive, in which case life becomes neither black nor white but a nice, cosy, indistinct grey.'

'But surely you want me to love you for ever?' Lorna asked, bewildered.

'Of course, you infant—I was talking generally at that moment, not particularly about our marriage. I was just wondering what you'd do if I disillusioned you.'

'You couldn't.'

'Again, you're so sure. Lorna, dear, you ought not to marry someone like me—I'm the wrong sort. I shall never value highly enough the things you consider invaluable, or perhaps indispensable. Quite frankly, I'm not quite certain if I know what sin is—while you, I imagine, could tell me very fully what you think both sinful and evil. You ought to marry someone like your doctor friend—he's the direct "pukka sahib" sort of chap that you'd understand.'

'But I don't want to marry Michael,' Lorna said breathlessly, 'I want to marry you. Why are you trying to paint yourself so black?'

'I'm not. I was making rather a feeble effort to tell the truth. I'm even trying to warn you that if you valued your future happiness you'd throw me over. If I'd the strength of will I believe I'd do it myself.'

'Jimmy! How can you say such things! I don't understand. Don't you want me? Then why are you marrying me?'

Jimmy pushed his hat back off his eyes and sat up.

'Darling,' he said, 'I'm talking a lot of rot. I'm marrying you because I want you—and I want you more than I deemed it possible ever to want anyone—therefore marriage is inevitable. But having won you I am merely trying in honour bound to point out that you are too good for me.'

'I've never heard such nonsense!' Lorna said. 'Why, the boot's on the other foot. Have you ever thought that I may make you a very bad wife? I don't know what you like in the way of wives, but I feel it's not a person like me at all—not as I am at present anyway. You'll have to help me to be smart and witty and up-to-date—in fact all those things that people will expect from Mrs. Jimmy Braith.'

'Kiss me,' Jimmy said suddenly.

Lorna looked up at the house and hesitated.

'I don't care who's looking,' he said. 'Kiss me.'

She did as she was told and her lips clung to his for a long, ecstatic moment.

'There!' he said as he released her. 'That's to tell you that I don't want any more suggestions about you altering yourself. You're to stay as you are—understand?'

'Aye-aye, sir. I see that you are going to bully me.'

'I'm not really, but I shall be very jealous if I see too many young men hanging around. That dimple at the corner of your mouth is the most provocative thing I've ever seen!'

'Is it?' Lorna asked, putting her fingers up to touch it.

'You know it is, and I bet a great many people have told you so.'

'You're the only one.'

'What? Hasn't even the doctor chap remarked on that?'

'Who—Michael? Of course not.'

'I don't know why you should be so vehement about it,' Jimmy said, watching her through half-closed eyes. 'You're hardly going to pretend that he isn't in love with you?'

Lorna made no reply.

'Isn't he?'

'I suppose so.'

'I wonder why you don't marry him?'

'Why do you keep talking about him? I'm not in love with Michael. I told you the truth when I said that I looked on him as a brother. I always had until the other day.'

'When he asked you to marry him. Was that before or after my arrival in these parts?'

'After.' Lorna was looking down, plaiting a long piece of grass round her fingers. Jimmy whistled.

'So I was the pebble that started the avalanche, was I? And why did you refuse him?'

'Because, as I've told you, I've never thought of Michael in that way, and because I think I was already in love with you.'

'Well, we'll be kind and let him dance at the wedding. When are you going to tell him the joyful news?'

Lorna got rather hastily to her feet.

'To-night, I suppose,' she said, 'when he comes to see Beth. That reminds me, I'd better go and see if the child wants anything. I won't be long.'

'I shall be furious if you are,' Jimmy threatened, and he watched her walking towards the house.

Michael didn't come to see Beth until late. He telephoned to say that he would be out all the afternoon, but would come in either just before or just after dinner. Minnie took the telephone message and gave it to Lorna at tea-time.

There was a sudden silence at the tea-table, and Lorna felt that they were all thinking the same thing—when Michael came there was something he had to be told—something which, even if he had expected it, was bound to make him unhappy.

She was aware with a sudden clarity of vision how everyone reacted to the situation. Minnie was resentful; her father was sad—he was unworldly enough to make no comparison between Jimmy's possessions and Michael's meagre income —he wanted his daughter's happiness and would rather she had found it with the boy they had known all their lives; the twins were frankly pleased that Lorna's choice would be of advantage to them; Jimmy was triumphant.

Yet, when the moment came, it was not half as difficult as Lorna had feared. Michael examined Beth, informed Lorna that there was nothing to worry about, and followed her out of the patient's room.

At the top of the stairs she hesitated; the twins were in

the sitting-room and her father was in the study; she wondered where it would be best to break the news.

'There's something I want to tell you.'

'There's no need,' he replied, 'I've guessed it already. My dear, I hope you'll be very happy.'

'How did you know?' Lorna asked in surprise—at a loss for words now that those she had planned to say were unnecessary.

'You're face is very expressive,' Michael answered. 'To-night you look like someone who's gained their heart's desire.'

'Does it really show as obviously as that?'

'It does to me, and I want to say that Squadron-Leader Braith is the luckiest man in the world.'

'I hope he'll always think so.'

Michael put out his hands and took hers.

'God bless you, my dear. If anyone deserves happiness you do.'

He dropped his hands and started down the stairs.

'You're not going?' Lorna cried. 'Daddy will want to see you and the twins are in the sitting-room.'

'I am very busy.'

Somehow she knew this was not true.

'Don't go, Michael,' she called, hurrying after him. 'I want to talk to you about so many things.'

'But isn't the Squadron-Leader here?' Michael asked, stopping as he reached the hall and turning to watch Lorna come down the last flight.

'He won't be back until nine o'clock at least,' Lorna replied, and added, 'Lady Abbott presides at dinner and she likes it to be a lengthy conversational ceremony.'

'Poor devils! Well, I'll stay for a bit, if you really want me. Let's sit here,' Michael said, seating himself on a sofa by the empty fireplace.

'Why here?' Lorna asked in surprise.

'I'm staying,' Michael answered, 'to talk to you. I don't feel particularly social to-night.'

Lorna put her hand on his arm.

'Oh, Michael dear,' she said, 'you don't mind frightfully, do you? You know how I'd hate to hurt you.'

Michael laughed. It was a harsh sound without much humour in it.

'You're old enough, Lorna, my child, to know that you shouldn't pull the legs and wings off a fly and then ask him if it hurts! Let's leave my feeiings out of it. If there's anything I can do for you I'm yours to command.'

Lorna felt suddenly miserable. Michael was being horrid to her—was being cruel in a subtle way. She looked at him and quick tears sprang to her eyes, and then suddenly his hands were on her shoulders—hands which gripped her almost brutally, and Michael—a strange Michael, with steely eyes and a grim, angry, mouth—was saying :

'Hurts! Of course it hurts! What do you expect, you little fool? But you're to be happy—you've got to be happy, do you understand me—and if you're not I'll wring that young man's neck for him with the greatest pleasure!'

Lorna was too surprised to say anything, she could only stare at Michael, bewildered and speechless. Then abruptly he let her go. He got up and walked towards the front door before she could recover her composure.

'Good night,' he said.

She had one last glimpse of his face and it seemed to her very tense and white—the face of a man driven beyond his strength.

For a long time Lorna sat where Michael had left her, then she forced herself to get up and go into the sitting-room. The twins were talking in low voices; as she drew near they stopped.

'What time is Jimmy coming back?' Peter asked.

'About nine, I suppose.'

'We'll go and meet him then. He usually comes across the fields, doesn't he?'

'Yes, always.'

Lorna felt tired. She wished suddenly that Jimmy was not

coming to-night, that she could be alone with the family just as she had been in the past. She went up to Beth's room, and sat beside her. She had only been there a few minutes when the door opened and Peke and Peter came in.

'Aren't you coming down?' Peke said. 'Jimmy's here, but he won't come up because a nurse has told him that you can get measles twice.'

'It's very exceptional,' Lorna replied.

'Well, he says he isn't risking anything. He wants to look his best on his wedding day.'

'How ridiculous he is!' Lorna laughed. 'What about me, I'd like to know?'

'Oh, you can cover your face with a veil,' Peter replied. 'My Heavens! Beth needs one at the moment, doesn't she?'

'You don't look so hot yourself, even without measles,' Beth retorted crossly. 'If you've come up here to make personal remarks you can go away.'

'I quite agree,' Peke said, for once siding against her twin. 'She can't help looking awful and it's nothing to what you looked like with chicken-pox. Poor old Beth! Is there anything we can bring you?'

'Muscat grapes, peaches, and a huge box of chocolates!' Beth said.

'What a hope!' Peter ejaculated, then his eyes and Peke's met and they both had the same idea at the same moment.

'Jimmy!' they exclaimed together.

'We'll ask him to get Beth something really nice—calves' foot jelly and chicken in aspic,' Peter went on.

'You're to ask him nothing of the sort,' Lorna interrupted.

'Oh, yes we can.'

'He says that now he's one of the family we aren't to hesitate to ask him for anything,' Peke explained.

'Well, I forbid it,' Lorna said crossly. 'I won't have him "sponged on" just because he's got money.'

'Good Heavens! What's his money for?' Peter asked. 'You shouldn't have false pride, you know.'

'Anyway, we're not going to have any!' Peke said.

'I haven't got any either,' Beth interposed. 'Do you think he'd give me a silver fox fur?—I do want one so much.'

'No, of course he wouldn't,' Peter said. 'He'll only give you sensible things—who wants a dead animal slung round their neck, anyway?'

'I'm going straight downstairs to warn Jimmy that he is not to give you greedy, mercenary children one single thing,' Lorna said with dignity. 'I'm ashamed of you.'

She went out of the room and shut the door. There was silence for a moment after she had gone, then Peter and Peke looked at each other.

'Shall we tell her?' Peter asked.

Peke nodded.

'As she's ill—let's!'

Beth's eyes glistened.

'What is it?' she asked. 'Do tell me.'

It was seldom the twins confided in her sufficiently to tell her one of their many secrets. This was obviously an occasion! They settled themselves down on either side of the bed.

'Listen, Beth,' Peter started in a low voice . . .

II

'Cold tongue?' the Vicar asked, as he took up the carving knife. 'It looks delicious.'

'I hope it is,' Lorna replied. 'Minnie and I felt very guilty about opening it—it's out of our store which is ready against an invasion—but we haven't had a minute all the morning. The sitting-room is as clean as a new pin. If anyone so much as dares to breathe in it before Lady Braith arrives I shall faint!'

'I shouldn't worry too much,' the Vicar said mildly. 'She will be looking at you, my dear, not the house.'

'I know,' Lorna answered. 'Isn't it a frightful idea! I feel like a remnant from the sales and that she'll say—"I don't think Jimmy's got much of a bargain—there were much better to be had"!'

'She won't say it to me, at any rate.'

'Bless you! You're looking absolutely fierce. I believe you're quite agitated about your eldest duckling taking to the water.'

'I'm afraid I am,' the Vicar admitted, 'but after all, it isn't a thing that happens every day of one's life. Perhaps by the time we get to Beth I shall be used to the experience.'

'That reminds me—you're helping Beth now. Don't give her too much—Michael said only a small amount of solids.'

The Vicar took a small slice of tongue off the plate.

'Will that do?'

'Perfectly.' Lorna put the plate on a tray which was waiting on the sideboard. 'I'll take it up to her.'

'What's happened to the twins?'

'Oh, they ought to be here at any moment,' Lorna replied. 'I expect they're loitering on the way home as usual—unless Mr. Maidstone's been unusually severe and kept them in. I should help them now, darling, and then they won't interrupt your own meal. I shan't be a moment.'

She disappeared down the passage carrying Beth's tray. As she came downstairs again the telephone rang.

It was Mr. Maidstone. Lorna listened to what he had to say, then, with a white face, she turned towards the dining-room.

'Daddy!' she called.

Even as the cry left her lips, the front door opened and Peke came into the house. Lorna stood still.

'Peke!' she exclaimed. 'What's happened? Mr. Maidstone has just rung up to say that you haven't been there. I thought there must have been an accident or something.'

She suddenly noticed that Peke had been crying and that she was alone.

'Where's Peter?'

'He's all right.' The answer seemed to be dragged from Peke, her voice was low and husky.

'What do you mean?' Lorna demanded. 'Where is he? Why isn't he here?'

'He's all right, I tell you,' Peke repeated. She stared at Lorna sullenly and defiantly, then her self-control snapped. She gave a cry—a shuddering, inarticulate cry.

'He's gone,' she shouted, 'He's gone and you can't stop him! You won't understand—none of you will understand —it's this ghastly horrible war!'

She stopped, the words seemed strangled in her throat, and before Lorna could move or speak she turned towards the stairs, her breath coming in great gasping sobs. She reached the landing and rushed into her own bedroom; Lorna heard the door slam and the sound of the key turning in the lock.

For a moment she stood still, debating as to whether she should follow, but she knew instinctively that it would be wiser to leave Peke alone, at least for a little while. There was nothing for it but tell her father. She went back to the dining-room.

'Are the twins back?' the Vicar asked. 'I heard you talking to someone.'

'It was Peke. Peter hasn't returned.'

'Well, he's sure not to be long. Where the twins are concerned it's a case of "Mary had a little lamb . . . and everywhere that Mary went, the lamb was sure to go".'

The Vicar smiled whimsically at his joke—it was not a new one.

'For once that isn't true,' Lorna said quietly. 'Daddy, Peter's done it at last.'

The Vicar put down his knife and fork.

'You mean he's gone?'

Lorna nodded.

'Mr. Maidstone rang up to say that they had neither of them been there this morning, and now Peke's come home alone. She's very upset.'

'She would be. Poor child! The separation will be ghastly for her.'

'But Daddy, what are you going to do?'

'I don't know. To tell you the truth, my dear, I've really no idea. The point is—where's he gone? Has Peke told you that?'

'She didn't say very much,' Lorna answered. 'I'll tackle her later. Oh, I'd forgotten—Lady Braith's coming! How awful! Can't we put her off?'

'That's impossible,' her father replied. 'Jimmy was meeting her at Melchester at two o'clock—she should be here at half-past.'

'Well, she's not staying—that's one blessing. But Daddy, we must do something about Peter.'

'Shall I go up and speak to Peke?' the Vicar asked, half rising in his chair.

'No,' Lorna replied. 'Finish your luncheon first. She's locked her door and I don't think she'll let any of us in until she's stopped crying—you know how Peke hates to show her feelings. I'll get the pudding.'

She went into the kitchen and fetched the plums and custard which Minnie had dished up and left ready.

'I won't tell Minnie yet,' Lorna thought.

She knew how bitterly she would take it to heart and at that moment Lorna shrank from any more emotionalism. She carried the dishes into the dining-room, waited while her father helped Beth, and ran upstairs with the plate.

'What is it?' Beth asked as she came into the room. 'Plums again—I'm sick of them.'

Lorna put the plate down on her tray having cleared away the dirty one.

'Beth,' she asked, 'had you any idea that Peter was going away to-day?'

She asked the question without expecting a satisfactory answer, for Beth and the twins seldom had any knowledge of each other's plans, but the moment she had spoken she realised from the expression on Beth's face that she had known.

'Is Peke back?' Beth asked.

'She's just come in. Where have they been, Beth, and where's Peter gone to?'

'Why don't you ask Peke?'

'She's crying in her bedroom.'

'Crying!' Beth ejaculated. 'Oh yes, I suppose she would. She'll hate being without Peter, won't she?'

Lorna sat down on the bed.

'Tell me what you know?' she coaxed. 'You realise this is awful for Daddy and me. Peter's too young.'

'You can't stop him. He looks eighteen—nobody will question his age.'

'But Beth, you can't want him to risk his life! Can't you see that we'll do everything to help him when he's old enough? But not now, he must wait.'

'Don't worry, Lorna—he'll be looked after all right.'

'How do you know he will?'

'I do know,' Beth said mysteriously. 'It's been fixed up, so don't worry.'

Lorna looked at her suspiciously.

'I wish I knew what you meant,' she said. 'There's something behind all this, isn't there? Somebody must have . . .' She stopped suddenly. 'I never thought . . . the railway fare! Where did Peter get the money! He hadn't got a penny last week. Somebody must have helped him. Jimmy! Was it Jimmy?'

'I've promised not to tell,' Beth said primly, but Lorna knew by her face that she had stumbled on the truth.

It was Jimmy!

'But how could he—how dared he?—when he knew what we felt about it!'

She remembered Peter lingering in the garden with Jimmy on the day they got engaged; she remembered the twins telling her triumphantly that Jimmy had told them now he was one of the family, they could ask him for anything they wanted. Of course it was all plain now; but how could Jimmy have been so idiotic—so cruel?

She got up abruptly from Beth's bed.

'I didn't tell you, did I?' Beth asked anxiously as she reached the door. 'The twins will never trust me again if they think I gave them away.'

'No, you didn't tell me,' Lorna replied. 'I was a fool not to have expected it!'

She went downstairs to her father.

'It was Jimmy!' she burst out as she entered the room, 'Jimmy who helped Peter! Oh! Daddy, I'm so sorry! I can't think how he could have done such a mean thing!'

'Peter would have been very persuasive,' the Vicar said.

He had finished his lunch, and was turning his glass of water slowly round in an absent-minded manner. In the clear sunlight coming through the window Lorna suddenly thought he looked old—old and tired—and there was something else too, an air of fragility about him.

She felt her heart contract. Impulsively she walked round the table and put her arm across his shoulders.

'I'm sorry, Daddy, it's my fault; I ought never to have brought an airman into the house.'

'You couldn't help that. You mustn't blame yourself, my child.'

'If only he could have been a sailor or a soldier—anything except an airman. Doesn't it seem to you, Daddy, as if there's a kind of devilry in fate at times?'

'No, I don't think that,' the Vicar replied, 'but it does seem as if fate is inescapable—"what is to be, will be"—and nothing we can do can prevent it.'

'I shall be furious with Jimmy,' Lorna said. 'That is, if I see him for a moment alone. Oh, why did this have to happen to-day of all days?'

'I know, I know. Well, we can't do anything until your young man arrives.'

'No, we can only wait. I'll talk to Peke, but I imagine she will refuse to tell me anything. And now, if you've finished, I'll clear the table.'

'But you've eaten nothing yourself,' the Vicar protested.

'I couldn't swallow a mouthful,' Lorna replied. 'To tell the honest truth, I feel sick.'

She piled the plates on a tray and carried them into the kitchen, put them down on the table and then, as she hesitated for words in which to break the news to Minnie, she saw that the old woman was crying.

'She knows,' Lorna thought.

It was extraordinary how difficult it was to keep anything from Minnie. She knew almost instinctively if anything was wrong. Now, the door being slammed, or perhaps the small amount eaten of the first course, had given her a clue. Already she would have questioned Beth—or perhaps Peke.

'There's nothing we can do for the moment,' Lorna said gently, 'but Daddy is certain to get him back. Don't be upset.'

'He's made his choice,' Minnie said gruffly. 'He's no longer a child—you've tried to keep him one but you've failed. Now you'll have to grin and bear it!'

'Do you mean that?' Lorna asked in surprise. 'Do you really think that's the best thing to do.'

'I'm sure of it,' Minnie answered. 'He's a brave lad, bless him; all we can do for him now is to pray that, by the mercy of God, he'll be kept out of danger.'

Lorna felt the tears start to her eyes. There was something grand in Minnie's acceptance of Peter's departure. She knew how much the old woman adored him and how, in his moment of revolt, she had not failed him in understanding and sympathy.

'Perhaps you're right,' Lorna said slowly, 'but I'll never forgive Jimmy for helping him. After all, he's Daddy's only son.'

'The Squadron-Leader has certainly taken a lot upon himself,' Minnie said grimly.

'We mustn't judge him until we hear what he has to say,' Lorna said quickly, feeling she had been over-hasty in her remarks.

'Talking won't alter the facts,' Minnie answered, taking up the plates and putting them noisily into the bowl. Then she rubbed her eyes with the back of her hand.

'It seems only yesterday that I held him in my arms,' she muttered, 'and now he's a man.'

There was nothing more to say. Lorna left the kitchen and went up to her own bedroom. When she had changed into her best dress and done her hair she knocked softly on Peke's door. There was no answer. She turned the handle—the door was still locked.

'Peke, let me in,' she pleaded. 'It's Lorna.'

'Go away—I want to be alone. I don't want to talk to anyone, and I shan't tell you anything!'

Peke's voice was muffled, but there was no mistaking the tone of it. Lorna sighed and went downstairs.

She was desperately sorry for Peke in spite of feeling that

a great deal of this was her fault. She had egged Peter on, encouraged him, been in the plot, and now she was suffering. It was inevitable, of course, for Peke's life centred entirely round Peter.

Perhaps, Lorna thought, it might have been easier if they had not been brought up in such an unusual way; but the aunt who had practically adopted them at their birth had idolised them both and had always been there, ready to gratify any wish they might express.

They had always spent half their holidays with her— holidays in which they travelled abroad or stayed in luxurious surroundings, yet Peke and Peter had never been interested in the personal luxuries that wealth could buy— beautiful clothes, which Beth longed for and for which even Lorna had a craving at times, were of no interest to Peke.

She and Peter only wanted to play games, to ski, to win skating prizes—and now to fly!

'How diverse we are as a family,' Lorna thought, 'and I'm the one who seems to have no interest except domesticity— hardly a talent which will commend itself to Lady Braith!'

Jimmy's description of his mother had alarmed her, and standing in the spick and span sitting-room she thought of the type of mother-in-law she would like to have. Somebody gentle and motherly, someone who could, in a small degree, take the place of the mother she had lost.

But wishful thinking would not help—instead she must do her best to make Lady Braith like her. It was important —terribly important, Lorna felt—that Jimmy's relations should approve his choice.

There was the sound of a car in the drive outside and Lorna's instant reaction was one of horror. She would have given anything to run away—to bolt through the french window into the garden—to hide among the thick rhododendron bushes as she had so often done as a child! Instead, she forced herself to go into the hall, to smile politely in what she hoped was a welcoming manner.

Minnie had been waiting by the front door. She opened

it at the exact moment that Jimmy stepped out of the car, and helped his mother to alight.

'Hello, Minnie. Here we are. Mother, this is Minnie—she's nursed all the family since they were babies, including my bride-to-be.'

Lorna heard Lady Braith's voice for the first time and felt that its clear brisk tones were characteristic.

'And here's Lorna,' Jimmy went on, drawing his mother into the hall.

'It was nice of you to come.'

Lorna came forward with her hand outstretched. She wondered if Lady Braith would kiss her, then realised that such an idea would never have occurred to Jimmy's mother.

'It was not very convenient,' Lady Braith said, 'but I managed to fit it in. Jimmy always springs surprises on one at the last moment. You'll find that.'

'Shall I?' Lorna felt at a loss for words.

Jimmy had been right—his mother was overpowering. Physically, she was not a big woman, but her dominating personality tended to make other people feel insignificant.

'Oh Daddy, here you are!' Lorna turned in relief to her father.

'I'm afraid you must be very exhausted after such a long journey,' the Vicar said to Lady Braith, 'and it's such a hot day. Can we offer you anything—a cool drink, or some tea?'

'I had luncheon on the train, thank you,' Lady Braith replied.

'Well, shall we go into the sitting-room or would you prefer to sit in the garden?' Lorna asked.

'The sitting-room, I think,' Lady Braith said. She replied instantly to any question without hesitation.

'You needn't be sorry for Mother,' Jimmy said. 'She likes travelling—in fact she likes anything that keeps her on the go. Don't you?'

'I don't know quite what you mean by that,' his mother replied. 'I certainly have a lot of travelling to do and I have learnt that one does one's duty more efficiently if time and energy aren't wasted in disliking the doing of it. I am sure you agree with me?' she added, turning to the Vicar.

Lorna felt that no one, however brave, would dare to disagree with Lady Braith!

'Of course—quite . . .' her father said. 'And your husband? How is he? It's many years since we met.'

'You were at Oxford together, weren't you? He told me so after he had received your letter—a letter which I must say came as a surprise.'

'I think it has been a great surprise to all of us,' the Vicar said gently.

'Including me!' Jimmy interposed. 'As you know, Mother, I never meant to get married until I couldn't help myself. Well, the moment is here—my days of gay bachelorhood are ended!'

'I suppose we might be grateful for that, at any rate,' Lady Braith retorted drily.

Lorna, watching her closely, saw that her eyes rested on her son for a moment with a somewhat strange expression. It was as if, in spite of herself, she loved him, and yet when she spoke her voice was hard and without any inflection other than that of a somewhat sarcastic humour.

'Well, we won't have much time, so perhaps it would be wise to speak at once of future plans. My son tells me that he wishes to get married as soon as possible and he has asked me to persuade you, Vicar, to agree.'

'I am naturally in no hurry to lose my daughter.'

'That's understandable, but young people want homes of their own and we can't be expected to keep them tied to our apron strings for ever. With my children I always took up a very firm line. While they were young I tried to give them balance and stability—when they reached the age of eighteen I realised that I could do no more for them. They were individuals and must fend for themselves.'

'Unfortunately, our idea of fending for ourselves did not coincide with Father's,' Jimmy interrupted.

'That was to be expected,' Lady Braith replied. 'Your

father, perhaps, is somewhat old-fashioned in his outlook. He liked his children to be dependent on him, but you will remember that I always advocated your receiving an allowance from the time you left school.'

'I do remember,' Jimmy said with relish. 'You were extraordinarily sporting about it.'

'It's my idea that children should shoulder their own responsibilities, especially financially. Unfortunately, as far as Jimmy is concerned his sense of economic values is strangely undeveloped, as you will find out when you marry him.'

She looked directly at Lorna.

'I'm afraid I don't understand,' Lorna said, hesitatingly.

'Mother means I'm wildly extravagant,' Jimmy explained. 'Don't you worry, darling. I'll settle down as a good paterfamilias, and you'll be surprised how well we shall manage!'

'Where are you going to live?' Lady Braith asked.

'Well, that's still to be arranged,' Jimmy replied. 'Until I get back to my Squadron I can't make any plans. Just before I crashed there was some talk of moving; and, of course, there's always the chance of my being sent abroad.'

'Abroad!' Lorna whispered the word below her breath; but Lady Braith showed no sign of any emotion.

'That's one of the reasons,' Jimmy said, 'why I want to get married quickly. I shall get some leave and I want a honeymoon.'

'Where will you spend it?' his mother asked.

'I thought we might go to Cornwall. You could open The Towers for us, couldn't you, Mother?'

'I could,' Lady Braith answered. 'It will involve a certain amount of work, of course, but I'll do it.'

'Fine!' Jimmy said. 'And then we could come to you for a night or two before I report. If the Squadron stays put we can find a house in the neighbourhood. But we can't decide anything until I get back—plans are impossible in wartime.'

'They certainly are,' Lady Braith agreed. 'Well, that's settled then—you'll go to The Towers and then come to us. Now about dates.'

She drew a black morocco engagement book from her bag.

Lorna sat silent, feeling that this was a dream, but she knew she must agree to whatever was suggested. She felt as though Jimmy's mother sapped her will-power, made it impossible for her to do anything but stand on one side—an interested spectator—while her future was arranged by other people.

'Now, what day do you expect to leave the Home?' Lady Braith was asking.

Lorna heard Jimmy's reply, heard Lady Braith turn to her father and knew the die was cast. In a week's time she was to be married—she would be Jimmy's wife. For the first time the thought had no power to stir her; instead, she felt only awed and apprehensive. Could it be true?—and, if it were, could she ever make Jimmy happy?

She imagined that Lady Braith must approve of her. It hadn't taken her long, but then Lorna was sure she was a person who made up her mind instantaneously and never varied from it.

'Whatever happens now,' Lorna thought, 'I would never dare to disarrange her plans.'

'Well, that's settled,' she heard Lady Braith say, 'and now I've something to tell you. Your father and I, Jimmy, have considered it from every angle but we find it will not be practical for us to come to your wedding.'

'I'm sorry,' Jimmy said, 'but I expected it.'

'It is impossible for your father to get away for the whole day, and even if he could manage it the journey is too exhausting,' his mother continued as if he had not spoken. 'While, for my part, any time in the next three weeks is quite impossible; all the organisation of War Weapons Week falls on my shoulders. We are combining our three largest towns, Vicar, giving each town a week of its own, running the three in friendly competition, but uniting the results into a grand total.'

'Needless to say,' Jimmy interrupted, 'there's no one to do

anything except Mother. If there were she wouldn't let them!'

'Rubbish, my dear boy. I'd be only too pleased to have assistance,' Lady Braith said. 'Unfortunately, I have made myself a slave to the Country for so many years that they have grown used to depending upon me.'

It was difficult to imagine Lady Braith being a slave to anyone, Lorna thought. She caught Jimmy's eye, he winked.

Some of the tension she was feeling lessened. Whoever else might be afraid of Lady Braith it was quite obvious that her son held her in no awe and was quite prepared to be amused at her eccentricities.

'And now,' Jimmy said, 'Lorna and I will go into the garden while you tell the Vicar how lucky he is to get me for a son-in-law. Don't accentuate all my worst faults, Mother—leave him a few surprises!'

'All right,' Lady Braith said graciously, 'but keep an eye on the time. I must definitely leave here at half-past four.'

'I expect you'd like to have tea at four o'clock?' Lorna asked.

'That would be very nice, thank you.'

'Come on!' Jimmy slipped his arm through Lorna's. 'We're not wanted.'

Lorna let him lead her into the garden. As soon as they were out of earshot he said:

'Well, didn't I warn you?'

'She terrifies me,' Lorna confessed. 'Oh Jimmy!—do you think she likes me?'

'If she didn't she'd have said so long ago,' Jimmy replied. 'Between ourselves, I think she's delighted with you. The old people are both a bit straight-laced and I think they were in deadly fear that I'd marry a chorus girl or run off with a married woman. Father's after a peerage and he wants to keep the family escutcheon untarnished.'

'Does that mean you would have a title one day?' Lorna asked. 'If so I hope he doesn't get it.'

'Yes—don't you fancy yourself as Lady Braith? I

140

wouldn't mind betting that he gets what he wants in the next Honours List.'

'Things get more intimidating every minute.'

'No one shall frighten you, darling, while I'm about. All I aim at is to please.'

His facetious words jogged Lorna's memory.

'You don't!' she said quickly. 'Oh Jimmy, you've done a terrible thing! I'm furious with you. How could you do it?'

'Do what?' Jimmy asked. 'What are you talking about?' His air of innocence was not convincing.

'You know—of course you know what you've done. Oh Jimmy, where is Peter?'

'Now don't get fussed,' Jimmy said soothingly. 'The boy's all right—I'm looking after him.'

'But Jimmy, where has he gone? I can't tell you what a worry it is for Daddy! We are both so terribly upset.'

Jimmy whistled.

'Phew! I'd forgotten about the old man. Is he annoyed?'

'No, but he is very sorry that it has happened.'

'Quite honestly, darling, I'd never given him a thought. Of course, now I see . . . only son and all that sort of thing! But Peter talked to me about joining the Air Force—well, as you know, he's talked about nothing else ever since I've been here—and I thought—let the kid have his chance. Why not? Life's too short to sit fretting and being miserable. So I gave him some money and a letter of introduction to a pal of mine and he'll be as right as rain.'

'But why didn't you consult us first? We can't let him go like that. Don't you understand? Daddy will have to fetch him back.'

Jimmy thought for a moment.

'I wasn't going to tell you where he'd gone,' he said, 'but I suppose if your father made a point of it, it would be rather difficult for me. All the same, I'd hate to let him down. I tell you what—I shall say I lent him some money but I'd no idea where he was going.'

'You can't lie about it.'

141

'Can't I? Peter's going to keep in touch with me and we'll know exactly how he is and what he's doing, but if you are all going to be difficult about it I shan't pass on the information. I shall just keep mum.'

'Jimmy, I could hate you for this!'

'Oh, no you couldn't! Your brother doesn't mean all that to you and I mean a good deal. Look at me, darling, and dare to tell me you hate me! You know it would be impossible.'

Jimmy, turning suddenly, cupped Lorna's chin with his hand. He tilted up her face so that he could look deep into her eyes.

'Go on!' he urged. 'Tell me you hate me and make it sound convincing!'

She couldn't, and he held her prisoner for a long moment before he pressed his lips against hers. . . . The world of problems and difficulties receded . . . what did anything matter? . . . how could she worry as long as Jimmy loved her and she loved him? . . . He released her and stood laughing down at her.

'There's something extraordinarily exciting in making you give in to me,' he said. 'You make me feel a "Helluva fellow". Perhaps that's why I love you so much.'

'Perhaps one day you'll get bored with such easy conquests. I shall have to stop myself becoming a "yes" woman!'

'I shall beat you if you don't obey me.'

Lorna dimpled at him and turned towards the house.

'I'm not afraid of you, and now we'd better go and see about tea for your mother. I warn you, you're in Minnie's bad books at the moment!'

'I expected that. I can't say it will give me many sleepless nights.'

'The funny thing is, I think she agrees with you. She feels that Peter's grown-up and must do as he thinks right.'

'Of course he must! Now look here, darling, don't you worry about it. I think the best thing will be for me to have a talk with your father and make him see sense.'

'I expect he sees it already. It's I who mind—for his sake and for Peke's.'

'Well, stop worrying about anyone except me,' Jimmy commanded.

'Don't you think you are rather egotistical?' Lorna asked, half-serious, half-joking.

'Where you are concerned—yes. I want you for myself and I want you soon.'

They were walking along the narrow path which led between high bushes to the back door. Jimmy suddenly caught her to him.

'Damn all this marriage business! I'm sick of hanging about, of making plans, of waiting . . . I want you now . . . at once . . . to-night!'

He held her tight against him and kissed her greedily . . . she felt his lips on her hair, her eyes, her neck, and her mouth. . . . There was no checking him, no resisting him, and she let the tide of his passion sweep over her as she stood quivering in the fierceness of his hold.

12

Lorna came out of the house, walked across the lawn, and opening the gate into the churchyard, passed between the ancient gravestones.

In the church the candles on the altar cast a golden light which glittered on the tall cross and on the vases of white and crimson flowers which Lorna herself had arranged the day before—flowers chosen lovingly for her wedding.

She knelt down in the ancient carved oak pew which she had known ever since she could remember. There were only two or three other people in the church; vague, bowed figures whom she recognised but to whom she did not give a second thought. Her father, in his vestments, entered the chancel.

Never, Lorna thought, had the Communion Service seemed so mystic and so inspiring. It seemed to hold a special message for her, a message of hope and sanctification. She dedicated herself to the service of love—a love which she truly believed was an echo of the Divine Love she worshipped.

'Please, God,' she prayed, 'help me to make Jimmy happy.'

The service ended, she slipped away before anyone else moved. She did not want to speak, did not want to listen to congratulations or good wishes. For the moment she wanted to be alone, alone with her own thoughts and feelings, an entity in herself perhaps for the last time.

'In a few hours,' she thought, 'I shall be part of Jimmy and he of me. This is "Good-bye" to my old self.'

She went into the Vicarage garden and walked towards the orchard. Under the cherry tree where she had first met Jimmy she stood still, letting the peace and beauty of the morning envelop her. Now the sun was reaching out pale delicate fingers of quivering gold.

Lorna felt as if they caressed her, bringing her an indefinable joy. She wanted to hold out her arms in love to the whole world. She wanted to pour out her happiness, to give it and share it.

'I'm so lucky,' she told herself, 'so terribly lucky!'

At last she knew she must go back to the house. There was so much to do, so many things to see to, and yet it was hard to cast off this mood of spiritual ecstasy and take up the burden of mundane reality again. But it had to be done.

She passed through the sitting-room, where there was an almost overpowering fragrance of flowers. All yesterday Lorna and Peke had arranged great bowls of roses, delphiniums, lupins, and scented stocks; the room was transformed, its shabbiness hidden and forgotten.

Lorna went upstairs to her bedroom. While she had been out Minnie had tidied the bed and laid out her wedding dress. Lorna looked at it and felt a quick throb of pleasure. It was very lovely—the loveliest frock she had ever possessed. Aunt Julie had sent it to her, with several other dresses, coats, and a collection of exquisite lingerie.

'This is my wedding present, dear Lorna,' she had written. 'Luckily, I remembered that you are exactly the same size as the mannequin who models for Sylvia—these clothes are models and conveniently labelled second-hand. You can therefore spend your clothing coupons on hardwearing, sensible underwear for the family—I believe that will give you more pleasure than any wedding gift I could envisage.'

Lorna had laughed when she received the letter, but she looked with awe at the dresses which looked as if nothing save fairy fingers had ever handled them. All the things were from a famous Court dressmaker, and all of them so perfect in material and line that Lorna felt she would never dare to wear them save on very special occasions.

What a contrast to the garments she was wearing at the moment! One of her old dresses, out of shape and faded, and a shabby straw hat which she had worn for three summers!

She touched the soft blue chiffon of her wedding dress and the pale brown fox cuffs on the coat that matched it. There was also a little cap of soft blue feathers and even gloves of the same colour—Aunt Julie had thought of everything.

'It's all too magnificent,' Lorna murmured. 'I shan't feel like myself at all.'

Later, when she was dressed, she stared at herself in amazement. Clothes did make a difference! The exquisite person reflected in her looking-glass was hardly recognisable as the Vicar of Little Walton's eldest daughter. Peke and Beth stared at her.

'You do look smart,' Peke said at length. 'I shouldn't know you if I met you in the street.'

'Well, let's hope that Jimmy will recognise me,' Lorna retorted. 'It would be a pity if he stopped the service because he thought he'd got the wrong woman!'

'It's the loveliest dress I've ever seen!' Beth enthused. 'Oh, I do wish I were coming to the church—I think it's beastly of Michael to stop me.'

'You're lucky that he'll let you come downstairs. If we were having a proper reception he wouldn't.'

'I'm going to have some champagne, anyway. Jimmy's promised me that.'

'Well, don't drink too much,' Lorna begged. 'I should feel disgraced for ever if you were drunk at my wedding.'

'Don't you worry,' Beth replied. 'To tell the truth, I prefer ginger-beer, but I must drink your health in the real stuff.'

'I wish Peter were here and then he could have given you away,' Peke said wistfully.

'It was nice of him to send a telegram,' Lorna said. She

looked again at Peter's message propped up on the mantel-piece.

'Happy landing. The top of the world to you both.'

She planned that she would write him a long letter at the very first opportunity. Everyone was resigned now to letting him have his own way. Jimmy had been clever about it, Lorna thought, for the Vicar had not really blamed him for being instrumental in Peter's departure.

It had, too, been impossible to resist a long apologetic letter from Peter—'I just had to go,' he wrote—and Lorna knew her father could never humiliate him by bringing him home.

'Now, have I got everything?'

'Your flowers!' Beth cried. 'They came this morning—haven't you seen them?'

'I just peeped into the box,' Lorna replied. 'Get them quickly, Beth—how awful if I'd forgotten them!'

Jimmy had sent her a huge spray of purple orchids. They were very lovely against her dress and when she had pinned them on she looked at herself admiringly.

'I do look grand,' she said. 'I can never be grateful enough to Aunt Julie.'

'Don't forget to let us have all your clothes when you're tired of them,' Beth said.

'Of course I won't,' Lorna said, 'and I'll send you new ones, too, with every penny I can spare—but only on one condition.'

'What's that?'

'That you won't forget to write long letters. Peke, you will let me know everything that happens in the house, won't you? I want to hear every detail—what you have for lunch, who comes to see you, how Daddy is, when you hear from Peter, what's going on in the village . . . don't omit anything. I'll telephone whenever I can, but you know what the lines are like these days.'

'I won't forget,' Peke said, 'but I wish you weren't going. I shall hate having to do it all.'

'I'm afraid you will,' Lorna said, 'but do look after Daddy. You know how careless he is about changing his shoes when they get wet, or remembering to put on a cardigan when it's cold. Do try to remind him, Peke.'

'I'll do my best.'

Peke was looking pale, and even thinner than usual. It was obvious to everyone that she had never recovered her spirits since Peter left.

'I must ask Michael to give her a tonic,' Lorna thought, 'she needs something to buck her up.'

'And Beth,' Lorna went on, turning to her younger sister, 'you will be good, won't you? As soon as Michael says you are all right you are to go back to school and work really hard; and do try to leave the young men of the neighbourhood alone.'

'All right,' Beth said solemnly, then quite suddenly she began to cry.

'Don't, Beth!—don't!' Lorna forgot about her dress and, crossing the room quickly, knelt down beside her sister and put her arms round her.

'I can't help it!' Beth sobbed. 'I don't want you to go away. It'll be beastly here without you—absolutely beastly!'

'I wish I weren't going,' Lorna said and her voice trembled. 'I've a very good mind not to get married, it's all such a fuss, and I can't think how you'll manage without me.'

Beth stopped crying and looked at her open-mouthed.

'You mean you'd chuck it up now!' she asked. 'Oh Lorna, you couldn't! Why, everything's ready, and you would have to send back your dresses.'

'I suppose it's impossible,' Lorna said, weakly. 'We've got to be sensible; but don't cry, Beth, I can't bear it!'

Beth wiped her eyes and gave a loud sniff.

'I thought weddings were gay,' she said, 'but I feel absolutely miserable about this one.'

Minnie opened the door. She was wearing her hat and coat and a large button-hole of white roses.

'I'm going across to the church now, dearie, and the Vicar said I was to ask you to come downstairs as they're all waiting.'

'Jimmy must be here,' Lorna said. 'Come on, Peke, and you too, Beth. You might as well wait in the sitting-room until we come back.'

'What about Muriel?' Peke asked.

'Oh, I expect she's ready,' Lorna answered, 'but go and see, there's a dear!'

Peke went along to the spare room. Lorna was alone in her room for a moment and her eyes rested on her bed and the photograph of her mother which always stood beside it. It seemed to her that she said good-bye to her childhood and to her girlhood, then with her head held high she walked slowly downstairs.

The church was only half full. Lorna had sent out no invitations; only their closest friends had come as a matter of course. The Squire was there to give her away, and the Miss Piggotts; while Lady Abbott, resplendent in flowered satin and a large picture hat, had come from the Hall; otherwise there were just the village people who had known Lorna since she was a baby.

There was no choir, only the organist to play softly as Lorna and Jimmy walked unconventionally up the aisle together. The sunlight, glinting through the stained glass windows, made a halo of light behind her father's head as he came forward to meet them.

Jimmy's voice was firm and strong as he repeated the marriage vows; Lorna spoke softly but none the less steadily. She felt his hand grip hers, and then the ceremony was over and they were in the vestry signing the register.

'May I be the first to kiss my wife?'

Lorna raised her face to Jimmy's. He kissed her on the lips and she turned to her father.

'God bless you, my dear. May you be very happy!'

'Thank you, Daddy. I am happy.'

Peke and Muriel came in to sign the register and then the

bride and groom were walking down the aisle, the villagers crowding after them, anxious to shake them by the hand and wish them all possible blessings.

It was some time before Lorna and Jimmy could escape into the Vicarage garden. They found the Vicar waiting for them with a few people he had asked to come in and drink their health. Lady Abbott, unfortunately, was one of them.

'I really feel quite responsible for this,' she told the Vicar coyly. 'I expect you don't know whether to be grateful to me or to feel annoyed that I have been instrumental in making you lose your pretty Lorna?'

'So long as she's as happy as she is to-day,' the Vicar answered, 'I shall always be grateful.'

'Dear young things!' Lady Abbott gushed. 'The simple ceremony brought tears to my eyes. War weddings are always a little sad, don't you think?—so hasty and unceremonial. It must have been a sad grief to your dear parents, Squadron-Leader, that they could not be present?'

The last remark was to Jimmy but, anxious not to be drawn into the conversation, he pushed his sister forward.

'They have been well represented by my sister. I don't think you've met her. Muriel, you have heard me talk of Lady Abbott's kindness to me while I was in her Home.'

'Your brother has been a model patient. I'm simply delighted to meet you,' Lady Abbott enthused.

Jimmy put his arm through Lorna's and drew her away.

'I can't stand the old chatter-box. I need a drink. Let's go and get one.'

'We mustn't offend her.'

'Can't help it if we do. Come on.'

They started off for the house in advance of the others. Beth met them at the door and kissed them both affectionately.

'Did it go off all right?' she asked. 'Jimmy didn't drop the ring or anything ghastly?'

'There wasn't a hitch,' Lorna replied. 'And you've been all right?'

'Perfectly. I only nibbled one or two of the sandwiches to keep my strength up.'

'You are a pig! If there aren't enough to go round you'll have to cut some more yourself.'

'Let's go and see how much damage she has done,' Jimmy said, leading the way to the dining-room.

'Where's Michael?' Lorna asked suddenly. 'I didn't see him in church.'

'He wasn't there,' Beth replied. 'He's only just come. He's washing his hands—he's come straight on from a case.'

'Well, I do think he might have come to my wedding,' Lorna said in a hurt voice.

'I can't see that it's very important,' Jimmy said.

She looked at him quickly and realised that he was jealous.

'How ridiculous!' she thought. 'Fancy being jealous of Michael.'

It amused her and gave her a sense of power so that when Michael came into the dining-room a few minutes later she held out her hands to him with perhaps a more exaggerated welcome than she would have proffered him in the ordinary way.

'Michael dear, wish me luck! But I'm furious you didn't come to the wedding!'

'Couldn't get away,' Michael said gruffly.

Lorna knew it wasn't true.

'Morning, Davenport,' Jimmy said. 'The arm's behaving well—a bit stiff, but otherwise O.K.'

'I'm glad,' Michael said. 'Don't put any strain on it for a few days, will you?'

'Lorna will have to remind me.'

'Oh, I will! I'm a very good nurse, aren't I, Michael?'

'I don't know—you've never nursed me.'

'Michael! How ungallant of you!' Lorna complained. 'You've seen me nurse hundreds of people and you've always said how good I was.'

'I'm sorry—I seem to have missed my cue.'

'It's getting quite a habit of yours,' Jimmy interposed.

The two men exchanged a glance. Lorna felt as if there was an underlying meaning to all their remarks to each other. It was something she did not understand, but there was no mistaking an atmosphere of antagonism. Nervously she tried to change the subject; the Misses Piggotts were standing near and she started to talk to them.

'Where are you going to-night?' the elder of the two asked.

'To Cornwall,' Lorna replied. 'That's why we had to be married so early. We're going to lunch on the train, we reach Kingsbridge about tea-time, and will motor the last thirty miles from there.'

'How delightful! I have the most charming memories of Cornwall. We were there in 1903—or was it a year later?—and my sister and I . . .'

Lorna was not listening. She was feeling that this was a dream . . . the laughing voices . . . the chatter of tongues . . . the antagonism she had noticed between Jimmy and Michael. . . . It was all part of some fictitious fairy-tale into which she had drifted to find herself playing the leading part. She felt strange, half bewildered, as if she were watching herself move upon the screen of a cinema.

At last it was time to go and a sense of unreality still held her, so that without tears, without any emotion, only a queer numbness, she kissed her family farewell—clung for a moment to Minnie—then was in the car driving away with Jimmy.

She turned round, waving through the small window at the back, but still half convinced she was only acting a part. A silly jingly rhyme kept running in her head; she could only remember one line—

'Lawks-a-mercy, this is none of I!'

'I think weddings are hateful!' As the car disappeared from sight Beth turned away from the door petulantly, but

Michael saw that her lips were trembling and that she was not far from tears.

'You'll enjoy your own,' he said soothingly. 'Come out of the draught, Beth, I don't want you to get a chill.'

'I don't care if I do!' Beth retorted, but she obeyed him.

'I tell you what we'll do,' he said. 'Find a quiet spot where we will not be disturbed and I'll fetch you some sandwiches and something to drink. I don't expect anyone in this house had a sensible breakfast this morning.'

He guessed that Beth was likely to feel particularly depressed by Lorna's departure. She had never had much in common with Peke who had been completely absorbed in Peter. Beth was the 'odd man out' of the family and Michael knew that the aftermath of an attack of measles was also likely to prove depressing.

'Poor child!' he thought, as he took a plate of sandwiches from the dining-room table, at the same time avoiding Lady Abbott's eye—she was looking for another victim on whom to inflict her never-ceasing flow of small talk. He found Beth curled up in the window-seat of her father's study.

'Sandwiches, shortbread, and a large slice of cake,' he said. 'How's that?'

He put the plate down in front of her and produced a bottle of ginger beer and a glass from his pockets.

'Lovely!' Beth said. 'I wish the cake were iced, though.'

'You can't have everything in wartime. Now eat it up and you'll feel better.'

'I feel all right. It's just that I hate Lorna leaving us.'

'We all hate that.'

Beth nodded.

'I know you do. Oh Michael, I wish she'd married you instead of Jimmy!'

Michael's lip tightened for a moment, then he smiled.

'Thank you, Beth.'

Beth looked at him with serious eyes.

'You know I've been thinking a lot since I've been ill,' she said, 'and I see that I was wrong about love and marriage. I

153

thought it would be awfully exciting and thrilling, but I never realised it could be an unhappy thing too—that it could hurt you and make you miserable.'

'It can affect us in many ways.'

'I see that now. I expect you think I'm stupid, but I didn't think of it like that before.'

'You've got plenty of time to get wise before it's your turn.'

'I suppose so, but I don't like to think about time—it passes so slowly and growing-up is a very lonely feeling.'

Michael put out his hand.

'I'm lonely too, Beth. We'd better make a bargain to try to keep each other cheerful.'

Beth flushed.

'Oh Michael, do you mean that? It would be wonderful if you did. You see, I've got no one to talk to now—in fact I have never had anyone particularly. Daddy's always adored Lorna, the twins have had each other, and then there was me—rather a nuisance, it seemed.'

Michael felt his heart contract. This explained so many things—Beth's desire to attract attention, her precocious craving for young men—it was the need to be loved.

'Now listen to me, Beth,' he said. 'I know just what you are feeling—I've felt it myself time after time. I'll help you —and you must help me. We're friends. If you want someone to talk to, you come to me! If I'm feeling blue I shall come and tell you my troubles—and there's something else.

'There's a nursery being started for the evacuated children. Will you come and help me there? I know you can only get off on Saturdays and Sundays, but if you could put in an hour or two it would be of great assistance.'

'But what can I do?' Beth asked.

'Play with the children, for one thing,' Michael answered, 'and afterwards you can tell me what you think about their reactions to ordinary interests. You'd be an excellent person to judge—not too old to join in their games, and not too young to form a definite opinion as to their well-being.

'Some of them are desperately nervous—those are the

154

ones who've been bombed night after night, or have perhaps been buried for several hours. Will you do it, Beth?'

'Of course I will, Michael, if you really think I can help?'

'I know you can.'

'Oh Michael, I think it would be marvellous to have a real job! You'll make Daddy agree?'

'There'll be no difficulty about that.'

Beth put the last piece of cake into her mouth, and licked her fingers appreciatively.

'I shall write and tell Lorna about it at once, and I shall tell her that you're the nicest man in the world.'

'I shouldn't overdo it. Your new brother-in-law might be jealous.'

'Do you really think he would? What fun! Let's make him!'

'Better not,' Michael cautioned.

Beth pushed the plate out of the way, and moving across the window-seat, slipped her arm through Michael's.

'I'm going to show Lorna that I can be good when she's not here,' she said. 'I'm going to work hard with you and not be silly any longer.'

'That's fine! You'll help me and I'll help you—we're "a mutual assistance company." I won't let you down.'

'I don't think you'd ever do that to anyone,' Beth said, speaking with greater wisdom than she knew. Then, with a sigh of content, she rubbed her cheek against Michael's shoulder.

'Do you think,' she asked, 'there's just the bare possibility of your finding me another bottle of ginger-beer?'

13

Lorna was lying on the awning-shaded verandah wrapped in a white bathing robe.

She watched her husband coming up the sandy beach; he was only wearing bathing shorts, and his athletic body, tanned by the sun, reminded her of the statues she had seen of the old Greek heroes. He was amazingly good-looking—there could be no two opinions about that.

She smiled up at him as he reached the verandah and threw himself down on one of the gay chintz-covered mattresses arranged invitingly on the wooden floor.

'It's hot, isn't it?' she said. 'I couldn't bear the glare another moment—that's why I came in.'

'You're getting thoroughly lazy. What have you got there —the post?'

'Yes,' Lorna replied. 'It's just come. A long letter from Daddy full of news, and telling me all the things I wanted to know—what the village thought of our wedding—and pages of local gossip. He also enclosed a letter for you. It was sent to the Hall, but Lady Abbott brought it to the Vicarage with her own fair hands, and asked Daddy to forward it on. It's from Sally, I think—I'm sure I recognise her writing?'

'Oh!' Jimmy didn't sound very interested.

'I expect it's congratulations. Shall I open and read it to you?'

'If you like. . . . No—throw it across. It's a mistake to let you get into the habit of opening your husband's correspondence—you might discover the secrets of his guilty past!'

Lorna laughed.

'Let's be cautious by all means. I should hate to stumble upon the skeleton in the cupboard!'

She threw him the letter. It fluttered through the air, and fell a foot or two short of where he was lying. Jimmy reached out for it and slit the envelope open with his fingers. There was only a single sheet of notepaper inside. He read it, and looked across at Lorna.

'Curious?'

'Of course. It is from Sally, isn't it?'

'You're right, as usual.' He threw the letter back to her and lay down again, closing his eyes.

Lorna picked up the note which fell on her lap. There were only a few lines of writing.

'This is just to wish you happiness, both now and always. With rosemary for remembrance—Sally.'

'What does she mean—"rosemary for remembrance"?'

'Can't imagine. Some sort of joke, I suppose—a reference to my gay, irresponsible bachelorhood. R.I.P.'

'Do you mourn its passing?' Lorna challenged.

'Good Heavens, no! Actually, I never think about the past, so I never have any regrets. I'm not that type of person.'

'Yes, I'm sure that's true of you.'

'I hope so, at any rate.' Jimmy stretched his arms above his head. 'All the same, I wish there was a Casino in this benighted hole.'

'A Casino!' Lorna echoed in surprise.

'A Casino,' Jimmy repeated firmly. 'This is Eden without the apple—or should I say the serpent?'

'What do you mean? Why do you want a Casino?'

'Something to do, my poppet. If things were normal we'd have spent our honeymoon in the South of France—Cap d'Antibes, perhaps, and when we were bored we could have gone on to Biarritz. I'd like to have watched you gambling—it would have given me a thrill, and it would have been fun showing you off in the evening, watching the other chaps thinking what a lucky fellow I was. Damn this war!—it's a nuisance.'

'Do you find it dull here alone with me?' Lorna asked in a small voice.

'Of course I don't. How you trip a fellow up! I'm enjoying myself a hundred per cent. At the same time you can't say it's exactly an amusement park.'

It was impossible to blind herself to the fact that Jimmy was getting restless. Lorna already understood him well enough to realise that swimming, lying about in the sun, and making love, were not enough in themselves.

Jimmy wanted action, he wanted people—crowds, and entertainment. For the first time since she had been married Lorna felt a tiny cloud on the horizon of her happiness.

'Couldn't we motor somewhere this afternoon?' she suggested.

'Don't expect we've got enough petrol.'

'What about the car that brought us here? Couldn't we hire that?'

'What for? There's nowhere to go and nothing to see. Don't you worry—we'll eat a huge lunch and swim it off afterwards.'

His words were consoling, but his tone was sharp as if he were irritated. Lorna looked out over the perfect blue of the sea with troubled eyes. To her this spot was paradise.

Yet now her joy was impaired. Jimmy was bored, and she had the sense to realise it was not any disparagement of her but rather that he had no experience of entertaining himself. He expected amusement to be provided by outside sources from which he could take his choice.

Lorna was no fool. She knew how deadly Sally and other gay friends found Little Walton. After a few hours at the Vicarage they would complain bitterly of the lack of cinemas, ask if there wasn't a local dance, and nearly faint when they discovered that the Overton family did not possess a wireless.

Jimmy was like them, he had been brought up in a world where people were afraid of solitude and bored with their own thoughts. Just for a moment Lorna was afraid for the future. How few interests they had in common!

For one thing, Jimmy, apparently, did not care for reading. Lorna had questioned him as to his favourite authors, and he had not been able to name one.

'But don't you ever read?' she asked.

'Of course I do,' he replied. 'What an extraordinary question. But naturally I don't have much time for novels. I read the papers, and when we're waiting for orders to take off we look at the weekly magazines, the *Tatler, Picture Post,* and all that sort of thing—but books aren't much in my line of country.'

Lorna let the remark pass. It was no use trying to explain to Jimmy that her ideal of enjoying herself was to read a book. Now she found herself wondering despairingly how they would be able to fill in the next three days of their honeymoon.

There was a step on the verandah and the butler appeared with something on a silver salver. He handed it to Jimmy.

'A telegram, sir. It has just been sent over the telephone.'

'Thank you, Burton.' Jimmy looked at it and sat up.

'The Air Ministry!' he exclaimed. 'I wonder what's up? Burton, we'll have to catch the afternoon train. That means leaving here immediately after lunch. See that they start packing our things right away.'

'Very good, sir.'

The butler disappeared, and Jimmy got to his feet.

'The Air Ministry wants to see me at noon to-morrow. Do you think it's promotion or the sack?'

He smiled down at Lorna, and she realised that all his irritation had vanished. He was alert—vividly and vitally alert.

'You don't think you are being sent abroad?' Her voice faltered.

'Who knows?' Jimmy shrugged his shoulders. 'But don't

worry, darling, it's much more likely to be something quite unimportant.'

'I hope so. I'd better go and get dressed. I shall hate leaving here—it's the loveliest place I've ever seen.'

'You've been happy?'

'Terribly!'

She got to her feet, feeling unusually small in her heelless sandals as she looked up at Jimmy. He put out his arms and drew her to him.

'You're very sweet,' he said. 'It's been a lovely honeymoon.'

He kissed her carelessly, then pulled the bathing robe from her bare shoulders.

'Jimmy!' Lorna exclaimed. 'Someone might come.'

His hands grew more possessive, and he held her tighter.

'Who cares?' he asked. 'You're my wife, aren't you?'

Lorna struggled, but she was helpless against his strength.

'Won't you learn?' he asked triumphantly as he held her prisoner, flushed and dishevelled.

'Let me go,' she pleaded, 'we shall miss the train.'

'Kiss me, then,' he commanded.

She did as she was told and he released her. As she ran upstairs to her bedroom she heard him whistling joyously.

'He's glad to be going,' she thought with a pang, and yet she understood. Jimmy could not be inactive, even in happiness.

It was a long and tiring journey, and they only reached Mountley Park just before ten o'clock. The Braith's house was only fifty miles from London, and Jimmy had thought it better to go straight on to his parents, rather than risk staying the night in London, and being caught in a bad raid.

It was not yet dark as they drove up the drive, and Lorna saw a massive mansion of grey stone, turreted, and surrounded by ornamental gardens.

When they arrived they were shown into a blue and gold drawing-room, where it seemed to Lorna that a very large crowd of people were talking and playing bridge. Shy and embarrassed, she was thankful that little was required of her save to shake hands and murmur polite thanks to the greetings and congratulations she received.

'Your train's late,' Lady Braith said. 'Was there a raid on in London?'

'The sirens had gone,' Jimmy replied, 'but nothing seemed to be happening. Father, this is Lorna. It's time you met my wife—we've been married for four days.'

'Quite a long time for this generation,' someone joked in the background.

Lorna held out her hand to a tall, severe-looking man whom she would never have imagined could possibly be Jimmy's father. There were deep, sardonic lines running from Sir Douglas' nose to his tight-lipped mouth; he was very thin, and although his hair was not grey he gave the impression of never having known youth—a monument more than a human being.

He stared at his daughter-in-law beneath bushy eyebrows but he said nothing. Lorna was to learn later that his 'two-minute silences' were famous.

'I'm sorry you couldn't come to the wedding,' she said, nonplussed by his silent regard and feeling that some sort of remark was required of her.

'Unfortunately it was impossible,' Sir Douglas replied. 'Have you had dinner?'

'On the train,' Jimmy answered, 'and exceedingly nasty it was!'

'You should have waited till you got here. I'll order sandwiches and drinks.'

'Oh, please don't bother!' Lorna said quickly, but Jimmy replied.

'Thanks. I can do with a drink.'

Lorna was introduced to the other people in the room. There were two Members of Parliament; several efficient-looking women of uncertain age; half a dozen local dignitaries who had brought their wives to dinner; and Muriel, whom Lorna was genuinely glad to see again.

She had not had a chance to get to know Jimmy's half-sister well, for Muriel had arrived at the Vicarage very late the night before the wedding, but now, shy of so many strangers, Lorna clung to her as if she were an old friend.

'I expect you want to wash,' Muriel suggested. 'Would you like to come up to your room?'

'Yes, please,' Lorna replied, and they moved together up the broad, soft-carpeted, oak staircase to the next floor.

'You're in here,' Muriel said, pushing upon a door leading into a huge room in which a maid was already unpacking. There was a fine four-poster bed in an alcove and high mullioned windows hung with cherry-coloured damask.

'How did you like Cornwall and The Towers?' Muriel asked.

'I adored it,' Lorna answered. 'It's the loveliest place I've ever seen.'

'I love it too,' Muriel confessed. 'But we seldom get down there, even in peace time. Mother's so busy and she likes me to help her.'

It was strange to think that Muriel was nearly forty, she gave an impression of being much younger, still behaved as if she were a young girl with no independence of action.

Her clothes were expensive and well chosen and yet nothing Muriel wore could give the impression of being really smart or make her look anything but insignificant. Yet is was impossible not to like her and Lorna felt their strongest bond was that she, too, adored Jimmy.

Lorna took off her hat and coat, revealing a pretty flowered dress—one of the many frocks given her by Aunt Julie.

'That is pretty,' Muriel said admiringly, 'but anything you wore would look nice. I thought your wedding dress was lovely.'

'So did I,' Lorna confessed frankly. 'I'm so glad you liked it. I've never had clothes like this before and, do you know, they give me confidence. I was terrified as we came up the drive just now, but the feeling that I looked nice gave me courage and made me feel less shy.'

'Are you shy?' Muriel asked. 'I can't think why you should be. It's different for me—people never notice me and when Mother abruptly calls their attention to me they are covered with confusion—and so am I! I can't tell you how awful it is sometimes—I wish I could sink through the floor!'

'Oh, I've felt like that, too,' Lorna said, 'but you've always lived like this and among a lot of people—surely it can't be so bad for you? You've seen my home—it's a contrast, isn't it?'

'I loved your home,' Muriel said gently. There was a ring of sincerity in her voice.

'Did you really? Why?'

'It was so cosy and cheerful,' Muriel replied. 'It's just the sort of house I'd like to have if I married—but then, I never shall.'

'Oh, you will one day.'

Muriel shook her head.

'I've got lots of good friends, but I'm not the marrying sort.'

They were alone in the room, the housemaid had left. Muriel suddenly put out her hand and laid it on Lorna's arm.

'I didn't get a chance to tell you on your wedding day, so I want to say it now. I'm glad—very, very, glad—that you've married Jimmy, and so pleased to think that I shall have a sister. I've always wanted one.'

'Thank you.' Lorna put her hand over Muriel's and then impulsively bent forward to kiss her cheek. 'I'll do my best to make Jimmy happy.'

'I know you will. Oh, I'm so glad he's married you. I was afraid that it might be your cousin. I think she liked him very much and when they were here the week-end before last I was anxious about it.'

'The week-end before last?'

'Yes, didn't you know? They came here for Saturday and Sunday night.'

'I'd forgotten,' Lorna said quickly, conscious that Muriel was looking apprehensive in case she had been tactless. 'Sally had been staying with us.'

'That's right,' Muriel said in a relieved tone. 'She motored Jimmy up to London.'

Lorna's brain was working fast. She remembered Sally's departure while she had been out with her Girl Guides; she remembered, too, Beth saying that she had seen Sally before she went to school and had taken her the papers and the telephone book. It was funny how the words came back to her.

At the time they had meant nothing; but, of course, the local telephone book would have been of no interest to Sally unless she had wanted to ring up someone in the neighbourhood. But what did it mean? Why had Sally come here with Jimmy, and why had he not told her about it?

Lorna felt doubts and suspicions creep upon her, then resolutely she tried to force them away. There must be some explanation—there must!

Muriel was chattering on.

'Your cousin's very pretty, but she's the type of girl who aways overpowers me. She makes me feel about fifteen and ridiculously ignorant.'

'I know what you mean,' Lorna agreed absently.

'But of course I needn't have worried. So many girls have been enamoured with Jimmy at one time or another. It isn't surprising, for he's so good-looking; but I might have guessed he had enough commonsense to choose someone like you.'

Lorna forced herself to smile.

'I hope you will never be disappointed in me.'

'I'm quite sure that would be impossible. Are you ready now? Shall we do down?'

It was after midnight before they came up to bed. Jimmy had been drawn into a game of bridge and Lorna, after talking to her mother-in-law for a little while, was taken by Sir Douglas into his study.

'I want to get to know my new daughter-in-law. Come and talk to me.'

She followed him obediently through the hall and into a huge booklined room. There was a large desk in front of the window, piled with papers and bearing several telephones.

'Is this where you work?'

Sir Douglas smiled.

'Sometimes,' he answered. 'I have an office as well.'

'Do you like it?' Lorna asked. She saw the surprise in his face. 'I'm sorry. That sounds a silly question, but Daddy was telling Jimmy how much you enjoyed life at Oxford, how gay you were and how good at cricket, and so I wondered how it felt now to be the head of a vast business with thousands of employees dependent upon one?'

'It's a heavy responsibility,' Sir Douglas said. 'At Oxford I never dreamt that this type of life would be mine. I was a young fool and I wasted most of my opportunities of learning.'

'But you were happy?'

Sir Douglas gave a sharp, humourless laugh.

'Happiness and a career don't always go hand-in-hand, my dear, or perhaps I should say happiness and ambition—it's a better definition.'

'Can't one have both?'

Sir Douglas looked at her.

'An ambitious man,' he replied, 'is generally too busy to be emotional. That, I imagine, is what is wrong with my son —too many emotions and not enough ambition.'

'He's very keen about his job,' Lorna said quickly.

'What job?' Sir Douglas growled. 'Flying is his pastime. His job is to take over from me when I get too old to carry on. At the moment, he's about as capable of doing that as my office boy! Perhaps you'll be able to instil some sense into him—I can't!'

Lorna felt that it was extremely unlikely that she would

165

alter Jimmy. He was irresponsible and light-hearted, yet at the same time it was obvious that he had much of his parents' strength of character and determination.

'I'll try, she said, 'but I'm not very optimistic.'

Sir Douglas laughed again.

'You're frank, at any rate. I like frankness. When the war is over you and I will have to put our heads together.'

He turned towards the door and Lorna knew that this strange interview was at an end. She felt that Sir Douglas had considered her rather as he would a candidate for employment; she had passed the test; she had been accepted. She could not help a small feeling of gratification, even while she was slightly nonplussed by his manner.

Sir Douglas, however, had nothing more to say. He took Lorna back to the drawing-room and left her.

'Good night,' he said gruffly, and she gathered that neither she nor any of his other guests would see him again that evening.

When she and Jimmy went up to bed she waited until he had undressed. When he came into her bedroom she was sitting at the dressing-table brushing her hair.

'What do you think of the old homestead?' Jimmy asked. He stood in front of the empty fireplace smoking a last cigarette before he got into bed.

'It's rather overwhelming,' Lorna confessed. 'I'll reserve my opinion until I've seen more of it.'

'You've made a hit with the old people. I heard Mother singing your praises to the Lady Mayoress.'

'That's an exaggeration!' Lorna challenged, but she was pleased, nevertheless. Then she put down her hairbrush and turned round. 'Why didn't you tell me that Sally motored you up to London last Saturday week, and that you stayed here?'

Jimmy bent to flick his cigarette ash into the fire-grate.

'Didn't I mention it? I'm sure I did.'

'Don't be ridiculous! You know you never said a word. Why be so secretive?'

Jimmy looked across the room at her.

'I never gave it a thought, but I think Sally had some ridiculous notion that you might be jealous. She didn't want you to imagine that she had deliberately snooped your young man.'

There was reason in this, Lorna thought. She might have guessed that Sally would not have been deceived as to her real feelings about Jimmy.

'All the same,' she said, 'I think you might have told me.'

'Who let the cat out of the bag?'

'Muriel. She thought I knew.'

'I shouldn't make a good criminal, should I?'

'I'm afraid not, but I wish you'd told me.'

Jimmy threw away his cigarette.

'You can't be angry,' he said, coming across the room. 'It was before I was married. Now I've turned over a new leaf.'

'So far as I can gather, it was about time!'

Jimmy picked her up off the stool.

'If you're going to be impertinent, I'm going to be rough.'

Lorna reached up her arms and put them round his neck.

'I'm tired,' she said softly. 'Let's go to bed. It doesn't matter about Sally.'

'Of course it doesn't,' Jimmy agreed.

He lifted her high against his heart and kissed her mouth, then whispering words of love, he carried his wife towards the big four-poster.

14

Lorna was writing a letter to her father. Through the window she could look on to the ornamental garden with its big lily ponds laid out between clipped yew hedges, leading the eye to where, flanked by two great herbaceous borders, there rose the white columns of a summer house built in the classic style of a Greek temple.

It was all very beautiful, yet Lorna felt a sudden wave of homesickness for the overgrown confusion of the garden at home.

Here, in spite of the war, everything was tidy to the degree of perfection. It was a garden, she felt, where one might walk in a gracious manner, indulging in polite intellectual conversation, but it was a garden where one would not expect to hear the joyous laughter of happy children.

The house was just as awe-inspiring. After breakfast Muriel had escorted Lorna from the big oak-panelled dining-hall into the picture gallery and she had wandered round looking at the fine works of art which Sir Douglas had collected since he had become an eminently successful man.

There were new portraits, too, of Sir Douglas himself, of Lady Braith, and one of Jimmy as a small boy, looking unnaturally solemn and rather bored.

'It was done by Sargent,' Muriel said.

'I suppose it's very valuable,' Lorna asked.

'Oh, I suppose so,' Muriel replied. 'Although nothing is of

much value nowadays when a chance bomb might destroy it at any moment.'

'Wouldn't it be safer to put the pictures in the cellar?'

'I think so, but Father's a fatalist. At least, he says he is. Personally I think it's just obstinacy and a kind of queer defiance—as if he dared Hitler to disturb the even tenor of his life!'

Lorna laughed.

'Sir Douglas struck me as a very formidable person.'

'He's kind at heart,' Muriel said. 'I'm sure a lot of his sternness is put on because he's shy. You wouldn't think it, would you? but I believe deep in his heart, although he would never admit it, Father hates these big parties and the crowds of people he has to entertain. I feel certain that his abruptness, and what at times amounts to sheer, downright rudeness, is just a façade behind which he hides his real self.'

Lorna looked at Muriel with interest. She had not imagined her to be so perceptive.

'It's clever of you to know all that,' she said. 'I'm always so shy and frightened myself that I never think that other people might be experiencing the same emotions. I suppose that's egoism.'

'You must remember,' Muriel said with a smile, 'that I've had the opportunity of studying Father for a great many years. Besides, as you know, he's not my real father.'

'And I suppose you were naturally inclined to be critical of anyone your mother married. I know I should be.'

'Oh, it is nice having someone to talk to,' Muriel said impulsively.

'But you must have lots of friends.'

'A few, but that's rather different. You're one of the family—I can discuss Father and Mother, and even Jimmy, with you without feeling disloyal.'

'Tell me about Jimmy as a boy,' Lorna suggested.

'He was a little terror!' Muriel answered quickly, and they both laughed.

Muriel was called to the telephone and Lorna went to the writing-desk and started the letter to her father. There was so much she wanted to tell him. She had wired him yesterday that they were leaving Cornwall and going to Mountley Park. Now she described Sir Douglas, the house, and the people staying there.

'I don't know yet why the Air Ministry has sent for Jimmy,' she wrote. 'He's gone to London this morning and has promised, either to come back as soon as possible, or to telephone. I'm terrified that he might be sent to the East, but when I say anything he tells me "not to cross my bridges until I come to them". I'm sure he's right, but I can't help being anxious and imagining things.'

Lorna put down her pen.

'I will leave the letter open,' she thought, 'and finish it when Jimmy returns.'

At that moment Muriel came into the room.

'Whom do you think that was?' she asked.

'Jimmy?' Lorna questioned quickly.

Muriel shook her head.

'Oh no, he'd have asked for you. It was Sally, and she's coming down here this evening.'

'This evening!' Lorna echoed. 'Why?'

'Well, when she was here before Mother persuaded her to ask General Garthwaite—you know she drives for him— if he would speak during our War Weapons Week; so he's coming to-night and Sally's coming to stay as well.'

Lorna received this information with mixed feelings. She was fond of Sally; at the same time she always felt over-shadowed by her and she remembered all too vividly her feelings of being an outsider when Sally and Jimmy were together. She chid herself, however, for such reasoning.

After all, she was married to Jimmy now—he was hers as she was utterly his—things were very different, she told herself, from when Sally had stayed at the Vicarage. Besides, Lorna remembered, she was under a deep debt of gratitude to Sally's mother.

The lovely clothes she was wearing were due to Aunt Julie's generosity—it would be ungracious, to say the least of it, if she were to repay her by being resentful towards Sally.

'How nice. I shall be glad to see Sally again,' she forced herself to say to Muriel, conscious that she had hesitated rather too long to sound convincingly enthusiastic.

'I couldn't very well refuse to have her, could I?' Muriel asked anxiously.

'Of course she must come,' Lorna said. 'Whatever made you think of such a thing? Jimmy will be pleased to see her and so shall I.'

Nevertheless, there was a tiny dissatisfaction in her mind which remained with her all day—even after Jimmy returned in the early afternoon with the news that his interview had been extraordinarily satisfactory.

'It's really rather exciting,' he told them all, the moment after he had come striding on to the terrace where the house-party were sitting out after luncheon enjoying their coffee. 'I'm to be in charge of a new Squadron—one that's been given by and named after a certain place in the Empire. I'm not allowed to mention it as yet. They're American planes, absolutely the very latest thing. And are they good! You wait until we get into the sky—it'll give the Huns something to think about, I promise you!'

His excitement and enthusiasm were infectious. It was funny, Lorna thought, how his vitality stirred people. They had been sitting relaxed, rather limp and quiet, but Jimmy galvanised everybody into life.

The sound of voices rose, took on a higher note, as Jimmy received congratulations, answered questions, and reiterated again and again his own satisfaction.

'What's more,' he went on, 'I've been posted to a new aerodrome, and—hold your breath—it's only ten miles from here! That's lucky, isn't it? Lorna can live here and I can nip backwards and forwards whenever I get the chance. You'll have her, won't you, Mother?'

'Of course,' Lady Braith replied. 'But if you're going to

live here you'd better have the suite in the West Wing—it will give you a sitting-room of your own. Will you see to it, Muriel?'

'Yes, Mother.'

Lorna sat silent. She was obviously not to be consulted, but she had heard the news with a throb of dismay. She had looked forward to finding a cottage or a tiny house near Jimmy's aerodrome; she had wanted to be alone with him there, to make him a real home.

Already she had imagined herself cooking him delicious meals and running the house with perhaps the help of a local charwoman. She was disappointed and a little apprehensive, too, as to whether she could bear to go on staying at Mountley Park indefinitely.

When she broached the subject to Jimmy later in the afternoon he looked surprised.

'But good heavens, Lorna, surely you don't want to live in a cottage! It's absolutely impossible to get a decent house of any size near these aerodromes, especially in the London area. If it had been necessary we'd have managed somehow, but this arrangement is perfect. You'll be comfortable and happy here, and, I must say, when I do get a bit of time off I like my luxuries! I suppose I'm fond of the place too, in a way. After all, it will be mine one day.'

'Will it?' Lorna could hardly contemplate the idea of herself as mistress of such magnificence.

'Of course it will, stupid!' he said laughing at her disconsolate face. 'You might as well get used to the idea right away. You've got a position to keep up now, you know.'

'Oh Jimmy, I hope I shan't fail you.' She felt suddenly afraid, and very insignificant.

Jimmy kissed the top of her head.

'Don't be idiotic! Come on, I'm going to change. I want someone to play a really hard set of tennis with me. I shall get fat if I don't take more exercise.'

'Wait a minute.' Lorna put out her hand. 'I've got something to tell you. Sally's coming down here this evening.'

Jimmy stopped and turned abruptly.

'Good Lord! What on earth for?'

He sounded annoyed. Lorna explained, conscious of a feeling of delight that he had not been pleased, that he obviously did not welcome the idea of seeing Sally again. She had been afraid that he might have been eager to see her and now she was glad—so glad, that the pangs of jealously which had been nagging at her all the morning faded away.

'Well, it can't be helped,' Jimmy said, 'but I should have thought that Sally would have . . .' He stopped. Lorna wondered what he had been going to say, but he didn't finish his sentence.

'I don't expect she knows we're here,' she suggested.

'Yes, she does,' Jimmy replied. 'I sent her a wire yesterday in answer to her letter.'

There was nothing unusual in this, for Jimmy had sent telegrams to everyone who had congratulated him. When Lorna had exclaimed at the expense, he explained that he loathed writing letters.

'It's quicker to telegraph, less trouble, and people are delighted by my good manners,' he had told Lorna with a disarming smile.

So Sally, having received the wire yesterday evening, had telephoned Muriel this morning. Was there any connection between the two? Lorna wondered—or was it just chance?

When they came in to tea, Sally had just arrived. She was looking amazingly smart in her uniform, she had taken off her cap and her beautifully arranged hair fell silky and smooth almost to her khaki-covered shoulders. Her skirt was hardly regulation cut either in width or length—but it did not fail to reveal an exquisite figure and even more exquisite legs.

The General was a nice old man with courteous manners and a sense of humour.

'I promised Lothe I'd keep an eye on his daughter,' he told one of the Members of Parliament who teased him about choosing the prettiest chauffeuse in the A.T.S. 'Well, I'm keeping my word, but it doesn't leave me much time for running the war, I can promise you!'

They all laughed; but Sally, taking a cigarette out of her gold case, said in her clear insistent voice:

'Don't you believe a word he says! Hitler would have been in London a year ago if it hadn't been for the General. Why, I should be shot at dawn if I so much as endangered a hair of his head!'

The General was pleased at the compliment. Lorna could see that, and she thought how clever Sally was. How skilfully had she engineered this visit of the General's to coincide with another meeting between herself and Jimmy?

'A match, please.' Sally held out her cigarette and spoke to Jimmy.

As he lit it she gave him a long, lingering look from under her dark, fringed lashes.

'You've had a very short honeymoon, haven't you?' she asked.

She was speaking to him alone. Lorna, standing a little apart, could just hear what they said.

'The Air Ministry sent for me.'

'How convenient! A honeymoon cancelled is better than one regretted!'

'You're wrong about that.'

Lorna was feeling breathless, a little ashamed of herself for eavesdropping. She turned away, and at that moment Jimmy slipped his arm into hers.

'I want my tea.' He was smiling down at her and she felt happy and secure again.

Jimmy played more tennis when tea was over and, so far as Lorna was aware, he had no chance of talking to Sally alone before they went up to dress for dinner.

'We might dance to-night,' Jimmy said through the open door of his dressing-room. 'What do you say to that, Cherry Ripe? Do you realise I've never danced with you?'

'I hope I shall be up to your standard,' Lorna replied. 'We

174

didn't get much practice in Little Walton.'

'What on earth did you do with your time?' he asked.
'Play "Postman's Knock" with the eminent doctor?—or
should I say "Kiss in the Ring"?'

Lorna wrapped her dressing-gown round her and went
and stood in the doorway.

'I believe you're jealous of Michael,' she said, 'you're
always so nasty about him.'

'I bet he's nasty about me, too,' Jimmy answered.

'Of course he isn't. Why should he be?'

'For one very good reason known in some circles as—
Lorna.'

'He'd never be unkind because I love you. Michael knows
how to lose.'

'A sportsman, of course,' Jimmy said with a sarcastic note
in his voice. "Let the best man win." God! How I hate
people who are so inhuman! He's the sort of man who would
be a schoolgirl's hero.'

'Jimmy, you're being thoroughly nasty!' Lorna protested.
'I can't think why you should have such a down on Michael.'

'I can't stick the chap. You should have heard him talking
to me. . . . "Eric, or Little by Little" wasn't in it! I can't
think now why I didn't kick him hard—it was what he was
asking for.'

'When was this? What was he talking to you about?'

'You, of course.' Jimmy was tying his tie and looking in
the glass to see he got the bows precisely even.

'About me! What did he say?'

'That excites your curiosity, doesn't it? Well, I shan't tell
you!'

'Tell me,' Lorna pleaded, going into Jimmy's room and
standing beside the dressing-table. 'Please tell me, Jimmy.'

'Trust a woman to want to hear about herself,' Jimmy
said. 'It makes me mad even to think about it. Every time
you mention Little Walton now I think of Davenport and
see red!'

'But whatever did he say?'

'He had the impertinence to inform me that if I wasn't going to marry you, he was.'

'Michael said that!' Lorna ejaculated in an astonished voice.

'He further informed me,' Jimmy went on, 'that I could make up my mind right away, or he'd have me transferred to another Convalescent Home. Think of the damned cheek of it! I believe I could report him to the Medical Council for unprofessional behaviour—I've a jolly good mind to try!'

'But Jimmy, when did this happen?'

'When I came back from London, after I'd seen old Snooks, or whatever his name was, about my arm. I got back about lunch time, and your doctor comes puffing around about six o'clock for the report and the first thing he has the impudence to ask me is—if I'd been to see you.

'If I'd had any sense I'd have said, there and then, it was my business, and what the Hell had it got to do with him?—but you know my nice friendly nature. I said "No," but that I might pop in during the evening—and then he started! I thought I was back in the Victorian era!

'You should have seen his face when I told him I was, that I intended to marry you and damn quick about it. Looked as if he didn't believe me for a moment. I wish I'd seen his face when you told him we were engaged!'

Jimmy laughed and Lorna was curiously silent. After a moment she turned towards her own room.

'Hi! Where are you going?' Jimmy asked.

'I've got to hurry,' Lorna answered in a stifled voice. 'I shall be late otherwise.'

'Right-oh. I'll go down and get a cocktail.'

Jimmy looked through the door.

'I say,' he asked, 'you're all right, aren't you?—not upset or anything?'

'I'm quite all right.'

But when he had gone she sat staring in front of her for a very long time. She was trying to piece together Jimmy's story, trying to understand it, to see the truth and to answer some of the wild questions which raced through her mind. Why had Michael interfered?

Was it because of her unhappiness? Or because his own emotions were so deeply involved? Had his interference spurred Jimmy on to an action he would never have taken otherwise? Those were questions she could not answer.

She hid her face in her hands. It was a warm evening but Lorna was shivering. Only four days ago she had felt so safe and secure. In giving her whole life into Jimmy's keeping she had believed that she would be protected from any further heartaches, yet now she felt more bewildered and more lost than ever before.

She looked at the clock on her dressing-table and realised it was nearly eight o'clock. Hurriedly she finished dressing, putting on a frock of white chiffon which, in exquisite contrast to her sunburnt skin and fair hair, made her look unusually lovely.

To Lorna it would have been the same if she had been fastening a piece of sackcloth round her! Automatically, she combed her hair, put a finishing touch of powder on her nose, and turned towards the door.

The gong was booming as she came down the stairs. There was something ominous in the sound—it was like the rumble of thunder before the approaching storm.

15

Dinner was a long and formal meal. In spite of rationing and the difficulty of obtaining extra luxuries, there seemed to Lorna to be a great number of courses, but she did not enjoy the meal because she found it hard to concentrate on the conversation.

Her own thoughts kept intruding, and her replies became more and more vague and monosyllabic. She was glad when Lady Braith gave the signal for the women to leave the dining-room.

She did not follow her mother-in-law into the drawing-room where she knew coffee was waiting. Instead, she murmured to Muriel that she wanted to fetch a handkerchief and went upstairs to her own bedroom.

She had not been there more than a minute when the door opened and Sally came in. Sally had been sitting next to Jimmy at dinner and more than once Lorna had found herself watching them.

Her cousin was looking particularly attractive this evening; she was wearing a dress of black satin which moulded her figure and made her appear even more exotic than usual; she wore sandals of silver and green and there were emeralds flashing in the lobes of her small ears and a heavy bracelet of the same stones on one thin wrist.

'I thought you'd be in this room,' Sally said, walking towards the long mirror set in the wardrobe.

She looked round the room, at the great four-poster, at

the wide dressing-table littered with Lorna's personal belongings, and at the open door leading into Jimmy's dressing-room.

'How do you like it?' she asked. 'Somewhat of a change from the Vicarage?'

There was something in the tone of Sally's voice which told Lorna that the comparison was meant unkindly, but she checked the hasty words which rose to her lips, and instead said gently :

'It's nice to see you, Sally. Have you been working hard?'

'On and off,' Sally replied, 'but let's talk about you. You're the one who seems to have been having all the fun. The Cinderella story up-to-date!'

'You could hardly call Peke and Beth the ugly sisters,' Lorna suggested, smiling.

'King Cophetua, then. And how does the beggar-maid like being married?'

Lorna got up from the dressing-table.

'I'm very happy—thank you.'

'It would be surprising if you weren't at the moment. Is it five or six days since the momentous ceremony took place?'

'I think we'd better go down to the drawing-room!' Lorna moved towards the door.

Sally, however, sat down in an armchair and took out her cigarette case.

'There's no hurry, my dear. Your mother-in-law is taking the rest of the party round the Picture Gallery. I'm sure you've seen it already.'

'I'd like some coffee,' Lorna insisted.

She felt a sudden dread of having to stay here with Sally. She wanted to escape, wanted at any cost to avoid further conversation. The air was charged with electricity—she felt that Sally intended to be difficult.

'There's plenty of time,' Sally said. 'Have you got a match?'

Lorna picked up a box from beside the bed and took it across to her. Sally lit her cigarette, then lay back in the

179

chair extending her arms with a sensual gesture.

'Well,' she said slowly, 'you haven't told me anything yet. You know I'm dying to hear how you did it?'

'How I did what?'

'Caught the elusive Jimmy, of course!'

'Isn't that rather an unnecessary figure of speech?' Lorna asked. She spoke lightly, but with an effort. 'Jimmy fell in love with me and I with him!'

'And propinquity did the rest, I suppose?' This time the sneer was unmistakable.

'What does that mean?'

'Propinquity is what happens when a man and a woman see a great deal of each other. It's the reason why invalids marry their nurses and business men their typists.'

'It's hardly applicable in this case,' Lorna said quickly, 'for Jimmy proposed to me the day after he had returned from spending the week-end here with you.'

For the moment Sally was taken by surprise. Lorna could not help but be pleased that her thrust had gone home. Sally's eyes widened, then narrowed again. There was a pause before she spoke.

'So he told you that I motored him up to London and that we came here?'

'Of course,' Lorna replied smoothly. 'Why not? Surely there was nothing secret about it?'

Sally got up to press her cigarette into an ashtray.

'Nothing, of course. All the same, I hope, my dear Lorna, that you have been wise. Marriage is a tricky undertaking for the best of us.'

'Do you think you are qualified to judge?' Lorna asked.

She was being rude, but she didn't care! There was something behind Sally's insolence which infuriated her—something, too, of which she was vaguely afraid.

'Not of marriage as a whole, perhaps,' Sally answered smoothly, 'but, shall we say, I do know something about the particular sort of life into which you have stepped so blithely. For your own good I'm warning you to watch your step.'

'Perhaps it would be easier,' Lorna said in an unusually quiet voice, 'if you came into the open and told me exactly what you do mean. I'm afraid I don't understand these queer insinuations. What are you trying to suggest to me? I'd like to know.'

Sally did not look at her directly. Instead she walked towards the mirror and sitting down at Lorna's dressing-table started to powder her nose.

'Perhaps I've expressed myself badly,' she said after a moment or two. 'What I've been trying to convey is my surprise at finding you married to Jimmy.'

'That's obvious, I think,' Lorna replied. 'It was a surprise for a great many people.'

'When I was at Little Walton, it didn't seem to me that there was anything in your attitude to each other which might suggest marriage.'

'Perhaps you weren't looking for it,' Lorna replied. 'Actually we were already in love with each other.'

Sally snapped her vanity case shut with a sharp click.

'It's ridiculous,' she said, 'utterly ridiculous! And if you want the truth I can imagine no one more unsuitable for Jimmy's wife!'

'I'm sorry you should feel like that,' Lorna retorted, 'but it's a little late now, isn't it?'

'That's the pity of it,' Sally replied. 'However, there it is!' She shrugged her shoulders and moved towards the door. This time Lorna stopped her.

'I've listened to your insults, Sally,' she said, 'now I think you owe me an explanation. In the past I thought we were friends—certainly I have always been very fond of you— perhaps you will be kind enough to tell me what all this means? Why have you changed so suddenly? Why should you speak to me in this manner?'

Lorna was trembling and her words were coming quickly between her lips, almost falling over themselves in her agitation.

'My dear child, don't be so theatrical,' Sally answered

coolly, her voice deliberate and unhurried. 'I assure you my interest is quite impersonal. Your marriage or Jimmy's is nothing to me.'

'That's not true!' At last Lorna saw the truth and understood it. 'You're jealous. I'm not such a fool as not to realise that. You're jealous of me because you wanted Jimmy yourself. You're in love with him.'

The expression on Sally's face told her that she had hit on the truth. Just for a moment the girl was tense, then with an obvious effort she relaxed.

'What a ridiculous idea!' she said, but Lorna had turned away.

She walked towards the window. She was no longer angry. For some minutes she looked out on to the garden, seeing only the sadness of a friendship lost, a relationship ruined, and through no fault of her own.

'She can't help loving Jimmy,' Lorna thought quickly. 'I must be kind to her.'

But when she looked round Sally had gone—she was alone in the room.

Lorna picked up the white chiffon handkerchief it had taken her so long to get and went slowly downstairs. When she reached the drawing-room the men had already joined the ladies and there was the sound of music from the big radio-gramophone.

Everyone was dancing and as Lorna came through the door she saw Sally in Jimmy's arms, her face upturned to his, her dark hair sleek and silky against his shoulder. Lorna felt a sharp pang of jealousy and fear, then she told herself it was unimportant. Jimmy belonged to her.

Why should she care? Why, indeed, should she worry?

And yet as the evening wore on it was impossible for her to be unaware that Sally was being deliberately provoking, deliberately tantalising. As each dance ended she would keep Jimmy on some pretext or another by her side.

Once or twice it was a demand for some special record which had to be looked for in the big green leather-covered boxes which housed them; another time her bracelet came unfastened and Jimmy was still trying to manipulate the catch when the music started again and Sally crept back into his arms.

Finally she drew him through the open windows on to the terrace outside.

'It's so hot,' Lorna heard her say. 'I must have a breath of air or I think I shall faint.'

'I mustn't mind. I must be sensible about this,' Lorna told herself, but it was difficult to concentrate on what people were saying, to laugh in the right places, to make appropriate remarks to the partners who claimed the privilege of dancing with the bride.

Lorna felt that it must be obvious to everyone that Sally was behaving outrageously, but no one seemed to be noticing anything unusual. No one else seemed to be aware of the fact that during the two hours since dinner Jimmy had never once danced with his wife.

At last Lorna could bear it no longer. As time passed and Sally and Jimmy did not return from the garden she found it almost impossible to keep her eyes from the curtains swinging lightly in the breeze over the open windows. Surely they must come back!

Any moment Lorna expected to see Jimmy's hand pull a curtain aside. The time dragged by in slow, long-drawn-out minutes and still they did not come. Lorna went to Lady Braith.

'Do you mind if I go to bed?' she asked. 'I have a slight headache.'

'Of course. Go up at once,' her mother-in-law replied. 'Do you want any aspirin? I'll tell Muriel to bring you some.'

'I don't want one, thank you. It's nothing—just the heat, I expect.'

'Is Jimmy going with you?' Lady Braith asked abruptly. 'I wanted him to make a four at bridge.'

'I'm sure he'd be delighted,' Lorna said, then fled before Lady Braith could inquire as to her son's whereabouts.

'If she wants him she'll find him,' Lorna thought.

She hurried to her bedroom and dragging off the white chiffon dress threw it in a crumpled mass on the floor. She felt as if she hated the lovely clothes that had been a present from Sally's mother! All the doubts and fears that she had experienced earlier in the evening came back a thousand-fold to taunt and frighten her. Perhaps Sally was right, perhaps she was utterly unsuitable to be Jimmy's wife?

Lorna wrapped her dressing-gown round her and sat down on the floor disconsolately, with her head bowed on the arm-chair.

'I want to go home,' she thought, and hot tears pricked her eyes.

The door opened and before she could move Jimmy came in.

'Why are you sitting there? Are you all right?' he asked. 'Mother told me you'd got a headache—but I don't know whether to believe it.'

Lorna got to her feet.

'It is the truth,' she replied. 'So I thought I'd come to bed.'

'But you can't do that!' Jimmy exclaimed, 'the evening's only just started. Why, you haven't danced with me yet.'

'Have you only just realised that?' Lorna said. She could not help speaking bitterly.

Jimmy strode towards her, and putting his hand under her chin, tipped back her head so that he could look into her eyes.

'Look at me,' he commanded. She quivered in his hold but was forced to obey him.

'You're jealous!' he said accusingly. 'Jealous of Sally. My precious darling, how silly of you. Come downstairs and we'll dance until our shoes are worn out!'

'I won't!' Lorna struggled but he would not release her. Then he bent and kissed her.

'You're adorable, but you're not to be cross with me. I can't help it.'

'Can't help what?'

Jimmy hesitated as though he found the question difficult to answer.

'. . . playing the perfect little host in my own home,' he replied, but she knew that was not what he had been going to say.

'Put your dress on and come down again.'

Lorna shook her head.

'Don't make me,' she begged. 'It's half-past eleven and I never was any good at staying up late. Your mother wants you to play bridge and you know I don't play.'

'I want to dance with you,' Jimmy said obstinately.

'No you don't,' Lorna replied. 'I'm a rotten dancer. Go and play bridge and come to bed as soon as you can get away.'

He hesitated, and then, as if some argument other than hers convinced him that the suggestion was a reasonable one, he kissed her again and turned towards the door. As he reached it he looked back and she knew that he was not quite at peace within himself.

'You're not angry with me?'

'Of course not.'

His smile was the quick responsive grin of a small boy.

'Bless you, darling. Don't dare to be asleep when I come up!'

He was gone, and Lorna with a sigh started to undress. She wondered if she had been wise. Would it have been better to have done as Jimmy wished, to have gone down again, to have faced Sally triumphantly, to have let her know that Jimmy had come to fetch her and wanted her at his side.

It was too late now.

Whatever harm Sally was trying to do must have failed. She had had her opportunity in the garden with Jimmy and he had come hurrying back to look for his wife. Perhaps she had been clever without knowing it, but somehow it was all very wearisome. The idea of fighting and manœuvring for Jimmy's affection, of holding him against the wiles of another woman, was new and strange.

To her marriage had meant an end to doubts and heart-aches—not the beginning of them.

She was not asleep when, an hour or so later, she heard Jimmy come into his dressing-room. The light shone through the half-closed door and she heard him moving about and finally, he pushed open the communicating door and came into her bedroom.

'Are you asleep?'

He spoke in a low voice and for a moment she played with the idea of not answering, of closing her eyes and feigning slumber; then her usual honesty got the better of her impulse.

'No, I'm awake.'

Jimmy came across the room and stood close beside her. The light from the door did not reach the shadows of the curtained bed—she could see him, but she was in darkness.

'Did you win any money?'

He hesitated a moment, then said abruptly :

'I didn't play.'

'What did you do, then?'

Lorna tried not to ask the question, and even as she said it, knew that she did not want to know the answer—would give much not to know—but it was too late. The question was asked and Jimmy was answering her.

'Sally wanted to go out on the lake. The rest of the party were too engrossed in their bridge to accompany us, so we went alone.'

There was a tiny note of defiance in Jimmy's tone and suddenly Lorna understood that this was an effort on his part. For the first time in his life he was having to account for his actions and, even while he was behaving as in duty bound, he was resenting it; half fearful, half scornful of what her attitude might be.

Her own problems and her own miseries paled. This was Jimmy's problem—she could see is as clearly as if she had no personal part in it.

Quickly she put out her hand and touched his.

'It sounds nice,' she said, 'but I hope you haven't caught cold. There's a nasty wind to-night—I felt it just now when I was opening the windows.'

She heard Jimmy draw a quick breath, then he bent and kissed her.

'Between ourselves I'm jolly tired. I've had a long day.'

'You have,' Lorna agreed, 'and an exciting one, too. I'm so thrilled about your new Squadron.'

'It's wonderful, isn't it?' He turned out the light in his dressing-room and shut the door.

'Can you find your way?' Lorna asked. 'Shall I put on the light?'

'No, it's good practice. It's one of the things we're going to take on—night flying.'

He bumped against the bedpost and swore softly.

Lorna laughed and was surprised at the sound. The thick fog of misery which had encompassed her was clearing, she felt natural again and, for the moment, at ease. Here in the darkness with her husband it seemed impossible that Sally could matter, that difficulties and miseries could assume such terrifying proportions.

Jimmy got into bed, and she felt his arms reaching out for her, drawing her towards him.

'I love you, Cherry Ripe,' he murmured. 'There is no one in the world but you.'

16

Lorna awoke feeling limp and listless. As Jimmy got up, talking eagerly of the pending visit to his new Squadron, she felt that she could not make the effort required to face Sally again and talk politely to her and to the other guests who might appear at the breakfast table.

'Will it matter if I have breakfast in bed?' she asked Jimmy.

'Good Lord, no! Ring and ask for what you want. But you aren't ill, are you? You look a bit peeked.'

'I'm all right. Just a bit under the weather.'

'I should take things quietly, then. Don't let Mother drive you too hard. She won't really care if you help her or not.'

'What does Jimmy feel—about me—about Sally—about life?' she wondered as she heard him whistling in his dressing room after a bath.

'Does he feel anything? Is anything of supreme importance to him?'

If Sally attracted him—and there was no reason for Lorna to doubt it—why hadn't he married her. She was far more suited to this type of life.

Sally was right about that. She would have enjoyed spending Jimmy's money, she would have taken for granted these luxurious surroundings, she would have liked what Jimmy laughingly called 'a position to keep up'. To Lorna it was all alien and frightening.

She had to face it; although she loved her husband deeply and passionately, they were still poles apart. She loved him, with an unreasoning love. He had merely to touch her, to smile at her with that peculiarly charming, irresponsible smile, and she felt her heart turn over within her breast and knew that she could not withstand him, could only surrender herself without reservation into his arms.

The intensity of her emotions was frightening. Where was it leading her? Was it likely to bring them greater happiness, to deepen the joy they felt in each other? Surely, Lorna thought, they should have some kind of plan, should look ahead where the future was concerned and not be content to drift day after day, taking things as they came without thought for the morrow?

'Good-bye, darling. I've got to go now.'

Jimmy came into her room. He was in uniform and she thought he had never looked more handsome. She loved the way his hair brushed sleekly back from his forehead, waved slightly at the temples in spite of his efforts to make it lie smooth; she loved the blue of his eyes, a colour deepened to-day by the reflection from his blue tunic. As he stood beside her she reached up and touched the wings on his chest.

'Good-bye,' she said softly, 'and take care of yourself. I shall be thinking of you.'

He bent and kissed her mouth.

'Don't do too much,' he admonished. 'I'll tell Mother she's to do her own dirty work and leave you in peace.'

'Don't you dare do anything of the sort,' Lorna protested. 'I'm going to get up in a few moments.'

Jimmy kissed his fingers to her from the door and then she heard him stride away, whistling as he went.

She closed her eyes, aware that she was glad to have these moments to herself, yet spurred on by a guilty conscience to remember the time.

'Sally will have gone by now,' she thought, 'I might as well go downstairs.'

She had just finished dressing when there was a tap on her door.

'Come in,' she invited, and turning, saw it was Muriel.

'Are you better?' Muriel asked. 'I was awfully sorry about your headache. I ought to have come to see you last night, but it was late by the time we finished playing bridge and I was afraid you might be asleep.'

'It's much better now,' Lorna said. 'I don't often get headaches. Has everybody gone?'

'Yes. Jimmy went off nearly an hour ago, and Sally and the General about the same time. There are two people to catch the mid-day train and three others arriving at twelve-thirty.'

'Heavens!' Lorna exclaimed. 'Do you ever have a moment to yourselves here?'

'Not often,' Muriel confessed. 'I'm afraid you won't like living here—you'd much rather have a home of your own, wouldn't you?'

'It sounds rude,' Lorna replied, 'but like George Washington, "I cannot tell a lie".'

'But, of course, I quite understand,' Muriel said, 'although Mother won't. She thinks it's an excellent arrangement and has already planned several things for you to undertake in the County.'

'I won't do any of them!'

Muriel laughed.

'It's no use, you'll have to. The best thing is to agree, and hope that after a time Mother will feel how much better she could do the things herself and so take them away from you.'

'What does she gain by all this activity?' Lorna asked.

Muriel shrugged her shoulders.

'I can't think, unless it's forgetfulness.'

'Forgetfulness of what?'

'Herself, I suppose. Don't you believe that those who have a lot to do are happier than those who are lazy? They don't have time to think, they don't have time to worry, they just have to go on doing things—working against time.'

'I suppose that's one way of looking at it,' Lorna said. 'But it doesn't sound a very happy way of living.'

'Is there a happy way?' Muriel asked. 'Permanently, I mean? Don't you think that happiness comes in patches and if you haven't got a lot of work to do when happiness fails you, you are apt to suffer more?'

'What about you?' Lorna asked. 'What makes you think about these things?'

'It's my way of being busy, I suppose.'

Muriel looked wistful, and Lorna had a sudden desire to see her really happy, to fill her life with the really important things—a husband—children—and a home of her own.

It suddenly seemed to her so unfair that someone like Sally who had no depth, only a lovely body to offer the world, should be fêted, run after, and desired; while Muriel, because she was not particularly attractive to look at, should be left alone, unwanted and unnoticed.

'You aren't to do so much introspective thinking,' Lorna said impulsively, putting her arm round Muriel's shoulders and giving her an affectionate hug, much as she might have embraced one of the children. 'In future we'll talk it over together.'

Muriel's face flushed.

'You're sweet, Lorna, but I'm not complaining. I'm really very contented.'

'I think you're a splendid person. If I had to do all the things you do I should complain bitterly.'

'Indeed you wouldn't!' Muriel replied. 'Look at what you did at home! Your father was telling me the morning of the wedding how much they'd miss you in the parish.'

'I hope they will. I have an awful feeling at times that they have already forgotten about me.'

'Aren't you stupid? And now, if you're ready, we've something to do.'

'What is it?'

'I want to show you your new rooms in the West Wing. Your things will be moved in there to-day and Mother says, as it's to be your home, you must alter the rooms as you please, change them around or ask for anything you want.'

'How kind of her,' Lorna said. 'But I'm sure they are perfect.'

They walked together down the long corridors until they reached the West Wing. The windows looked out, not over the ornamental gardens, but over smooth green lawns which sloped down to the lake. The rooms themselves were not so formal as the ones Lorna had just left, and were decorated in coloured chintzes.

'It's quite lovely!' Lorna exclaimed.

'I'm so glad,' Muriel said. 'The housekeeper will be bringing some flowers up later. I don't think anyone has used these rooms since they were done up, so it will be like having a new flat all of your own.'

'It is kind of your mother,' Lorna said, trying to be enthusiastic, trying to put the thought of a home of her own out of her head, to accept without regret the idea of living here as Jimmy's wife.

'Mother took a great deal of trouble over these rooms,' Muriel was saying. 'She had the bedspread made by women in the Distressed Areas—she has taken a personal interest in them. Don't they do beautiful work?'

Lorna bent over the bed to look. The stitching was perfect on the peach satin which matched the rest of the room.

'What a lovely smell there is in here,' she said suddenly. 'I thought it must be from flowers when I first came in, but there aren't any. What is it?'

'Everybody asks that,' Muriel replied. 'It's one of Mother's housekeeping secrets. It's a special pot-pourri she makes and puts among the bed linen instead of lavender. Actually the main foundation of it is rosemary.'

'Rosemary!' Lorna repeated the word strangely, then she felt as if a sudden darkness encompassed her. She saw Sally's letter, heard her own voice repeating—'Rosemary for remembrance. What does she mean?' Now she had discovered the meaning for herself. . . .

She must have uttered some sound, for Muriel turned towards her, concern on her face.

'You look pale,' she said. 'Are you all right?'

Lorna put up her hand to her head.

'I feel a little faint. Do you think I could have a glass of water?'

'But of course. I'll get some at once. Sit down here. You do look ghastly—I think I'd better get some brandy.' She hurried towards the door. 'I won't be a minute.'

Lorna hid her eyes. The shock had for a moment numbed her—now she felt, not faint, but sick. It was horrifying, and yet at the same time one part of her brain seemed to be saying over and over again—I must be sensible . . . I must be sensible about this.'

No wonder Sally had been surprised at the news of their marriage—no wonder she had taunted her last night in bitterness and in anger! Was it surprising, too, that she, Lorna, should feel as if the whole foundation of her world had given way beneath her, had crashed leaving her dazed and bewildered in a place she could not recognise?

She thought of how in her first realisation of her love for Jimmy she had felt as if divinity had touched her, how her ecstasy had raised her to undreamed of heights. It had sanctified her, making her, through love, a creature apart. And now what could she feel save degradation and dismay?

Muriel came back with a wineglass of brandy and a jug of water.

'I won't have any brandy,' Lorna said. 'I feel better now.'

Muriel touched her hand.

'But you're cold,' she said, 'your hands are like ice. It will do you good—drink it.'

Lorna let herself be persuaded to take a sip or two, and the fiery liquid coursing down her throat did indeed disperse that feeling of nausea and dizziness which still threatened to overcome her.

'I think you ought to go back to bed,' Muriel said. 'You must have got a touch of the sun yesterday.'

'I shall be all right in a moment,' Lorna replied. 'Please don't tell your mother.'

'Well, we haven't got anything to do this morning, anyway,' Muriel said. 'Nothing important, that is. I've got a few letters that I must finish by lunch time, if you won't mind my leaving you?'

'But of course not,' Lorna felt a sudden craving to be alone . . . alone or at home! The idea suddenly came to her. She must go back . . . she must be with her family, must recover her poise by leading her normal life again. This was all unreal; her happiness with Jimmy had only been a dream which now had changed into a nightmare.

Events, suspicions, discoveries, were all closing in on her with that relentless nightmare quality which makes escape seem impossible. She thought of her father, of his straightforward honesty; she thought of the children, and of Michael's reliability and frankness.

She was homesick for them with a yearning which was indescribable, she only knew that it seemed to tear her soul asunder—it was a fierce desire which she could not control.

She was suddenly aware that Muriel was looking at her, waiting for her to speak.

'I'm all right,' she repeated. 'Let's go downstairs.'

They walked in silence down the corridor and then, as they were coming down the main staircase, a footman came hurrying up towards them.

'I've been looking for you, Madam,' he said to Lorna. 'You're wanted on the telephone.'

'Is it from the aerodrome?' Lorna asked. Jimmy had said that he might telephone later in the day and now she felt a great reluctance to speak to him. Wildly she wondered if she could send Muriel—could make some excuse to avoid hearing his voice just yet.

'I don't think so, Madam,' the footman replied. 'It's a personal call—long distance from Melchester.'

'It's from home!'

Lorna ran down the stairs. There was nobody in the morning-room; she shut the door behind her and picked up the receiver; after a moment there was a click and she was connected through to the main line.

'Hello.'

'Is that you, Lorna!' It was Beth's voice.

'Darling, what is it? I tried to ring you last night but I couldn't get through.'

'Oh, Lorna, listen. Peke is hurt—terribly hurt . . . she's had an accident . . . We were going to our lessons this morning and she was run over by the gate . . . I've been trying to get through to you for hours . . . Michael's here . . . They haven't told me anything but it was awful, Lorna, a lorry hit her . . . we were hurrying because we were late and we never saw it coming . . .' Beth's voice was high and hysterical.

'One minute, Beth,' Lorna interrupted. 'Where's Daddy? Is he there with you?'

'No, we can't find him . . . He's gone over to Copland, I think, but we don't know where he is . . .'

'But Michael's there?'

'Yes, Michael came at once . . . Martha telephoned him as soon as we carried Peke back here . . . she was bleeding . . . and her leg was crushed . . . she looked white . . . and silent . . . and dead . . .'

Beth was crying now. Lorna's voice was steady.

'Listen, darling, I'm coming to you. I'll start now. Try to be calm and do exactly what Michael tells you. I'll be with you as soon as it's humanly possible.'

'All right, Lorna, but you will hurry, won't you? . . . It's so frightening here and nobody tells me anything . . .'

'Be brave, darling. I'll take a taxi out from Melchester so don't attempt to meet me.'

Lorna put down the receiver. She found Muriel in the hall and tried to explain to her.

'It's my sister—Peke. She's had a bad accident. I've got to go—I must get to them. Can I have a car to take me to the station or would it be quicker to motor through to London? If I could possibly catch the midday train to Melchester I could be home by three o'clock.'

Muriel looked at the time.

'You'd better motor to London,' she said. 'I will ask if we have enough petrol; if not, we can hire from the local garage. I'll fix that. You go and tell the maid what you want packed.'

'I'll do it myself,' Lorna said.

The car was round in ten minutes and, carrying her own suitcase, Lorna came running down the stairs. She kissed Muriel good-bye.

'Explain to Jimmy,' she said, 'and to your mother.'

'You'll telephone, won't you?' Muriel asked.

'If I can, but one can't always get through.'

She did not look back as the car drove her away down the drive. She had only one idea in her mind—to get home.

Never had time seemed to pass so slowly. The drive to London was full of anxiety—watching the clock, wondering if she could do it in the time. She reached the station five minutes before the train left, and then there was the long, uneventful journey to Melchester.

It was the best train of the day, but it was late and delayed at several of the stations. When at last she reached Melchester Lorna felt as if she had passed through an eternity of waiting and worrying.

All the way she was wondering if she would be in time, telling herself that Beth had exaggerated hysterically, and yet terrified that she had spoken the truth and that Peke might be dead or dying.

It took her some minutes to find a taxi outside the station that would take her as far as Little Walton; but when at last one agreed to make the journey they rattled along at a good speed. At last they reached the outskirts of the village, and with Lorna giving directions to the driver they came finally to the Vicarage itself.

Lorna jumped out, paid the taxi, then, carrying her own suitcase she opened the door and entered the house. She had only taken a few steps into the hall when Beth came hurrying out of the sitting-room her arms outstretched.

'Oh, darling, you're here at last! I couldn't believe it was really you when I heard the car outside. Thank goodness you've come!—I've been frantic!'

'How's Peke?' Lorna put down her suitcase and pulled off her hat.

'Michael's still here. There is another doctor, too, from Melchester, and a nurse. I don't know what they're doing. They talked at first of moving Peke and then they thought it was too dangerous. I think they have had to operate.'

Lorna stood still. She could smell the faint, sickly scent of ether.

'Where's Minnie?'

'Helping them,' Beth replied. 'They wouldn't let me. They've been boiling things, taking bowls, sheets, and all sorts of things along to Peke's room and moving the furniture about too. Oh Lorna, it's all so frightening. I'm glad you are here.'

'It's all right, darling. Where's Daddy!'

'We don't know. I remembered afterwards that he was going to lunch with the Squire, but of course I didn't think of it until after two o'clock and when I rang up he had just left.'

'Well, perhaps it's better that way. We don't want him upset.'

Lorna took off her coat and put her things down on a chair.

'Have you had any lunch?'

Beth shook her head.

'I couldn't have eaten a thing even if anyone had remembered it.'

'Well, you're going to have something now. As a matter of fact I've had nothing myself. We'll make some tea and toast. I daresay the doctors will want something later.'

'That's a good idea,' Beth said. 'Shall I lay the table in the sitting-room?'

'Yes, do,' Lorna replied.

The strained look was fading from Beth's face and the note of horror from her voice.

'I must keep very calm,' Lorna thought to herself. 'Whatever happens Daddy must be saved from as much anxiety as possible.'

She went into the kitchen. Beth came hurrying after her.

'Don't spoil your new dress,' she said. 'Shall I run upstairs and get you an overall?'

Lorna shook her head.

'I'll be careful.'

'Oh, I'm so glad you are here,' Beth said again. 'I've been so scared.'

'It was very sensible of you to telephone me.'

'It was the first thing I did as soon as we had got Peke upstairs and Michael had come. I tried to help but they told me to go away. It was awful! I thought Peke was dead and I was all alone with no one to talk to. I put through a call to you and waited and waited for the bell to ring—and then just after we had finished speaking it rang again, and who do you think it was?'

'Who?' Lorna asked. She was cutting a piece of bread ready for toasting.

'It was Peter! He said—"I want to speak to Peke"—and I said—"You can't. She's had an accident." He said—"I knew it. Where is she?" I told him she was here and that Michael was with her and then, just as I began to tell him about the accident, he rang off. Wasn't that strange?'

Lorna put down the bread knife.

'Oh Beth, I hope you didn't say too much?'

'I didn't get a chance,' Beth replied. 'But wasn't it queer, Lorna? Do you think he felt that Peke had been hurt? You know that the twins always think the same as each other. Do you imagine they feel the same, too?'

'I don't know,' Lorna answered, 'but it's worrying. I wonder if I could telephone him.'

'I've got his number somewhere, it was on his last letter. Shall I get it?'

'It might be a good idea. We could put through a personal call; but we will wait until I have seen Michael, and then

I can tell him the very latest news.'

'Supposing Michael says she won't live?' Beth asked in a whisper and the tears welled into her eyes.

'Hush! We won't think about it.' Lorna picked up the tray. 'I'll take this into the drawing-room. Watch the toast and don't let the kettle boil over.'

As she reached the hall she heard the sound of a car coming up the drive. She wondered who it could be, then realised it was not a car but a motor bicycle. She heard the engine stop and someone come striding across the gravel. She put the tray down on a table and went to the door.

'I'd better see who it is,' she thought. Peter was standing in the porch.

'Peter! We were just talking about you.'

Lorna would have kissed him, but he made as if to push past her. He was in uniform, but he was hatless, his hair covered with dust, and his face streaked and dirty.

'Where's Peke?'

'Upstairs, but you can't see her yet. Michael's with her and I haven't yet heard how she is. I think they are operating.'

'I've got to see her!'

'Of course you shall,' Lorna said soothingly, 'but not at this moment. You must wait, dear.'

Peter put his hand across his eyes and Lorna saw he was half dazed.

'Come and wash,' she said gently, 'and then I will give you some tea. You must be exhausted. Did you ride the whole way?'

'Yes, I came straight here.' Peter spoke with difficulty, forcing his voice through his dry lips.

'I'm so glad you could get leave.'

Peter looked at Lorna, and then his eyes darkened and his expression changed, as if some new and strange idea had suddenly presented itself to his benumbed brain.

'But I didn't get leave . . .' he stammered. 'I just came straight here after I'd talked to Beth!'

17

There was the sound of a door opening. Lorna and Peter turned quickly, their eyes raised to the upper landing. Michael, wearing a white coat, came to the top of the stairs. He looked down on them, and then, before Lorna could move or speak, Peter had run up to meet him.

'How's Peke? I've got to see her!'

Michael put his arm round the boy's shoulders in a gesture both affectionate and protective.

'She'll be all right,' Michael said quickly. 'You can't see her yet—she's not properly round from the anæsthetic.'

They walked slowly down the stairs linked together; as they reached the hall, Michael held out his free hand to Lorna.

She took it impulsively in both of hers. Her eyes were full of tears and she was battling for her self-control. She knew now how anxious she had been, how apprehensive of what the verdict might be. For a moment they said nothing; they were united by an understanding which made words superfluous.

Then Lorna released Michael's hand.

'There'll be some tea for you in a moment,' she said. 'I'll bring it into the sitting-room.'

She turned away and hurried towards the kitchen. Beth was pouring boiling water into the tea-pot.

'Peter's here,' Lorna said abruptly, 'and Michael's just

come downstairs. He says Peke will be all right.'

Beth made a convulsive sound and started to cry. Lorna took the kettle from her and, putting it down on the range, said :

'It will be all right, darling. You mustn't give way now—there's so much to do.'

'I know. . . .' Beth sobbed, 'but I thought she was dead. . . . There was such a lot of blood . . . I had no idea anyone could bleed so much and still live. . . .'

'Don't think about it,' Lorna commanded. 'Come and talk to Michael. There's so much I want to hear.'

Beth wiped her eyes.

'You won't tell him that I've been such a coward?' she asked. 'He'll despise me. . . .'

'But you have been very brave,' Lorna replied, 'and you've done everything in your power. Come on now—bring the toast.'

Beth did as she was told and followed Lorna into the sitting-room. Michael was sitting in his favourite chair by the fireside; Peter was on the sofa, bending forward, his head in his hands.

'Don't get up,' Lorna said hastily. 'You both look as if you need a cup of tea.'

'That's exactly what I do need,' Michael replied.

'And what about the other doctor?' Lorna asked. 'Beth said that someone else was here.'

'Oh, he's all right for the moment,' Michael answered. 'He gave the anæsthetic and now he's packing up. Besides, Minnie will look after him and the nurse. I needn't tell you that she has been invaluable.'

'Minnie's always a tower of strength. Now here's your tea —and Peter, here's yours.'

Peter raised a white face and as he put out his hand to take the cup Lorna saw it was trembling. She looked at Michael and raised her eyebrows; but Michael made no response, although she was well aware that his keen eyes had missed nothing.

'Won't you tell us about Peke?' Lorna asked. 'How badly is she hurt?'

Michael took a long drink of tea, then put down the cup.

'To be quite frank with you,' he said, 'when I first saw Peke I was anxious. I was afraid of some really bad internal injury but, after examination, I can now assure you that there's nothing so seriously damaged that it can't be mended by time and patience.

'I have done a good deal of patching and, we've set her leg in plaster of Paris; now we can only wait, hoping that the shock will not have affected her too deeply. Thank goodness her face was quite untouched and, though her body is badly bruised, there were no other bones broken. And now, Beth, tell me how it happened? I've got a good idea, of course.'

Lorna saw that Beth was on the verge of tears. Quickly she interrupted the first stammering words which fell from her sister's lips.

'Let's hear about that later,' she said. 'There's plenty of time. First of all, I want to say how thankful I am that you were here, Michael.'

'I shall always be here if I'm needed,' Michael replied. 'And what about you? Did a magic carpet bring you? I've never been so surprised in my life as when I saw you and Peter standing in the hall.'

'Beth had the good sense to telephone me. I just managed to catch the midday train, otherwise I shouldn't have been here for hours.'

'I'm more than thankful that you managed it,' Michael said. 'I had every intention of ringing you up myself and asking you to come home, but Beth—clever girl—wasted no time.'

He smiled at Beth as he spoke and she tried to smile back, but it was a tremulous effort.

'And now, Peter my lad, what about you?'

Peter was looking better, there was some colour in his face and his hands were no longer shaking. He looked first at

Michael and then at Lorna in a somewhat shamefaced way, before he blurted out the truth.

'I knew something had happened to Peke. I can't explain how I knew, but I was sure of it. I suddenly felt I had to speak to her. I got through on the telephone and Beth told me she'd had an accident. I took a motor-bike out of one of the sheds—there were several there—I've no idea to whom it belonged—and I just came straight here, hell for leather!'

'He didn't ask for leave,' Lorna explained. 'What shall we do, Michael? We've got to do something about it.'

'You'd better speak to your C.O., hadn't you?' Michael asked.

'Oh, I couldn't, he'd never understand!' Peter got up abruptly and walked towards the window. 'I shall get browned off for this all right!'

'We must offer some explanation,' Lorna insisted.

'Would it be any good if I told him the facts?' Michael suggested. 'Or would he listen to your father?'

'What excuse can you make?' Peter asked. 'He'll think we're all crazy—and it isn't surprising.'

'Why not get Jimmy to put in a word for you?' Beth asked. Peter turned round.

'That's an idea. Lorna, call him up and tell him what's happened.'

'I don't think I can. . . .' Lorna began, and then she stopped.

There was no possible reason she could give for not asking Jimmy's sympathy and co-operation. She could not tell them, with Peter's eyes pleadingly upon her, with Beth and Michael listening, that her one desire was not to speak to Jimmy.

This was not the moment to be selfish, and put her own personal feelings before her brother's career. She had got to help—the boy was in trouble.

'All right,' she said reluctantly, 'I'll telephone him.'

'That's topping of you!' Peter exclaimed. 'I know Jimmy

will do what he can for me—he's been so jolly sporting about everything.'

Lorna walked towards the door. She knew that Michael had been aware of her hesitation even if the children had not noticed it. She wondered what he thought.

It was with a feeling of bitterness and resentment that she picked up the receiver. The nausea and disgust she had experienced during the morning came flooding back to her.

As she lifted the telephone she thought of Sally standing here in this very place to telephone Jimmy; of the lies by which she had covered her departure; of the satisfaction she must have felt as she had driven away to pick up Jimmy at the Hall and to take him to London.

She remembered her own feelings that week-end. Recalling how slowly the hours had passed as she counted them until Jimmy's return. Now she asked herself whether, if she had known before how Jimmy had spent that week-end, she would have accepted him with such passionate joy.

The exchange answered at last. She gave them Jimmy's name and number and they said they would call her. As she finished speaking Michael came out of the sitting-room.

'I'm going up to Peke,' he said. 'Would you like to look at her?'

'Of course I would.'

'Wait one minute until I've been in.'

Lorna followed him upstairs and stood on the landing.

'How can I worry about Jimmy?' she asked herself, 'when Peke is so ill—when she is injured and suffering?'

But she knew that whatever was happening, if the whole world lay in ruins at her feet, she could not escape her own feelings towards Jimmy. She might run away from him to the uttermost corners of the earth but still he would have the power to hurt her.

Even now, though humiliated and shocked, she knew that one part of her ached for him. She was ashamed of her weakness but could not deny it.

'God, how I hate it all!' she said aloud; and, even as she

spoke, was conscious that Michael was at her side and must have heard what she said. He looked at her strangely but said nothing. Instead he took her arm and drew her towards Peke's bedroom.

'She has not quite come round yet,' he said. 'She won't recognise you. She's had a good deal of morphia besides the anæsthetic.'

The blinds were lowered, the room was dim, and there was the sickly sweet odour of ether hanging in the air. A nurse moved away from the bed as they entered and a shadowy figure in the other corner of the room was packing instruments into a leather case.

In the small white wooden bedstead Peke was lying very still. She looked so small and young. Lorna felt a throb of pity and tenderness. It was as if her own child lay there.

She had looked after Peke for so long that she had ceased to think of her as nearly grown-up; she was still a child—a child who had been hurt and who needed her love and care. She bent down and kissed Peke's hand which lay outside the sheets.

After a moment, Michael led her from the room.

'She'll be all right,' he said soothingly, 'you're not to worry.'

'How can I help it?' Lorna asked fiercely. 'I ought never to have left them! It's all my fault. She and Beth were late for school so they weren't looking where they were going. If I'd been here they'd have been on time and it would never have happened!'

'That's an absurd argument,' Michael said almost roughly. 'You've got your life to lead and they have theirs. You can't wet nurse them all their lives. It's unfortunate this thing should have happened—but it's certainly not your fault.'

'I ought never to have gone away,' Lorna said obstinately. 'Oh Michael, why did you let me go?'

She spoke pleadingly, and she made no attempt to veil the expression in her eyes. She meant him to understand, meant him to know that she was suffering.

Michael considered her with a very intent look; then, as she waited almost apprehensively for his answer, the telephone rang.

'That'll be your call to your husband,' Michael said abruptly.

Lorna's eyes fell before his.

'I expect so,' she replied, and walked downstairs.

It was Jimmy.

'Hello, darling, what's happened? I've just got back and Muriel tells me that there's been an accident?'

Lorna told him briefly what had occurred, and then she went on to explain about Peter.

'What a fool the boy is!' Jimmy explained. 'He had only to ask for compassionate leave and it would have been granted; but tearing off like that on somebody else's motor-bike will land him in the devil of a mess!'

'I know—he's just realised that himself. Will you help him, Jimmy?'

She hated to ask a favour, but Jimmy's quick response gave her no time for regret.

'Of course I will!' he said. 'I'll call up the aerodrome at once. As a matter of fact the C.O. and the Adjutant are both pretty good friends of mine and, if anyone can fix it, I can. Tell that young idiot he wants kicking, but he'll be let off this time.'

'Thank you,' Lorna said.

'He'd better give me an hour,' Jimmy went on, 'to get through and tell the tale, and then he can ring up himself and ask for orders. And, by the way, I go on duty to-morrow night. It's taking forty-eight hours off my leave, but they want me and I can't very well refuse.'

'I quite understand.'

'Yes, but when am I going to see you again, dear?'

'I can't possibly leave here—not yet, at any rate.'

'No. I suppose you'll have to stay—but it's pretty damnable all the same. I want you—I want you to be with me. I shall miss you badly to-night, Cherry Ripe.' Jimmy's voice was caressing.

Lorna shivered.

'I've no idea when I shall be able to leave here.' She spoke abruptly.

'You sound upset. Take care of yourself, darling, or you'll have me worrying about you.'

'I'm all right,' Lorna said. 'Good-bye, and thank you about Peter.'

'Good-bye, sweetheart. I love you.'

She slammed the receiver into place and knew that she was trembling, not with fear but with anger. She asked herself how he could dare to speak to her like that? Then remembered that he had no knowledge of her discovery, no idea that her feelings for him had altered since the morning.

But this was not the moment for introspection. In the sitting-room Peter was waiting for her. She gave him Jimmy's message and his face lightened.

'And I think you can go up to Peke for a moment,' Lorna said, 'but you must be very quiet. She won't recognise you, but you can see that she's all right.'

Peter put his arm round her neck.

'You're a brick, Lorna. I shall never forget what you've done for me—and Jimmy too. He's tip-top as a brother-in-law and you can tell him so from me!'

'I will when I get the chance,' Lorna said, 'but I'm going to stay here for a little while.'

'Are you really?' Beth asked, climbing off the window seat where she had been curled up, quiet and strangely un-obtrusive.

'Naturally I'm not going to leave you until Peke's much better,' Lorna replied, 'and it seems to me you will want looking after too. It's been a nasty experience, poor darling.'

'Everything will be all right if you are here,' Beth answered. 'I can't tell you how beastly it has been without you! At first I thought it was going to be rather fun not to have anyone to find fault with me. But I missed you tremendously all the time !'

'Well, here I am, back again,' Lorna said, 'so that's that !'

Beth looked at her in surprise.

'But you won't be able to stay long. Jimmy will want you. Was he awfully miserable at your coming away?'

'He quite understood,' Lorna replied, not meeting Beth's eyes, 'and he's joining his Squadron to-morrow so I daresay he'll get along all right without me.'

There was silence for a moment, then Beth, with her usual perceptive sharpness, said :

'You sound a bit queer. Don't you like being married? Isn't it as nice as you thought it was going to be?'

Lorna got up abruptly.

'Don't ask so many questions, there's a dear. We'd better take these things back to the kitchen.'

She was conscious that Beth's eyes were on her, that Beth was about to speak and ask questions which would make evasion and subterfuge difficult, when the entrance of the Vicar created a welcome diversion.

He cried out in surprise at the sight of Lorna. Then she was in his arms, explaining what had happened, and why she was here. She told him how thankful they all were that he had escaped the hours of anxiety when Peke's fate hung in the balance.

By the time Lorna had brought her father some fresh tea, Michael had come downstairs again.

'I'm going now,' he said, 'but I shall be back later this evening. Heaven knows what's happened to the rest of my patients—I suppose they'll either have died or recovered !'

'What about the nurse?' Lorna asked.

'I've told her to ask you for everything she wants,' Michael answered. 'She must have the bedroom next door to Peke's. It is nice to have you here, Lorna. I should be worried stiff if there was only this little scatterbrain to see to everything.'

He ruffled Beth's hair, and she made an affectionate grimace at him.

'If I hadn't such a sweet nature,' she said, 'I should take umbrage at that remark. As it is—I'm even more pleased to see Lorna than you are.'

'Shall we say we are all delighted to have her back,' the Vicar interposed. 'Lorna, my dear, I can't think how we've managed without you. We must be very grateful to Jimmy for sparing you.'

'Sparing me, nothing! I was wanted and so home I came —and here I'm going to stay!'

She spoke defiantly and looked at Michael as if challenging him.

'I only wish that were true,' he said in a tired voice, and, for some strange reason that she could not explain, Lorna felt ashamed.

18

Michael turned the car off the main road and driving up a small winding cart-track brought it to the summit of a low incline.

The track ended abruptly and he drove the car on to the grass. The countryside sloped away before them—green fields, red-brown patches of plough-land, waving gold of ripening corn, and the orchards with their lime-washed trees. It was all very quiet and very peaceful.

There was a hawk hovering high in the blue sky, a rabbit scampering into a sandy burrow, the wood pigeons rising and settling again, and the silver flash of plovers' wings as they wheeled and circled overhead.

Michael pulled out his pipe.

'Do you mind if I smoke?'

'Not if you talk to me as well,' Lorna answered.

'That's exactly why I've brought you here! I want to talk to you.'

She was silent. She had the feeling when he invited her to go driving with him that he had something special to say to her.

Michael got his pipe to draw, flicked the burnt match out of the window, then turned his face towards Lorna with a smile.

'Well,' she said. 'Am I to get a sermon or the third degree?'

'Neither,' he replied. 'As a matter of fact I only want to

ask you one question. When are you rejoining your husband?'

She looked at him in astonishment. This was the very last thing she had expected Michael to say! For the moment she hesitated, then answered in a voice which was half-provocative, half-defiant.

'Are you worrying about that?'

'As a matter of fact I am.'

Michael's tone was serious and Lorna felt rebuked. She did not look at him but gazed in front of her, seeing nothing of the view, feeling only irritation and bitterness, Michael put out his hand and touched hers.

'There's only one thing in the whole world I want,' he said gently, 'and that is, perfect happiness for you.'

'You shouldn't be so ambitious!' Lorna retorted in a hard tone. 'If we aim for something unattainable it merely makes us discontented.'

'Is it unattainable?'

Lorna shrugged her shoulders, and there was a long silence. In the stillness she felt her resentment ebbing away, to be replaced by a feeling of desolation and misery. She had expected Michael to be sympathetic, she told herself. No, that was not true.

She had wanted him to be loving, to sustain her pride by showing her that his affection was undiminished, that his love could withstand time and change—even the fact that she had married someone else. But now it appeared that Michael had deserted her.

Why should he be interested in her return to Jimmy? Surely he should want to keep her here, should be grateful for her presence?

Her emotions swelled in a flood tide and overcame her control.

'I hate everything!' she said unsteadily, and her voice broke on the words.

'Aren't you making things worse by running away from them?' Michael asked.

Lorna turned sharply to look at him.

'Why should you think I am running away?' she challenged.

Michael's eyes met her steadily.

'I am sure you are,' he replied. 'I'm right, aren't I?'

Lorna's eyes dropped before his. 'I suppose so.'

'Isn't that rather cowardly?'

'I don't know. Perhaps it is the easiest way to avoid trouble.'

Michael's hand tightened on hers.

'You can never avoid trouble by refusing to face it.'

'What do you know about my troubles?' Lorna asked impatiently.

'Very little,' Michael replied. 'But I had a letter from your husband this morning.'

'From Jimmy!' Lorna exclaimed in amazement. 'What did he say? Why did he write to you? How extraordinary!'

Michael released her hand.

'He asked me,' he said, and his voice was grim, 'to return his wife to him.'

'How could he? And what does he think I am?—a parcel, or something?'

Michael ignored her interruption.

'He has come to the conclusion that something has upset you. He frankly admits he has no idea what it is and he suggests that I make it my business to find out, as, to quote his own words, I am "more likely to know than anyone else".'

'I don't suppose he meant that as a compliment.'

'I understand that. But even without your husband's letter I have not been blind these past weeks. I knew that you were unhappy, but hoped that you might turn to me in your own good time. I was a pretty reliable "Father Confessor" in the old days, wasn't I?'

'Ever since I can remember,' Lorna replied, 'I have come to you with my troubles and you have never failed me—but this is different. It is not because I don't trust you that I have kept silent, it is not because I haven't needed your help, but because what is upsetting me is something which I could repeat to no one, would feel ashamed to discuss even with my nearest and dearest—and that, Michael, is you.'

Michael pulled steadily at his pipe; then he asked:

'In that case, what are you going to do about it?'

'I don't know,' Lorna said helplessly. 'I want to stay here with my family.'

'That's impossible!'

'But why? It is war-time—Jimmy is busy—what is more natural than for me to prefer to be at home where I am needed rather than trying to live a completely artificial alien life in my father-in-law's house?'

'And your husband? Isn't he entitled to some sort of consideration?'

Lorna was tense for a moment, then she said:

'The last time you gave me advice, you told me to open my wings and fly—but you didn't tell me to expect a hurricane round the corner!'

'Are you quite sure it is a hurricane?' Michael asked. 'We are all inclined to make mountains out of molehills; or, perhaps I should say, a hurricane out of a puff of wind.'

'Do you really think I am a hysterical person? The type of woman who would exaggerate small grievances—small difficulties?'

'I am quite sure you are nothing of the sort,' Michael replied. 'I believe, too, that you are big enough and strong enough to overcome any differences between yourself and your husband. When you married, you loved each other. He still loves you. Whatever has happened in the meantime, a solution can be found if you set your heart to it.'

'And why should I make the effort?' Lorna asked. 'I am the one who has been injured. I am not going to tell you how, but you must take my word for it. Jimmy is in the wrong— not I.'

'You are the one who must make the sacrifices,' Michael said. 'It may sound illogical to you, it may sound unjust; but my dear, you are a giver. The world is divided into people who give and people who take; and for the former there is only one happiness—in the unceasing effort of giving.

'Had you asked me if I could contemplate your marriage proving a failure, I should have answered that the only possibility lay in your husband not demanding enough of you—not asking enough.

'Frankly, I don't believe in your hurricane. If it were there you would face it bravely; you would even welcome it because it demanded so much of your strength.'

'You don't understand,' Lorna said desperately. 'I have certain standards, and ideals, also a sense of honour. These have been violated and besmirched.'

'Are you quite certain that these particular standards are so important?' Michael asked.

Lorna stared at him in amazement.

'But of course they are, they are the very foundations of my existence. They were given me by my mother and nothing you nor anyone else could say or do would convince me that they were not right.'

'Right for you—yes,' Michael said, 'but I imagine it is not your actions which have fallen short of them, but someone else's. Are you justified in judging everybody by your standards? My dear, you must learn not to be presumptuous where others are concerned. Your life is your own—other people have a right to theirs.'

Lorna remembered how often she had criticised Jimmy's light-hearted acceptance of everything that came his way. Michael's words echoed much of her own reasoning; for she knew that any sin of pleasure Jimmy committed would mean infinitely less to him than to the majority of people she knew.

There was logic in all that Michael said; but that did not seem to help much when emotions, and not cold reason, were involved!

'You are arguing without knowing the facts,' she said. 'However skilfully you present Jimmy's case for him, I am not convinced that I should let myself be persuaded into leaving home.'

'Your home is with your husband.'

Lorna remembered how her father had said that just before she married.

'Daddy and the children will always mean home to me,' she answered fiercely.

'We won't argue about that,' Michael said, 'not at the moment. Let us say instead that your place is with your husband—especially at a time like this.'

'He can look after himself. He doesn't need me.'

'That's not true, and besides—have you ever thought that one day you might regret that time you have wasted apart? Have you thought seriously of the dangerous work he is doing for his country—for us all—for you?'

Lorna sat very still. Supposing Jimmy were killed?—she thought, and her fingers slipped down to touch the unopened letter hidden in the pocket of her dress. A world without him! . . . a world which no longer held his smile . . . his infectious laughter . . . his lips seeking hers.

She fought against the return of the insidious aching need of him which she thought had disappeared for good, but which Michael's words had brought back irresistibly. She surrendered unconditionally.

'Very well, then, I will go back. You can write and tell him that I am coming.'

'Good girl!' Michael approved; but his voice was dull and it seemed to Lorna he suddenly looked very grey and tired.

'Michael,' she asked, 'why did you make Jimmy marry me?'

As soon as the words left her lips she would have given much to recall them—but it was too late.

'I didn't,' Michael replied. 'I merely told him that if he was not interested I was, and I wanted a clear field. If he had left you then it might have been in time—I might have made you love me.'

'Did you do it for my sake or for your own?' Lorna questioned in a low voice.

'My own. I loved you—I shall always love you.'

Lorna was only half convinced, but there was nothing more she could say. She could only bend forward and press her lips against Michael's hand as it rested on the steering wheel of the car.

As her lips touched him, slowly his hand tightened until the knuckles showed white. Then, without a word, he bent forward; switched on the engine; and, backing slowly, ran the car off the grass to where it could turn on the sandy track.

They drove home in silence; only as they went up the drive towards the Vicarage did Lorna look at Michael with the pitiable expression of a forlorn child.

'How soon must I go?'

'Anticipation is usually worse than realisation,' Michael replied. 'Wouldn't you prefer to get it over? Why not tomorrow?'

'I can't!' Lorna cried. 'I can't possibly!' But even as she spoke the question came to her mind—'Suppose Jimmy were killed?' It was no use—she could not escape him!

As the car stopped, she opened the door, saying :

'All right, I will go to-morrow on the two-thirty.'

She turned away quickly from the expression on Michael's face—it was that of a man entering purgatory.

It was very quiet in the house. The blinds were drawn against the hot afternoon sun. Lorna pulled off her hat and threw it down in a chair.

'I expect Daddy is in Peke's room.'

'I will go up and see her,' Michael said, 'although she's had my official visit for the day.'

'I'll get some tea.'

She turned towards the kitchen and then, suddenly, her self-control gave way—she felt the tears come flooding to her eyes. She expected Minnie to be out; but as she walked through the kitchen door, half-blinded, she saw the old woman sitting in a wicker armchair in front of the fireplace.

Lorna hesitated; then, as Minnie looked up at her in anxious surprise, she ran forward and, flinging herself on her knees, hid her face in Minnie's lap.

'What's the matter, dearie? What's happened?'

'Nothing,' Lorna sobbed. 'Nothing. Only I'm so unhappy —so utterly miserable!'

'There, there. You musn't take on like this.'

Lorna stifled her sobs and raised her head.

'I'm going away to-morrow. I'm going back to my husband.'

'And quite right, too. He'll be lonely without you, the poor man, and he must need someone to come back to in between harassing them Huns.'

'Minnie,' Lorna said in a whisper. 'Do you think I have made a mistake? Do you think I ought to have married Michael?'

Minnie put a warm, comforting arm round Lorna's shoulders.

'We have all of us got to follow our hearts, dearie,' she said, 'and it's no use gainsaying them, wherever they may lead us. Love's more powerful than all the arguments in the world, and all the common sense too. We may make a lot of mistakes because of love, but it teaches us to be mighty human and very forgiving.'

Lorna heaved a sigh.

'I am being a fool. I will try to be more understanding— but it's very difficult when one cares so much!'

'That's a sensible girl,' Minnie said approvingly. 'There's nothing that you can't forgive if you love a person, and nothing that you don't aim to understand sooner or later. Men are like little boys—they're always into mischief of some sort. But if you can't understand them and you won't forgive them, you aren't any sort of a woman.'

Lorna hugged her.

'You are more help than all the sermons in the world,' she

cried. 'I can't think what we'd do without you, you old darling!'

Minnie looked at the clock.

'It's your tea-time, I'll bring it into the sitting-room for you.'

'Michael's here.'

'There! Why didn't you say so before? I'll make him some hot buttered toast—I know he likes it. There's always something hindering me from getting my work done in this place.'

Lorna knew that Minnie grumbled to hide her feelings. It was a habit of hers, whenever moved, to busy her hands and speak resentfully of wasted time. She smiled at her a little tremulously from the doorway.

'I'm going up to powder my nose.'

In her own room she looked at herself in the glass and exclaimed at her general air of dishevelment. Then she pulled Jimmy's letter from her pocket and started to read it.

Whether it was Michael's influence or Minnie's she did not know, but, for the first time since she came home, she read her husband's letter with understanding. It seemed to her like the outcry of a child who has been unjustly punished; he was bewildered; he was slightly resentful; a little on the defensive.

'What have I done? What have I said?' he asked.

And through every phrase his longing for her appeared as an ever-recurring theme.

A sudden impulse made Lorna long to go to him now— at once! She felt a vague premonition of something unpleasant creep over her.

She looked at the clock. It was four-thirty. If she got ready immediately she could catch the train this evening. She would be in London by nine and at Mountley Park before ten o'clock.

'I'll do it,' she thought, 'why shouldn't I? I must go back and Jimmy really does want me.'

'But why not wait till to-morrow?' the voice of caution

suggested. 'You've been away so long, another twenty-four hours isn't going to make much difference.'

Jimmy's letter lay open on her dressing-table. It seemed to be calling her; she could almost imagine his voice speaking her name. By unreasoning instinct she answered to that call.

'I must go—I must!' she reiterated aloud.

And then she was packing—dragging her suitcase out of the cupboard at the top of the stairs—calling for Minnie and for Beth—getting them to fold her dresses and wrap up her shoes—changing swiftly into a travelling dress which had been part of her trousseau—combing her hair and trying to hide under cream and powder the tell-tale marks of recent tears.

When all this was done she had twenty-five minutes in which to catch the train. Michael would take her to the station—she had already made sure of that by sending Beth to ask him. She ran along to Peke's room.

Peke held out her arms, and Lorna put her glowing face against her sister's pale one.

'I am going now, darling,' she said. 'I have to go back to Jimmy. I can't stop to explain, there isn't time, but take care of yourself and get well—very quickly.'

'Must you go?' Peke asked, a little wistfully. 'It's been so lovely having you here.'

'Yes, I must go now,' Lorna said, surprised at her own firmness, 'but I will come back very soon—very soon. I will try to see Peter and let you know how he is.'

'That will be lovely.'

Lorna hurried down the stairs. Her luggage had already been put in the car. Michael was waiting at the wheel. She flung her arms round her father, and turned to Beth.

'Look after everything,' she said. 'You are in charge now Peke's laid up.'

'So I am!' Beth exclaimed. 'I hadn't thought of that.'

Minnie was standing in the doorway.

'Good-bye, you old sweet,' Lorna said as she kissed her. 'I shall be thinking of what you said to me.'

'Good-bye, and God bless you.'

'Good-bye, my darlings—good-bye.'

The voices rang out above the roar of the engine; and then she was off, waving as she went down the drive. Her heart was beating and her spirits soaring with joy which could not be gainsaid—she was going back to Jimmy!

19

The station taxi drew up at the door of Mountley Park. Lorna jumped out and ran up the steps. When the butler opened the door she saw a look of surprise on his usually immobile face.

'I suppose you weren't expecting me, Thompson. Didn't my father manage to get through on the telephone?'

'The wires are all down, Ma'am,' he replied. 'We had a land mine about two miles away last night.'

'How awful! Did it do much damage?'

'Rather a large number of casualties, I'm afraid, Ma'am. It fell near some council houses. Will you be wanting dinner?'

'No, thank you, I had it on the train. Where is everybody?'

'Her ladyship is out. She had a meeting at nine o'clock, and Miss Muriel has gone with her. Sir Douglas will not be returning until the late train. Mr. Jimmy, however, is here. I think he is in the West Wing, Ma'am.'

'I'll go up at once.'

'Very good, Ma'am.'

Lorna hurried up the broad staircase until she neared the door of the sitting-room, then moved more slowly. She had not anticipated that Jimmy would be at home; somehow she had been quite certain that he would be at the aerodrome and had meant to telephone him—to hear his surprise when she told him she was speaking from Mountley Park.

Now she felt both shy and nervous.

In the train she had rehearsed to herself the things that she meant to say to Jimmy; for she had told herself that if they were to live together with any kind of happiness she must be truthful and frank with him.

It was impossible for her to be secretive, it was not in her nature; and she could not contemplate taking up the threads of their life together without telling him what had been in her heart these past weeks.

The fear of the future where Sally was concerned troubled her. After all, she was her cousin and Jimmy's friend. It was going to be difficult to cut her out of their life, yet Lorna was determined that, if possible, neither of them would ever see her again.

'I must be sensible about this,' Lorna thought. 'I must keep Jimmy away from temptation, and that's impossible unless I have his co-operation.'

She had it all planned, catalogued and tabulated within her own mind. She meant to be cool, dignified, and very sensible as she told Jimmy what she had decided; but as she turned the handle of the sitting-room door her heart was pounding within her—her breath coming quickly.

Jimmy was sitting at the writing-desk. He looked up casually as the door opened, and for a moment was too surprised to move. Then he jumped to his feet with a shout of gladness.

'Lorna !'

'I've come back.'

'Oh darling, by all that's wonderful! When did you arrive? Why didn't you let me know?'

Lorna put her handbag down on a chair.

'They tried to telephone from home, but the lines are down.'

And then she could make no further explanation for Jimmy's arms were round her, he was holding her closely to him.

He pulled off her hat and tossed it away, then bent his

head, kissing her hungrily and fiercely until she felt as if the whole world swayed dizzily round her; until her lips were bruised; until passion swept over her, echoing his, and she clung to him while the flame-like ecstasy united them both. . . . . . .

It was a long, long time afterwards that Jimmy, looking down at her flushed, glowing face against the silk cushions on the sofa, asked :

'Do you love me?'

'I adore . . . you !'

There was a ripple of laughter in her throat at his asking such an unnecessary question. Vaguely she remembered that she had something to tell him, something to discuss, but it had retreated into the mist of unreality, while this was all-important, all-consuming.

'Why have you stayed away from me so long? Have you missed me?'

Jimmy's hands were on her throat, touching her hair, smoothing the softness of her skin.

'Of course I have . . . more than I can ever tell you.'

It was the truth—she had missed him. Now she was with him again, she knew how much.

'It's been absolute hell without you! Are you a witch, Cherry Ripe, that you can draw me to you so that I cannot escape, cannot forget you even for a moment? Always your spirit is with me, even when I am flying. When I shoot down a Hun I feel that you are beside me—at times it is difficult to prevent myself from turning to you and saying—"That was good, wasn't it?" '

Lorna reached up her arms and put them round his neck.

'I will always be with you,' she whispered, 'I will never leave you again.'

'But I'm afraid I have got to leave you, my darling.' He looked across the room at the clock standing on the mantelpiece. 'I must go now—in a few minutes.'

'Oh, must you?' It was a cry of disappointment.

'Yes. I've got to be on duty at eleven-thirty, and it takes

me a good twenty minutes to get to the aerodrome—going full out.'

'But I've hardly seen you. There's so much I wanted to say.'

Jimmy silenced her protests with a kiss.

'I'll be back to-morrow,' he promised. 'I'm not quite certain when I can get off and I can't telephone. Just expect me either for lunch or some time during the afternoon.'

He stood up, picked up his uniform jacket from the floor where he had flung it and put it on. Then he swiftly bent towards her again.

'That's how I like to remember you,' he said. 'Your face flushed and your eyes shining. You are lovely, my sweet—the loveliest thing I've ever seen.'

Once again he kissed her, his mouth lingering on the soft tiredness of her lips until with an effort he wrenched himself away.

'God! You excite me!' he exclaimed. 'I want to love you again and go on making love to you all night—but I've got to go.'

He walked towards the door, then looked back.

'Don't forget me, Cherry Ripe,' he said, 'and don't disappear again! I've had enough trouble to get you back this time!'

'I'll be waiting for you,' Lorna promised, 'and take care of yourself, my darling.'

She called the last words after him, for he was already in the passage; she heard his voice through the closed door and then she was alone.

For a long time she was still. Until, at last, she roused herself, but in those moments of quietness she had come to a decision. She would not speak to Jimmy about Sally, not unless some new crisis arose, not unless Sally made another attempt to break in upon their happiness.

At the moment the past seemed utterly unimportant. It was impossible for Lorna to doubt his love now, or to question his gladness at seeing her again.

'Why have I tortured myself like this?' she asked herself. It was like awakening from a nightmare.

The feelings of horror and fear had faded away; she could hardly remember them, they were lost in a kind of haze into which it was difficult to infuse reality.

'What a fool I've been!' she thought.

She heard sounds in her bedroom and went in, to find her suitcase being unpacked, her things laid out for the night.

'What time will her ladyship be back?' she asked as she tidied her hair in the mirror.

'I think she's expected any moment, Ma'am,' the house-maid replied, 'in fact, I fancy I heard the car a few minutes ago.'

'I'll go and see.'

As Lorna reached the top of the stairs, she saw Lady Braith and Muriel standing in the hall. There were exclamations of surprise and pleasure from them both. She told them that she had seen Jimmy, and Muriel remarked :

'I'm so glad that he hadn't gone. He has been awfully lonely without you these past weeks. It must have been a tremendous thrill for him—your unexpected arrival.'

'I couldn't come before,' Lorna said. 'My sister has been very ill indeed.'

This was not strictly true, for Peke had been out of danger for over a fortnight, but she was desperately anxious that Muriel and her mother-in-law should not imagine that any-thing had been wrong between her and Jimmy. Lady Braith's next words, however, told her that her absence had not escaped criticism.

'I am sorry about your sister, but I am glad you have come back to look after your husband.'

'I hope he has not been getting into mischief!' Lorna said, trying to speak lightly.

'On the contrary, he has been doing exceedingly good work,' Lady Braith replied. 'Air Vice-Marshal Raffery, who commands his station, was over for dinner the other night and he spoke most enthusiastically of Jimmy. I believe even his father was impressed!'

'I am so glad,' Lorna spoke lamely.

'So were we,' Muriel interposed, 'and Mother was as pleased as punch.'

'So am I,' Lorna said proudly.

They gossiped downstairs for a little while and then, without waiting for Sir Douglas's return, said good-night. Muriel linked her arm through Lorna's as they walked towards the latter's room.

'It's lovely to have you back,' she said. 'Have you given us a thought since you've been away?'

'Of course I have,' Lorna answered, 'but don't tell me you've missed me—I know that you've been far too busy.'

'I have missed you terribly,' Muriel replied, 'and as for Jimmy—he's been like a bear with a sore head! I would never have believed that anyone could have such an effect on him. It ought to make you proud—and sorry.'

'Has Sally been here while I've been away?'

Lorna couldn't help the question, it burst from her lips, forced out by the tumult of her feelings.

'No, we haven't seen anything of her,' Muriel replied, 'not since she came down with the General. But she did ring up one day. We were in the garden and Thompson came out to say she was on the telephone and wanted to speak to Jimmy. He said : "Damn the girl!" then made me take the call and say he was in the middle of a set of tennis!'

'What did Sally say to that?' Lorna asked.

She stared at her dressing-table, afraid lest Muriel should see how eagerly she was listening.

'I think she was rather piqued, to tell the truth,' Muriel said. 'You know what Sally's like—annoyed if she doesn't get her way in even the smallest things.'

'You don't know if Jimmy's spoken to her since?'

'Not as far as I know,' Muriel replied. 'Why? Are you . . . jealous?' She spoke the last word tentatively, afraid that Lorna might be angry at the suggestion.

Lorna hesitated, then told the truth.

'Yes, very.'

Muriel gave a little exclamation, and took Lorna's hand in both of hers.

'But you needn't be, dear Lorna,' she said earnestly. 'I know Jimmy so well—I have devoted myself to him ever since he was born—I know every twist and turn of his character, and I promise you that never, in all these years, have I seen him even begin to love anyone as whole-heartedly and devotedly as he loves you.

'He's had love affairs—he would be the last to deny it—but always they have been light-hearted, irresponsible episodes which have lasted a month or a week and then petered out into irritated boredom on Jimmy's part.'

Muriel paused then went on as if choosing her words carefully.

'There have been scenes and unhappiness—and, of course, I'm not saying that Jimmy is blameless by any means—but most of the girls with whom he has flirted have understood only too well the rules of the game. They have been neither innocent little misses nor straight-forward, gentle and loyal like you.'

'But I am none of those things', Lorna protested.

'Well, how else can I describe you?' Muriel asked. 'You know your cousin. She's the type that Jimmy has found amusing. She is sophisticated, smart, and up-to-date—you would be quite sure, wouldn't you, that she could look after herself? But you are different. There's never been anyone like you in Jimmy's life and that is why, when I first saw you, I was so happy.

'I had always been afraid that Jimmy might marry someone like Sally, someone who would cut me out of his life so that I should have nothing left save Mother's charities.'

Lorna impulsively put her arms round her sister-in-law's shoulders; for Muriel was speaking with a passionate sincerity, and her tone told Lorna almost more than her words how much she loved her half-brother, and how afraid she had been of losing him.

'I'm a fool, I know,' Muriel went on, and there were tears in her eyes, 'but every time Jimmy goes back to the aerodrome I am afraid. He is all I have ever had to love and if anything happened to him . . .'

'Don't!' Lorna interrupted. 'Don't say such things—it is unlucky . . . it's frightening!'

For a moment the two women clung to each other; then Muriel, making a gallant attempt to laugh gaily, said:

'Aren't we ridiculous! Especially you, to be jealous of Jimmy! Why, he's so jealous himself that I don't think you need have a moment's anxiety!'

'Is he jealous?' Lorna asked.

'Of course he is,' Muriel replied. 'He told me quite a lot about Dr. Davenport the other day. I met him at your wedding, of course, and I thought how nice he was, although we only exchanged a few words.'

'Michael's the most wonderful person in the world, but I don't love him. Sometimes I wish I could have done, it would have made life a lot simpler—but these things either happen or they don't.'

'That's right. And they've happened where you and Jimmy are concerned?'

Lorna smiled.

'Oh, yes!—and I see now what an idiot I have been about Sally.'

'I was half afraid you were upset the other night. Why didn't you tell me? I'd have stopped her coming here. I could have made an excuse of some sort to Mother.'

'I didn't feel jealous till after she'd been,' Lorna said truthfully.

'But there isn't anything between them—I assure you. She's an old friend of Jimmy's and it amused him to dance and flirt with her. She's a very good dancer—there's no denying that.'

Lorna was half tempted to tell Muriel what else she knew about Sally. Then she remembered Michael's words and she tried to see it from Jimmy's standpoint—to judge it from his standards, not hers.

She bent forward and kissed Muriel on the cheek.

'You're the most sensible person I know,' she said, 'and I am never going to be silly again. Next time I am worried about Jimmy I shall bring my troubles to you.'

'I wish you would,' Muriel replied. 'I should be so proud.'

'I've been so stupid,' Lorna thought, as she climbed into the comfortable bed and sank back on the soft pillows.

She could not sleep. Her conscience began to trouble her. She felt she had been unfair and unjust to Jimmy and wondered now how she could have let the weeks go by in bitterness and resentment.

She loved him; how could she ever have doubted it? How could she ever have believed that she could live without him? It couldn't be only physical attraction, she told herself, there must be something more; there must be something that united them spiritually; and yet if that were so—how could she have been so unforgiving? ... how could she have stayed away from him?

'It's easy for Jimmy,' she thought. 'He has known so many women, but there have been so few men for me to study or try to understand.'

Then she thought that perhaps, after all, there was a similarity in all men; they all needed sympathy and understanding; they all needed looking after; they all wanted to show off to someone who was proud of them and to whom they could turn for commendation.

Perhaps in Jimmy she would find a little of Peter, of Michael, and of her father. Her experience with them would guide her, would help her where Jimmy was concerned.

Other things, too, were important to marriage—unity of interests. She must make herself, she thought, keen on the things that Jimmy liked, such as aeroplanes and flying, and try to understand the jargon that he talked when he was with another airman. There were his sporting interests, also. She knew that Jimmy liked shooting, was a good golfer, and fond of ski-ing.

'He must teach me these things,' she thought; and wondered if he would reciprocate by trying, when he had time, to share her love of reading.

And then children—wouldn't they be one of the greatest joys in their lives? She had never discussed it with Jimmy and yet she felt somehow he would like children, would be both interested in them and at ease in their company.

No one could have been more understanding than he where her own family were concerned. Peter and Peke liked and admired him, and if he raised his little finger Beth would be his adoring slave.

'I can give him a child of his own!' Lorna thought triumphantly.

The night drew on. Just before midnight the sirens went. Lorna could hear them whining away, their wailing loud and clear from the nearest village.

Later there was the sound of bombs, not too near, but near enough for the vibrations of them to shake the house and rattle the windows. Far away in the distance there was the sound of gunfire; and later, the swift purr of the fighters sweeping through the skies to rout the enemy.

'Jimmy must have gone up,' Lorna thought.

She lay still and taut—willing, with all her power, protection towards him. It was almost an act of prayer, this projecting of her spirit into the ether to shield her beloved from harm.

Then, as dawn came, she fell into a fitfull slumber. After being called she felt extraordinarily tired; and, looking in the glass, saw tell-tale lines of sleeplessness beneath her eyes.

'I must look pretty for Jimmy,' she thought, and took more pains than usual over the making-up of her face.

She was nearly dressed when there came a tap on the door.

'Come in,' she called.

The door opened a few inches.

'It is Thompson, Ma'am.'

'Come in, Thompson,' Lorna said.

She got up from the dressing-table and walked towards him.

'Sir Douglas would be obliged, Ma'am, if you would go down to the study as soon as possible.'

'What is it? What does he want me for?'

'I am afraid I don't know, Ma'am. He just told me to give you that message.'

'I will go down at once.'

She picked up her handkerchief and, slipping it into the pocket of her linen dress, ran downstairs. What could it mean?—she wondered. It was a strange message to send before breakfast.

She opened the door of the study. Sir Douglas was standing on the hearthrug, and besides him was a man in Air Force blue.

'Come in, my dear,' Sir Douglas said. 'Raffery, this is my daughter-in-law.'

Lorna held out her hand, half bewildered, half apprehensive that something unusual had occurred. She noted the senior rank of the man with whom she shook hands, automatically registered the fact that he wore the D.S.O. and Bar—and then Sir Douglas spoke.

'The Air Vice-Marshal,' he said, 'has brought us bad news. You've got to be very brave, my dear.'

'Jimmy!' Lorna only whispered the word.

The Air Vice-Marshal did not relinquish her hand; instead, he held it tightly and his clasp was firm and comforting.

'He's alive,' he said quickly, reading the question in her eyes, 'but he is injured—badly injured, I'm afraid. I came over to tell you and Sir Douglas myself.'

'What happened?' Lorna asked. Her lips were dry but she spoke steadily and her voice was clear.

'Jimmy went up last night with the Squadron,' the Air Vice-Marshal said. 'We got the order for night fighters to go into action at about one o'clock. The raiders were overhead, aiming at the big munition works about twenty miles from here. I went along to the Operations Room and then went down and listened to my Wing Commander, who was at the inter-communications.

'As you know, we can speak to the pilots and they can reply to us. We heard your husband shoot down his first Hun. About three minutes afterwards he sent a second spinning down in flames; and then, as he got on to the tail of the third, a Messerschmitt 109 got him. It shot away part of his fuselage. We heard him say :

' "I am wounded and on fire. I'm at five thousand feet— coming in to base. Get the fire tenders ready"

'The Wing Commander said—"If it's bad, bale out."

'Your husband replied—"What ! and lose this aircraft?— not ruddy likely !"

'He got over the aerodrome, but as he started to land something went wrong—the plane crashed. It was a small inferno before the groundsmen reached him—before they could get him out. He was rushed to the hospital and I saw the doctor just before I came here. He will live, but I think you would like to know the truth. His eyes are damaged--I am afraid there is no hope of saving his sight.'

Lorna gave a little cry.

'Jimmy blind ! How will he bear it?'

'There is only one other thing I have to say,' the Air Vice-Marshal continued. 'It may be a little comfort to you later. I have personally recommended your husband for the D.F.C. He has been exceedingly gallant—not only on this occasion, but on many others—and there is no one under my command who deserves it more.'

20

Lorna sat looking out of the window. The sun was turning the trees to gold, the shadows were lengthening across the garden of the hospital. It was very still.

From the distant village there was the sound of children's voices as they came out of school, and there was a whisper of music from a wireless set turned low, so it should not disturb those who were ill.

The figure on the bed made a slight movement and Lorna turned round quickly. She waited anxiously, wondering if Jimmy would speak; but he lay still again, his bandaged head steady amongst the uncreased pillows.

It was a relief to see him thus, remembering the long days and nights when he had tossed restless and delirious; when it had taken more than one person to hold him down; when his voice, croaking and distorted, had screamed out in agony; and yet this immobility was frightening too.

It was so unlike Jimmy, just as the face at which she now looked was unrecognisable—his skin blackened by anti-burn ointment, his swollen lips grotesque and shapeless, while his eyes and head were concealed by bandages.

At times, when that hoarse croaking voice called her, when those burned hands with their bent fingers groped across the bed, Lorna wondered if this were in truth her husband—the being she had known and loved in all the strength and beauty of his manhood.

She sighed, and instantly there came another movement from the bed.

'Who's there?'

Lorna got up from the window.

'I am here,' she answered gently. 'Do you want anything, darling? Shall I call Nurse?'

'No, it's all right. I have been asleep.'

'Quite a long time. I expect it has done you good.'

'How long have I been here? I keep forgetting.'

'Nearly six weeks.'

'It seems longer.'

'I am sure it does, but you are better—so much better that I hope they will let us move you soon.'

'Where to?'

'I don't know yet—your home, I think. I heard Sir Douglas talking to Matron about it yesterday. You'd like that, wouldn't you—to be at home . . . to have your own things round you?'

'What difference does it make where I am?' The voice was utterly weary.

Lorna put out her hand to touch his, and then instinctively she stopped. The skin was still so tender, so fragile, that the slightest pressure could hurt.

'Don't talk like that,' she pleaded. 'We shall be together. I will look after you.'

There was silence and then Jimmy said :

'Describe this room to me.'

Lorna looked round her, taking in every detail of the monotonous conventionality of the hospital room. She sought for words—glad to be able to interest him in any way, and anxious to paint the picture as glowingly as possible.

'It is a nice room,' she said at length. 'Not very big, but it gets all the sun. You are high up, on the top floor in fact, so that you don't have noises overhead. All the private rooms are up here. The walls are white, of course, and your window looks out over the garden. It is not much of a garden, but there are flowers in it, and some of the more convalescent patients sit there in the afternoons with the nurses. There are dahlias . . .'

Jimmy interrupted her.

'Go on about the room,' he commanded. 'Is the window low or high?'

'Oh, about the ordinary height from the floor,' Lorna replied. 'It's a nice big window opening outwards—you know the type.'

'What's below?' Jimmy asked. 'Directly below?'

Lorna walked across the room and leant out of the window.

'Nothing very interesting. It looks to me like a solid piece of concrete—as if it might cover a tank, or something like that.'

'A solid piece of concrete.' Jimmy repeated the words after her.

'Why are you so interested?'

'I wanted to know.'

A sudden suspicion made her tense.

'Why do you want to know?' she insisted.

He did not answer for a long minute, then he said sulkily :
'I have my reasons.'

'Jimmy!' Lorna gave a cry. 'You are not thinking . . . of anything . . . stupid?'

'I don't know what you mean—and why shouldn't I?' he asked contradictorily.

'Oh, Jimmy, don't talk like that! Explain to me—you frighten me!'

She felt herself trembling; she felt helpless and impotent, staring at this strange figure in the bed whose face registered no expression and who bore no resemblance to anyone she had ever known.

'Jimmy!' she repeated, almost whimpering.

'Tell me the truth, the real truth—I want to know. There's no hope, is there?—none at all?'

'For your eyes?' Lorna faltered. 'I don't know. We hope...'

'You know that's not true,' Jimmy interrupted her savagely. 'You are trying to keep it from me, all of you, but I'm not a fool—I know what they thought the last time they examined me! Father got some big man down from London. He said very little, but I knew by the tone of his voice—and what's more he has never come again. If there had been any hope at all, don't you think he'd have been here again and that he would have ordered some sort of treatment?'

'They may want you to get stronger first,' Lorna suggested.

'For Christ's sake don't lie!'

Jimmy's voice was like a snarl—the snarl of a tortured animal. Lorna put her arms round his shoulders.

'Darling, you've got to be brave. It won't be too bad when you get used to it. I shall be there to help you—to see for you. If only I could give you my eyes I'd do it, but as it is you must just use me.'

'I can't bear it,' Jimmy whispered. 'Do you hear?—I can't bear it! I've got to get out—to escape. Do you think I want to live as an invalid?... Do you think I want to be beholden to anyone—an encumbrance—a poor creature to be pitied and to be led like a pet lamb on a string. I can't face it, I tell you, I can't!'

His voice rose.

'Don't!' Lorna begged. 'Please, Jimmy, don't!'

'Do you love me? Do you love me at all?'

'You know I love you. You are everything in the world to me, you know that.'

'Then help me.' His voice was low again, she could hardly hear what he said. 'Help me. I don't care how... through the window is perhaps the easiest, or a drug. They give me morphia. Find out where they keep it—give me an overdose.'

He was speaking quickly, craftily, and there was something sinister and frightening about him. Instinctively

Lorna drew away from him, standing straight and still by his bedside. But when she spoke her voice was broken with pity.

'I can't. Don't you understand, darling, I can't do that.'

'Then I'll get somebody else,' he said. 'I'll find a way somehow. You are like all the rest! You are trying to make me live—trying to drag me back into a hell in which no semblance of manhood will be left for me. Well, you'll fail, I promise you—I'll defeat you yet!'

'I'm not trying to fight you,' Lorna said desperately. 'Don't you understand that I want you?'

Jimmy gave a harsh sound which bore no resemblance to laughter.

'Want me!' he said. 'What use am I to you? Get yourself a pet of some sort—a monkey would be far more entertaining—I am useless. A blind man!—who wants him? You think at the moment that you will be very noble and self-sacrificing. In a year or two's time, when you are bored with nursing me, you'll find my blindness very convenient if you want to nip off with some other young man or have a discreet affair with the doctor.'

He was trying to hurt her, trying to make her angry. Lorna knew that, but her voice was steady when she replied :

'That's unworthy of you, Jimmy. Do you imagine that I only loved you for your looks or because you could see? Supposing it had happened to me?—supposing I had been injured?—would you have left me?'

'I expect so,' he answered brutally. 'I never pretended to heroics—I loved you because you were beautiful—because you were you. Why should I continue to love an entirely different creature? Why should you want to love a broken, repulsive-looking man with sockets where he once had eyes?'

'But darling, your face will be exactly the same in a few months' time. This new treatment for burns which they give you is miraculous. If you could see the men who had been burned by the flash of a thousand-pound bomb and some of them are almost unscarred now. The doctors tell me that in six months even the redness of the skin will have gone. It's like a miracle.'

'No miracle will give me back my eyes.'

'That's true,' Lorna said gently, 'but otherwise you will look exactly the same, I am sure of that. I wouldn't have believed it myself until I saw the other patients and knew that the doctor was telling me the truth.'

'All the same, what's the use of living when one can't see? Money . . . luxury . . . all the things that people say one is lucky to have? God! Why don't they impress on you that the gift of sight is far more valuable?'

'There are worse things,' Lorna pleaded. 'There's a man here who has lost both legs and one arm. He was run over by a tank in the Libyan Desert. They sent him here to see if there was any possibility of fitting him with artificial limbs, but it can't be done. He will have to be carried everywhere for the rest of his life.'

'What's that got to do with me?' Jimmy said savagely. 'Don't tell me! Don't try to make things sound better for me! Other people's suffering was never any antidote to one's own. Let him die too, and the quicker the better, even as I shall. I can't stand it! . . . I want to die, I tell you!'

Lorna felt helpless. She stood silent, with the tears coursing slowly down her cheeks.

'Go on,' Jimmy goaded her bitterly. 'Haven't you got anything else to say? Can't you think of any more convincing arguments?'

'What can I say?' Lorna asked. 'I can only tell you that I love you. If you had been killed while you were flying I think it would have broken my heart. If you kill yourself now because you are too much of a coward to face the future I think it will kill me too.'

'Too much of a coward,' Jimmy repeated. 'Yes, that's what I shall be. I'm not afraid to say it.'

'It will be a good example, won't it?' Lorna said. 'A Squadron-Leader and a D.F.C.—a man who has been commended for great gallantry, who has been looked up to and admired by all the men under his command. Can't you see the headlines in the papers?'

'It might appear as an accident,' Jimmy said weakly.

'Accidents of that sort are always found out,' she insisted quickly. 'Sane and sensible men don't fall out of open windows—or take overdoses accidentally.'

There was a long silence. Then, at length, Jimmy said, in a voice of utter exhaustion :

'All right, you win. Have it your own way—and be damned to you! I hope you enjoy dragging me about on a string . . . I hope you enjoy the days when I shall scream at you in fury and resentment . . . I hope you will enjoy the nights when I shall keep you awake when you are tired because day and night mean exactly the same to me . . . I hope you will enjoy being nothing more than a nurse, enjoy life with me when I have grown to hate you—hate you because I'm dependent on you !'

He was silent for a moment, then with his voice even more bitter, he asked—

'Have you thought what it means to live without amusement, without entertainment? No theatres, no dances, no travelling—for even places will all seem the same—I shan't know the difference between Venice and Manchester. What does it matter to me where we live or what sort of a house we live in?—it will all be in darkness as far as I am concerned !'

'There will be music,' Lorna said, 'music, the wireless and . . .'

Jimmy interrupted her.

'The wireless !' he scoffed. 'Yes, we shall be reduced to that ! The estimable B.B.C. will come into its own. I congratulate you, my dear, on the originality of your taste ! I shall learn to appreciate that in the long years when we shall be together. Well, it's up to you now to choose where we are to go and where we are to stay—it's immaterial to me. I must accept everything second-hand. Will you feed me too,

I wonder, or shall I be allowed to do that for myself? You will, of course, have to cut up my meat.'

His harsh bitterness hurt and wounded Lorna and she was thankful when at last the nurse came and interrupted them. She said good-bye tenderly, but returned to Mountley Park with the merciless taunts of Jimmy's last words still ringing in her ears.

All that night she lay awake wondering if his self-control would snap, and whether he would, as he threatened, take the easiest way out—through the open window. She had hesitated as to whether to speak to the doctor or nurse of his idea; then realised she could not bring herself to say the words—it would have been a betrayal of her husband's honour.

The weeks that followed brought to Lorna many hours of torture and misery. She suspected that, when she was not there, Jimmy used to lie thinking up things he could say which would wound and hurt her.

Every day he seemed to have something new—some fresh threat or some scoffing comment which would get beneath the skin, making her flinch so that her face whitened and she would sit listening to him with her hands clenched together to keep herself from crying out.

The fact that he was growing stronger daily and more normal in health and appearance, only seemed to increase the virulence of these verbal attacks on his wife until Lorna, sobbing in sheer desperation night after night, wondered if it would not be better for her to go away—her presence only seemed to aggravate him and make him worse.

Finally the climax came. She left Jimmy's room after a scene of unparalleled mental cruelty. Worse even than the others to which he had subjected her daily for the past two weeks. As she reached the entrance hall of the hospital it seemed as if her pent-up feelings suddenly overwhelmed her. She gave a gasping sob and the world went black. She felt herself sinking down . . . down . . . down . . . into some abyss from which she could not escape.

She opened her eyes, to find herself lying on the couch in the doctor's consulting room. She was given sal volatile, and, after a few words with the doctor, left the hospital.

That night she did not cry; instead, she lay awake staring into the darkness, pondering over many things.

It was raining when she went back to the hospital the next afternoon. The air was moist and misty and there was the faint chill of the first autumn coolness in the wind blowing from the east. Lorna was glad that she had put on a warm coat.

Jimmy was waiting for her. She had learnt to know by the angle of his head when he was listening intently, expectant—and ready, doubtless, with some new cruelty on his lips.

'It's a horrid day,' she said as the nurse was leaving the room. 'I'm afraid the summer has gone.'

'The summer of happy memories,' Jimmy sneered. 'The summer when we met and when . . .'

Lorna interrupted him. She knew only too well what was coming. Gradually he would lead up to the moment when he had his accident, to taunt her with his present misery in comparison with the happiness they had known when they first loved one another.

'Jimmy! I have something to say to you and you must listen. First of all, I love you. I have always loved you, ever since the first moment we met. Now this has happened I want, if anything, to love you more, to look after you, to care for you and to make a success of our life together. It is going to be hard—hard for you and perhaps a little hard for me, too; but we could do it—I know we could!

'No . . . wait!' she said as she saw that he was about to interrupt. 'Don't speak yet, I haven't finished. I am prepared to do anything you like, to go anywhere you want to go, but only if you want me, only if I can be of use to you and bring you some sort of . . . contentment.'

Her voice broke but she went on bravely:

'These past weeks I have been afraid—I have begun to

suspect that I am the wrong person in your life, to feel that I upset you rather than bring you any comfort. I would have gone on without speaking, but something has happened which has changed everything. Yesterday I fainted when I left you. I was ashamed of myself for letting you upset me until a few words from the doctor made me think otherwise.'

She paused, Jimmy was listening intently.

'This morning I went up to London on the early train and I saw a gynaecologist recommended by your mother. It is a little soon for him to be certain; but, so far as he can ascertain, he thinks there is every reason to believe that I am going to have a . . . baby.'

Lorna waited; and then, as Jimmy did not speak, quite suddenly she bent over him, her hands on his shoulders.

'Say something,' she cried desperately. 'Oh, Jimmy, say something . . . I want you to be pleased . . . I want you to be glad! Don't you understand how wonderful this is for us both? It gives us something to live for, something which is an interest beyond anything we had imagined. Oh, Jimmy, do speak to me!'

Jimmy's mouth moved but no sound came, and suddenly she understood. He was trying to find words, trying to express an emotion which had swept away his egotism and his self-centred bitterness with one swift blow.

He put out his arms and Lorna found herself close against his heart. He was talking brokenly, the words falling over each other through quick breaths which were near to sobs.

'My darling . . . my own lovely one . . . my Cherry Ripe . . . forgive me . . .'

When they were a little calmer she wiped her eyes and his cheeks and, with her head against his shoulder, said:

'Now we can make plans. They are going to let you leave here in a week's time.'

'In a week's time?' Jimmy echoed, then his arms tightened round her. 'I am afraid to go out. You will be ashamed of me.'

'I shall never be that.'

'I want to be alone with you. I can't face Mountley and all those people. Mother will promise that we shall be quiet and that she won't invite large parties, but after a few days she will forget and the place will be packed with people—strangers who will stare and pity me. I can't bear it, I won't bear it! I'd rather stay here—I'd rather be sent to some other hospital.'

'We won't go to Mountley, then,' Lorna said, speaking softly as one might to a frightened child. 'We will go anywhere you like. After all, England is open to us. We will take a cottage in the country, somewhere quiet.'

'But until we find it,' Jimmy said slowly, 'we could stay at the Vicarage. I wouldn't mind going there. I would like being with the children and your father.'

Lorna gave a cry of gladness.

'Do you mean that? Do you really mean that you wouldn't mind going home—to my home, I mean?'

Jimmy smiled as his arms held her very close.

'We will go home, darling,' he said gently.

21

'There—the last cushion's done! The men are going now —they've finished!' Beth cried. 'It looks absolutely magnificent, doesn't it, Peke?'

She looked round at the transformed sitting-room.

'Tell me about it,' Jimmy asked in a quiet voice from the fireside.

Beth ran across the room and, seating herself on the arm of his chair, put her arm round his shoulders.

'It's simply gorgeous! I can hardly wait to watch Lorna's face when she sees it! The material is a sort of coral coloured linen scattered with flowers, and I can't tell you how rich the sofa and chairs look covered with it; especially with curtains to match, reaching down to the floor. We've never been able to afford that before!'

'We haven't afforded them now,' Peke said from the sofa where she was lying, 'we couldn't have saved enough coupons in a hundred years for all this. If it hadn't been for Muriel we should still be surrounded by our rags and darns!'

'What about the bedroom?' Jimmy asked.

'The carpet's down,' Beth answered. 'It's a wonderful madonna blue, and the rest of the furniture with the huge four-poster, all gold, white and carved with tiny angels, arrived from Mountley at one o'clock. The men have arranged everything as you wanted. It looks fabulous, like the room of a princess in a fairy-tale!'

'That's exactly what it is!' Jimmy smiled. 'And the flowers, have they come?'

'How awful of me! I forgot to tell you,' Beth exclaimed. 'I did them this morning as soon as Lorna left. They are perfectly lovely! There's an enormous bowl of chrysanthemums on the table by the window, another by your side, and a vase of orchids on Lorna's desk just like the ones she wore when you were married. Oh, I'm so excited, I can't wait until to-morrow! It's going to be the loveliest Christmas we've ever had.'

'It's a pity I couldn't get out to buy you any presents,' Jimmy said sadly.

Beth looked at him quickly to see if he were telling the truth; there was a smile at the corner of his mouth which belied his words. There was no sign of his burns save that he wore dark glasses. He was, in fact, an extremely good-looking young man.

'I don't believe Lorna has gone to Melchester this afternoon just for the drive,' Beth said shrewdly. 'Besides, she had a shopping list a yard long—she wouldn't let me see it.'

'Although, of course, you did your best?' Jimmy questioned. 'Your curiosity will get you into trouble one day.'

'It will get me a lot of fun in the meantime, though,' Beth answered promptly, and he laughed in appreciation of her quick wit.

'Do you know what Michael's giving me?' Peke asked. 'A pair of crutches!—and isn't it funny to think I am more excited about them than if he were giving me a Rolls-Royce?'

'If it goes on snowing like this they will be useless,' Beth teased her, 'you'll need a toboggan—not crutches.'

'Is it still snowing?' Jimmy asked.

Both got up and walked to the window.

'It's not too bad now,' she told him. 'In fact, the sky is clearing a little. The garden looks lovely, especially the trees. I do wish you could see . . .' She stopped and put her hand across her mouth.

'What were you going to say?' Jimmy asked.

'I'm sorry,' Beth replied. 'Lorna told us we were not to say that, but I keep forgetting.'

'It doesn't matter a damn! I'm used to it now and I honestly don't care.'

'Are you sure?' Beth asked. She went back to his chair and put her arm round his shoulders again. 'It's lovely having you here, Jimmy, you make everything such fun. So you've got to have a wonderful Christmas too. Besides, you've done so much for us.'

'Bunk!' Jimmy replied. 'I haven't done a thing.'

'Ooh, what a lie!' Beth and Peke cried simultaneously.

'What about the car, and the curate for Daddy?' Beth asked. 'That huge wireless, the new bathrooms, the help for Minnie, two of them! And all the other money you've spent on the house—including this?' She looked round the room appreciatively. 'Oh, I do wish Lorna would come back! She's late.'

'What's the time?' Jimmy asked, and there was a note of anxiety in his voice.

'It's about . . .' Beth began.

A cry from Peke interrupted her.

'Here she comes!'—but when the door opened only Minnie appeared.

'Oh, it's you, Minnie,' Beth said in disappointed tones, 'we thought it was Lorna.'

'I came to see if Peke wanted anything,' Minnie answered. 'Are you all right, dearie? Not too tired?'

'Of course I'm not,' Peke answered scornfully. 'I feel as strong as a horse. If it wasn't for this stupid leg I should be skipping about.'

'That's all right, then,' Minnie said, tucking a rug closely round her, then stooping to put some coal on the fire.

'Lorna's late,' Beth sighed, 'and here we are, consumed with anxiety, waiting for her to see the room.'

'She'll certainly be pleased,' Minnie said, 'if the shock doesn't kill her! How we put up with those covers and cur-

tains for so long I don't know. Talk about threadbare!—
they were held together by hope!'

'You approve, then, of the innovations?' Jimmy asked. 'I
haven't dared ask you before, Minnie—everything in this
house depends on your august approval.'

'Go along with you, Mr. Jimmy,' Minnie said with something suspiciously like a giggle. 'You're only buttering me up
because you want a good Christmas dinner to-morrow.'

'Oh, I shall get that any way,' Jimmy replied. 'I know you
wouldn't let the family or your reputation down, and what's
more—if that turkey isn't as good as the one we had last
summer I shall go on hunger strike!'

'You'll eat it and like it,' Minnie retorted. 'You don't eat
enough as it is. Your wife was complaining to me only the
other day and saying that we must fatten you up.'

'I'm afraid of losing my girlish figure,' Jimmy replied. 'As
for my wife, she's a bully—as I've learnt to my cost. She
ought to be here by now. I wonder why she is so late?'

'Now, don't you start a-worrying,' Minnie said soothingly.
'The doctor will look after her—she'll come to no harm.'

'It's too much for her—trapsing round the shops when
she's . . .' He hesitated.

' "In an interesting condition," is the right phrase,' Beth
supplied.

Minnie snorted.

'That isn't the way to speak about your sister,' she admonished. 'And in my young days young ladies didn't mention
such things.'

'Oh, I know, I know, you old prunes and prisms!' Beth
said teasingly. 'In your day they found babies under goose-
berry bushes. Nowadays, we're practical and outspoken. If
you'd seen as much of children as I have in the Evacuee
Nursery, you'd know that most self-respecting women would
leave the babies where they found them if procreation had
been slightly better arranged.'

Peke and Jimmy laughed at Beth's nonsense, but Minnie
looked shocked.

'I hope you won't come out with such ideas at the smart finishing school Mr. Jimmy's sending you to,' she said, 'or my goodness!—they'll wonder where you've been dragged up!'

'Darling Minnie, I'll be a credit to you and the highest moral influence in the seminary. What's more—I will return the perfect lady!'

'It'll take more than one term's tuition to change you into that!' Minnie said grimly. 'Well, I'll go and get your tea.'

As she opened the door, there was the sound of voices in the hall.

'Here they are at last!' Beth said. 'Now don't say a word—look quite ordinary, as if nothing unusual had happened.'

They heard Lorna's voice greeting Minnie and then she flung wide the door.

'Here I am at last, darlings. Did you think I was lost? Why ...'

She stopped dead just inside the doorway, her arms full of parcels, her face glowing from the cold outside.

'What have you done? But it's lovely! . . . Tell me all about it . . . Is this a Christmas present for me? . . . Oh, Jimmy!'

She put down her parcels and moved towards the little group round the fireplace. Jimmy had risen to his feet. Lorna went to him putting her arms around his neck and bringing his face down to hers.

'Thank you, my sweetheart,' she whispered.

She turned to Peke and Beth, who were bubbling over with excitement.

'Where did it all come from?' she asked. 'How did you get the material? Who put the curtains up?'

They both told her at the same time. How Lady Braith had put the material away when the war started because she had cancelled the redecoration of certain rooms at Mountley Park. How Muriel had remembered this, and sent the great bale of coloured linen down to Jimmy when she returned home, after staying at the Vicarage a month ago.

Jimmy had sent the material to the best decorating firm in Melchester, and had arranged that the measurements should be taken and the finished result delivered when Lorna was out.

'It's perfect!—and the flowers, too, are a joy—you know I love them, Jimmy. I never suspected anything so marvellous was being planned for my Christmas present,' Lorna enthused. 'But of course it would be Muriel who produced the stuff like a rabbit out of a hat.'

'Did you remember to order the taxi for her?' Jimmy asked.

'I did, but Michael says he'll fetch her.'

'I've got to go to the station anyway to meet the mother of one of my evacuees,' Michael said from the doorway.

'Well, that's lucky,' Jimmy said, 'but you're in for a long wait—the train is bound to be delayed. By the way, talking of waiting, you son-of-a-gun, why are you so late? Have you been making love to my wife again? If so, it's pistols at midnight—I'm not giving you any advantage.'

'The snow held us up a bit,' Michael answered. 'I suggested that it would be a romantic setting for an elopement, but alas! Lorna wouldn't listen to me—she can't rise above domesticity these days, poor girl!'

'You're a couple of idiots,' Lorna laughed. 'Tell me what you think of the improvements, Michael.'

'I'm thankful the great secret is disclosed at last!' he answered. 'I've heard of nothing else for weeks. The atmosphere of secrecy and intrigue has been nerve-racking.'

'Oh Michael, you pig!' Beth exclaimed. 'You know it's been absolutely thrilling!'

'I found keeping a check on my own tongue and yours as well nearly as exhausting as our shopping this afternoon,' Michael said, sinking down into a chair and stretching out his legs.

'Was it very tiring?' Jimmy asked Lorna. 'Are you all right, my darling? You haven't done too much?'

'No, I saw to that,' Michael interposed, 'although we had almost a stand-up fight in Woolworths because I refused to allow her to make a third journey to the basement to get something she had forgotten.'

'He's been insufferable,' Lorna complained.

Jimmy groped for her hand and found it.

'He's obviously been very sensible,' he contradicted. 'I gave him strict instructions that you weren't to do too much.'

'He obeyed you to the letter.'

'He didn't dare disobey me. I threatened to change my doctor—and yours!'

'What nonsense! As though anyone but Michael could look after us!'

'Well, he must prove himself capable of this solemn trust. These country doctors have a monopoly, you know.' Jimmy spoke facetiously, then suddenly he was serious. 'All the same, it's about time someone took care of you—you've nursed us for long enough.'

Lorna looked at her husband with a smile of perfect happiness and understanding, then, withdrawing her hand, she walked across to the sofa and bent down to kiss Peke.

'If you could choose,' she said, 'what sort of Christmas present would you like best in all the world?'

Peke looked up at her with shining eyes.

'You don't mean that Peter . . .'

Lorna nodded.

'We met the telegraph boy at the bottom of the drive. He's got leave and he'll be here by noon to-morrow.'

'How marvellous!' Beth exclaimed excitedly, but Peke did not speak. Lorna understood that there are some things beyond words.

'What a Christmas it is going to be!' she said softly. 'All of us together. And Jimmy, I got Daddy a really nice dressing-gown. It cost a fortune, but I'm sure you will approve—it's as warm and woolly as a baby lamb.'

'Think of the coupons you've spent,' Beth groaned. 'I know I shall go naked by Eastertide!'

'Nonsense! You've had half mine already,' Lorna said, 'and some of Peke's—you're not to be greedy!'

'Not greedy—glamorous!' Beth corrected her. 'Never mind. When the warm weather comes I'll form the first Little Walton Nudist Club—all male applicants for membership must wear dark glasses so as not to be dazzled by my unveiled beauty!'

'Really, Beth!' Lorna ejaculated—and to the others, 'What am I to do with her?'

'I'll prescribe for her,' Michael said, trying to look severe.

'Too late,' Jimmy sighed. 'Only a major operation would help now; but we might get her certified.'

'For which nasty crack,' Beth cried, picking up a cushion . . .

'No, Beth, put it down at once,' Lorna commanded. 'These new things are worthy of respect—and mind my parcels, too.'

'What else did you buy?' Peke asked.

'Yes, tell us,' Beth pleaded.

'You'll know tomorrow,' Lorna replied. 'Help me carry these upstairs, Beth, there are a mass more in the hall. Then we'll have tea. Minnie's gone to fetch it.'

She turned towards Jimmy.

'I adore the present, especially the orchids, bless you,' she said softly, and raising herself on tiptoe kissed his cheek. As he put his arm around her she whispered in his ear. There was something radiant in Jimmy's sudden smile as he listened.

Then Lorna picked up her bag and several packages while Beth took the rest. Suddenly she stopped.

'It's no use,' she said, 'I must tell you now, although I meant to wait until Christmas. Jimmy, they've taken your play! We can listen to it on the air on January 10th.'

There was a moment of stupefied silence, then as Jimmy reached out to grip Lorna's hand until her fingers turned white, a babel of sound broke out from Beth and Peke.

'What play? . . . Do you mean we'll hear it on the wireless? . . . What has Jimmy written?'

With a smile of incredible pride Lorna answered:

'He's written a short play about his friends in the R.A.F. We kept it secret just in case they didn't want it. But they do . . . and it's so funny I couldn't write down what he said because I was laughing so much.'

'It's the most exciting thing I've ever heard.'

Beth threw herself against Jimmy and kissed his cheek.

'That's not all,' Lorna went on. 'The B.B.C. are sending someone down to see you after Christmas, Jimmy, to talk about a series.'

Jimmy let out a deep sigh as if some tension within him was released, like the bursting of a dam. Then he said with a chuckle:

'What about occupational therapy now, Doctor?'

Lorna looked across the room at Michael with a smile.

'Michael always knew you could do it,' she said softly. 'And so did I . . . but I didn't think you could be so ridiculously, absurdly funny!'

Jimmy put his arms round her and held her very close.

'There's nothing I can't do when you believe in me,' he said.

He put his cheek against hers and knew she was trembling with happiness.

'I adore you, Cherry Ripe,' he whispered so that only she could hear. 'We can produce anything together, even triplets.'

Lorna laughed, but there were tears of joy in her eyes.

'The only trouble is,' Beth interrupted, 'that it will be expensive. You'll want a bigger size in hats right away!'

Jimmy reached out to pull her hair, and in a moment they were wrestling together like a pair of school-children. Lorna, moving out of the way, watched them with a happiness in her face which was indescribable.

That Jimmy should find an outlet for his energy was what she had prayed for, but it was living at the Vicarage which had done more to cure his depression and turn him into a normal man than anything the doctors could have prescribed.

She knew now that what he had always missed in his childhood, what he had needed without realising it was the rough and tumble of family life, the feeling of belonging, of having other people dependent on him.

'We'll have a dozen children!' she promised herself, then said aloud :

'Come on, Beth, help me with these parcels, or the budding playwriter will get no tea. And Minnie's toasting crumpets for us as a treat.'

'Crumpets, Jimmy famous, Peter coming home and new curtains!' Beth cried. 'It's all too wildly exciting—wait until we tell Daddy and Muriel!'

'I must be here to see their faces,' Lorna cried. 'Hurry, Beth.'

Carrying her parcels she went towards the door. Beth hung back to whisper to Jimmy.

'She'll have a fit when she sees her room!'

'Don't forget to tell me exactly what she says,' he replied.

Michael was opening the door for Lorna.

'Take the stairs slowly,' he admonished, half seriously, half teasingly.

'Really, it's getting hopeless,' Lorna said in an exasperated voice. 'You and Jimmy treat me as if I were a piece of Dresden china. One day I shall "come apart in yer 'ands" from sheer nervousness!'

Michael shut the door after them and came back into the room.

'She's all right, isn't she?' Jimmy asked.

'Perfectly,' Michael replied. 'Don't worry, I didn't let her do too much.'

'Did you get her present?'

'Yes, it had arrived this morning from London. I think you'll be pleased.'

'What are you giving her?' Peke asked curiously.

'Something I've had made,' Jimmy replied. 'Michael helped me choose it. Give me the box, Michael, I want to feel it.'

Michael passed him the pink leather jeweller's case. Jimmy's fingers searched for the catch—it sprang open.

'Diamonds!' Peke exclaimed. 'I can see them glittering. Oh, what is it?'

Michael got up and stood beside Jimmy.

'Two clips,' he said, 'designed to resemble wings. When they are joined together as a brooch they are not unlike the R.A.F. badge—a pair of open wings.'

If you would like a complete list of Arrow books
please send a postcard to
P.O. Box 29, Douglas, Isle of Man, Great Britain.